"Good n[illegible]

With a hand [illegible] against the truck door. She put both hands on his chest with intentions of pushing him away, but she made the mistake of looking into his eyes. Lashes slowly closed to rest on his cheekbones and she barely had time to moisten her lips before she was swept away by a scorching hot kiss.

She should push him back but instead, her arms went around his neck and she touched his bottom lip with her tongue. He groaned and opened his mouth, deepening the kiss into fiery hot passion. She would have been there until daylight, but he finally stepped back, picked up her hand, and kissed her palm twice.

"One kiss for the Lila I remember, the other for the woman she's become. Both are very special." Then he turned and disappeared into the darkness.

High Praise for Carolyn Brown's

LUCKY PENNY RANCH SERIES

WICKED COWBOY CHARM

"A nice blend of warmth, down-home goodness, humor and romance. Lively, flirty banter and genuine, down-to-earth characters are the highlights of this engaging story... The flirty banter between Deke and Josie is amusing and heart-warming, and the chemistry between them sizzles."

—*RT Book Reviews*

"There's nothing more delicious, memorable and addictive as a Carolyn Brown story."

—Fresh Fiction

MERRY COWBOY CHRISTMAS

"Top Pick! Carolyn Brown writes about everyday things that happen to all of us and she does it with panache, class, empathy and humor. 4½ stars."

—Night Owl Reviews

"A captivating cast of characters fills the pages of this sweet and funny novel."

—*Publishers Weekly*

"Brown's modern storytelling and fun-filled plot will engage readers and wrap them up in this sweet, Southern holiday romance."

—*RT Book Reviews*

HOT COWBOY NIGHTS

"Humorous storytelling, snappy dialogue and colorful characters are the highlights of this story."

—*RT Book Reviews*

"Carolyn Brown manages to create a romance that's steamy, light and fun, while also a relationship with substance and heart... a character-driven delight for romance fans."

—Fresh Fiction

WILD COWBOY WAYS

"A breathtaking romance filled with soul-sizzling passion and a heart-stealing plot. A five-star hit!"

—Romancing-the-Book.com

"Heartwarming and funny... *Wild Cowboy Ways* will pull you in and won't let you go until the end. I loved this book and recommend it to everyone. 5 stars."

—BookJunkiez.com

"A perfect read to just curl up with. The book is light, sweet and just the right amount of humor and emotions to keep you reading along. Carolyn Brown will get you falling in love with the characters before you can blink…It made me feel like I was watching a classic Hallmark movie. *swoon*"

—OnceUponanAlpha.com

Also by Carolyn Brown

The Lucky Penny Ranch series

Wild Cowboy Ways
Hot Cowboy Nights
Merry Cowboy Christmas
Wicked Cowboy Charm

Toughest Cowboy in Texas

Carolyn Brown

FOREVER
New York Boston

This book is a work of fiction. Names, characters, places, and incidents are the product of the author's imagination or are used fictitiously. Any resemblance to actual events, locales, or persons, living or dead, is coincidental.

Forever
Hachette Book Group
1290 Avenue of the Americas, New York, NY 10104
forever-romance.com
twitter.com/foreverromance

First edition: May 2017

Forever is an imprint of Grand Central Publishing. The Forever name and logo are trademarks of Hachette Book Group, Inc.

The publisher is not responsible for websites (or their content) that are not owned by the publisher.

ISBNs: 978-1-4555-9744-4 (mass market), 978-1-4555-9743-7 (ebook), 978-1-5387-2741-6 (Walmart exclusive edition)

Printed in the United States of America

OPM

10 9 8 7 6 5 4 3 2 1

This one is for
Kimberly Rocha, Margie Hager, and
Janet Rodman
Who all love cowboys as much as I do!

Dear Reader,

Welcome to Happy, Texas! There really is a town by that name in the panhandle of Texas where the flat land reaches out for miles and miles until it meets the sky.

Starting a new series is always exciting, but *The Toughest Cowboy in Texas* was an emotional trip for me. Brody and Lila had just graduated from high school the last time they'd seen each other. That was twelve years ago and now she's back in Happy where everyone knows everyone, remembers all the silly things that happened in the past, and the gossip mill is never without fodder. Cross Canadian Ragweed has a song on the market titled "17" and it says that you're always seventeen in your hometown. That's the way Brody and Lila felt that summer, even if they were thirty-year-old adults. I can relate to both of them because when I go back home, everyone still remembers me as a seventeen-year-old kid, and I've been gone for more than fifty years.

Writing this book took a lot of hard work—sitting in front of the computer while Lila and Brody argued about how the story should go, getting the journey just right from their first meeting to the end of the book, waking up in the middle of the night to listen to the voices in my head. But I can't take all the credit for taking this from a raw idea to a finished product, so put your hands together and make a little noise for the whole Grand Central team.

Let's hear a few extra loud whistles and yelling for my fantabulous editor Leah Hultenschmidt. Keep the energy going for the Forever team members Melanie Gold in managing editorial, Elizabeth Turner in the art department, and Michelle Cashman for all her great publicity work. Add a few more yells for my agent, Erin Niumata, and Folio Management. And before you stop the noise, let's hear it for my husband, Mr. B, who has stuck with me through the sorrows and the joys of an author's world. And one more round for all my readers! Thank you for reading my books, writing reviews, and telling your friends about them. You are appreciated more than mere words can ever begin to tell.

As I finish this book, fall is pushing summer out of the picture here in southern Oklahoma. You'll be reading it in the summer, so pour a glass of sweet tea and grab one or a few homemade cookies to nibble on while you read. And when you reach the end, remember Kasey and Jace have already petitioned me to write their stories. There's more on the way—so don't take your boots off just yet.

Happy Reading!
Carolyn Brown

Chapter One

Order up!" Molly yelled from the kitchen.

Lila picked up a basket filled to the brim with hot French fries just as the door to the Happy Café opened. The hot western sun silhouetted the cowboy in the doorway, but she'd recognize Brody Dawson anywhere—in the darkest night or the brightest day.

The energy in the café sparkled with electricity and her chest tightened. She gripped the red plastic basket to keep from dropping it and slowly inhaled, willing herself to take a step toward the table where a couple of old ranchers waited for their order.

"Well, well," Brody drawled. He closed the door behind him and slowly scanned her from the toes of her boots to her black ponytail. "The wild child has returned."

"But not for long, so don't go getting your hopes up," she smarted off right back at him.

In a few long strides he slid into a booth and laid

his hat on the space beside him. He filled out the butt of his jeans even better than he had when they were in high school and his chest was an acre wide. Lord, why couldn't he have developed a beer gut and two chins?

She carried the order to the other end of the café and set it down between Paul McKay and Fred Williams, two ranchers she'd known her whole growing-up years.

"I'd forgotten that they called you the wild child, Lila." Paul grinned.

"People change," she said. "Anything else?"

Fred squirted streams of ketchup across the fries. "Nah, we're good for now. Might need some more tea before we go. You should wait on poor old Brody. He looks like he's spittin' dust."

"Yeah. I'm dying over here," Brody called from across the small dining room. "How about a glass of half sweet tea and half Molly's fresh lemonade?"

"Anything else, Your Highness?" Lila asked as she turned to face him and made her way to his table.

His sexy grin and that twinkle in his baby-blue eyes made every hormone in her body beg for attention. But then she reminded herself that she didn't have to impress Brody Dawson. She was not that girl anymore. Oh, but to kiss those lips one more time just to see if they still made her knees go weak. *No! No! No!* Yet her fingertips went straight to her lips to see if the memory made them as warm as they felt.

"Whatcha got?" His drawl broke through the haze surrounding her.

She quickly dropped her hand. "What?"

"You asked if I wanted anything else." He wiggled his eyebrows. "So whatcha offering?"

She reached across his booth to pick up a one-page menu stuck between the saltshaker and napkin holder. Her arm brushed against his chest and more sparks danced around the café. Hoping that he couldn't hear the breathlessness in her voice, she straightened to her full height and started reading. "We have chicken fried steak, grilled pork chops, breakfast served all day, burgers of all kinds, and today's lunch special is meat loaf and mashed potatoes. I think there's a little more left if you're interested. I really thought you might have learned to read down there at Texas A and M."

He laid a rough, calloused hand on her arm. Pure electricity shot through her body.

"Are you still as wild as ever?" he whispered seductively.

"Oh, honey, you can't even imagine what all you've missed out on in the past twelve years." The chemistry between them hadn't changed a bit—at least not for her. She pulled her arm back and looked down at the menu. "Want me to go on or have you heard something that appeals to you?"

He raked his fingers through his thick, dark hair. It needed a cut, but then maybe he wore it a little longer these days. "Just something to drink for now," he said.

She turned away from him and headed back to the drink station. With shaking hands, she poured the tea and lemonade, stirred, and carried it to his booth. When she set it down in front of him, he motioned toward the other side of the table.

"Sit with me."

"You're a few years late with that invitation," she told him.

"Ah, come on, Lila," he said.

Throw a plaid shirt over that dirty white T-shirt and he'd still be the boy who had broken her heart all those years ago. But she'd cried her tears and burned the bridges between her and Brody, so bygones be damned.

He nodded toward the other side of the booth. "You're really going to hold a grudge and not sit with me for five minutes?"

"I really am," she said.

"Hey, Lila, we could use some more tea over here," Paul called out.

The years hadn't changed Paul and Fred much. Fred was the shorter of the two and Lila had never seen him in anything but bibbed overalls and faded T-shirts. A rim of gray kinky hair circled his round head. He could put on a thousand-dollar tailor-made suit and in five minutes he'd look like he'd slept in it. With a thick head of salt-and-pepper hair, Paul was his opposite. Always in freshly ironed jeans and shirts, he was tall, lanky, and every inch a cowboy, right down to his well-worn but polished boots.

She carried a full pitcher to their booth and refilled both glasses.

Paul whispered out the side of his mouth, "Brody lost his grandpa and his daddy the same summer you and your mama left town. So he didn't go to college after all. Don't be too rough on him. He carries a lot of responsibility on those shoulders of his."

Fred laid a hand on her arm. "Don't listen to Paul. That boy needs someone to give him hell. I was enjoyin' y'all's fight, so put on the gloves and get back at it."

"I swear on a stack of Bibles, I don't know why I'm even your friend." Paul sent a dirty look across the table.

"Ain't nobody else in Happy who knows you like I do. Hell, I bet I know you better'n your wife does." Fred's wrinkles deepened when he smiled.

Paul turned his attention toward Lila. "I hear that you're a teacher now."

"That's right." She headed toward the counter.

"So why are you here if you're a teacher?" Brody asked from the other end of the diner.

"To get my horns trimmed. I was getting too wild," she said sarcastically.

"Well, darlin', I can't help you with that." He grinned.

"Why?" She took one pitcher of tea and one of lemonade to his booth to refill his glass and pulled over a chair to sit down at the end of the table.

He leaned toward her and whispered, "I liked you as the wild child too much to shave an inch off your horns. God, we had some good times, didn't we?"

"And now we're thirty, not crazy kids anymore," she said.

"Too bad. Being a grown-up isn't nearly all it's cracked up to be."

"No, it's not but we do have to grow up. How's your granny?"

"Alive, kicking and giving out advice like candy at Halloween. Things in Happy don't change much," he answered. "How long are you going to be here?"

"Probably through the summer. Maybe less. Mama decided to put the café up for sale instead of leasing it. So if someone comes along and buys it, then I'm out of here."

He picked up his hat and stood up. "There's not many businesses left in Happy. I sure hope it doesn't close for good."

When she rose to her feet, they were so close that one step would have put her in the position to tiptoe and kiss him smack on the lips. Brody was right when he said not much changed in Happy, Texas. The minute she crossed the county line, she had the urge to do something wild and now she wanted to give in and wrap her arms around Brody.

She'd had a crush on him from the time they were in kindergarten. Truth be told, she'd liked him from before that—one of her first memories was standing on the church pew and staring at Brody sitting right behind her and her parents. He'd been a pretty little boy, had grown into a handsome young man, and now was one damn fine sexy cowboy.

"Hey." He grinned. "Remember when you decided that riding a bull wasn't all that tough? Took four of us—me and Jace and a couple of other guys to lasso that big old bruiser out on the ranch. I can still see you settling down onto his back as you held on to one of his horns with your right hand and waved your left one in the air. You stayed on for the full eight seconds and when the ride was over, you whipped off a straw hat with a glittery headband and bowed while we all hooted and hollered for you."

"Of course I remember that night and lots more, but what comes to mind the most often is the night before Mama and I left Happy the next day," she said with a long sigh, remembering the feelings she'd had that day.

He took a deep breath and settled his hat on his head. "You married?"

"Nope."

"Are all the men crazy wherever you've been livin'?" he asked.

"I didn't give them an IQ test before I robbed banks with them."

"Once a smartass," he chuckled.

"Smart—whatever," she shot back. "Are you married?"

"Never have been and don't intend to be anytime soon." His phone buzzed and he took it from his pocket. "Looks like Jace needs help out on the ranch." He tipped his hat toward her and stopped beside Paul and Fred's table. "Gracie know you're having that big load of taters right here at supper time, Paul?"

Paul shook his head. "No, she does not and don't you dare tell her, neither."

Brody chuckled. "Cross my heart. I've got to get back to the ranch anyhow."

Lila couldn't help admiring his long legs as he strode across the café.

"See, Lila, everyone in Happy doesn't know everything." Brody ducked to get through the door without removing his hat.

"Don't bet Hope Springs on that," she called out.

She whipped a white rag from the hip pocket of her jeans and wiped down the table where he'd been, spending extra time on it so she could watch him cross the parking lot. His distinctive swagger hadn't changed a bit and even from that distance she could see every ripple in his abs through that sweat-stained T-shirt. Her heart raced so hard that she was winded when she tucked the cloth back into her pocket.

Well, crap! So much for time, distance, and a broken heart erasing all the old feelings for that cowboy.

Brody left a trail of gravel dust in his wake, but then that was the story of her past. Always trying to impress him—always hoping that someday he'd go against his family and the whole town of Happy to ask her to go out—just the two of them. They'd sit side by side. His arm would be around her and he'd look deep into her eyes without caring that she was the girl with the worst reputation in Happy, Texas.

"His granny Hope turned the ranch over to him and Jace this past spring," Fred said. "Then Kasey and her three kids came to live on the ranch with them, and Hope moved out into the foreman's house. You remember Cooter Green, the foreman they had at Hope Springs?"

Lila nodded. "He had a couple of kids about my age. Melanie and Lisa, right?"

"Yep," Paul said. "They got married and moved out to Arizona. So Cooter retired and went out there to be with them."

"Last spring Hope turned the business over to the boys and then talked their sister into coming back to help out. So all three of the Dawson kids are living out there," Fred said. "Hey, we're out of fries. Would you get us another basketful and refill these tea glasses one more time?"

"Where's Adam? Didn't he and Kasey get married after high school?" Lila pinned an order on the spinner.

"He got killed in one of them secret missions overseas. I heard they couldn't tell Kasey nothing about it. Had the funeral here but the casket stayed closed," Fred answered.

Molly peeked out through the serving window and tucked a strand of short gray hair back behind her ear. With a round face, gray eyes set in a bed of wrinkles, penciled black eyebrows that made her look as if she were perpetually surprised, Molly hadn't changed much in the twelve years since Lila and her mother had left town. Not just in looks, either. Her attitude was the same too—she didn't take guff off anyone. The whole town would miss her sass when the café sold and she retired.

Molly crooked her finger at Lila. "You come on back here. I got something to say."

Lila glanced at the parking lot. No more customers were on their way inside, so she pushed through the door into the kitchen. What she got was a wooden spoon shaking her way, Molly's dark brows drawn down in a frown and her mouth set in a hard line.

"I heard what Fred and Paul was sayin'."

"And?" Lila asked.

Molly put four big handfuls of potatoes into the deep fryer. "Brody did step up and take on responsibility. He's turned into a pretty fine man when it comes to ranchin' and all, but that don't mean his attitude about bein' better than you has changed."

She'd heard it all many times before. She wondered if Brody had made it home yet and was hearing the exact same words. Without much effort, she could imagine Valerie Dawson threatening him with a wooden spoon as well.

"He's always thought he was a cut above you, girl. I'm not tellin' you nothing new. He broke your heart right before you left here and he'll do it again," Molly growled.

"That was a long time ago. So he didn't go to college like he planned? What's he done at the ranch?" She should be heeding Molly's warning, maybe even dropping down on her knees and thanking her, instead of defending the boy who had broken his date with her on the last night she was in town. For the first time ever, he was going to take her out to dinner and a movie. But he hadn't shown up and she'd cried until her eyes were swollen.

Another shake of the spoon and then Molly went back to fixing two meat loaf dinners. "I told your mama I'd watch out for you and that I'd see to it you didn't fall back into those wicked ways that got you that nickname. When you leave at the end of the summer, the only nickname you'll have is Lila. Why your mama named you Delilah after that wicked woman in the Bible is a mystery to me."

Lila threw an arm around Molly's shoulders and gave her a quick hug. Molly and Georgia had both worked for her mother from the time Daisy started the Happy Café. Then they leased it from her when Daisy and Lila moved to Pennsylvania to help Daisy's sister open a café there. Now, Georgia had retired and moved to Florida. Even with her sharp tongue, Molly had always been Lila's favorite and she was glad that she got to work with her again.

"It was my great-grandmother's middle name. Bessie Delilah was her full name. Do I look like a Bessie to you?" Lila giggled.

Molly shrugged her arm away but her expression had gone from sour to sweet. "Better that than Delilah. You might have been a preacher or a missionary with a name like Bessie. Now get these fries on out there to Fred and Paul before they get cold. Ain't nothin' worse than greasy, limp fries 'cept cold gravy."

"Miss Molly, I've changed from that wild child I used to be and I've been takin' care of myself for a long time." Basket in hand, Lila headed out of the kitchen.

"Yep, but that wasn't in Happy. Person comes back here, they turn into the same person who left."

Lila would never admit it, but Molly was right—the moment she hit the city limits sign in Happy the evening before, she'd had the urge to go out to Henry's barn, drink warm beer, and get into some kind of trouble.

* * *

Brody sang along with the radio the whole way back to Hope Springs. Seeing Lila again brought back so many memories. Nothing had been the same after she'd left town. Happy, Texas, didn't have a movie theater or a bowling alley or even a Dairy Queen, so they'd had to drive all the way to Tulia or Amarillo to have fun. Or they would stay in town and Lila would come up with some kind of crazy stunt that sent their adrenaline into high gear.

Like surfing in the back of my old pickup truck. It's a wonder we weren't all killed but the adrenaline rush was crazy wild. He chuckled as he remembered the two of them planting their feet on skateboards in the bed of the truck and then giving Jace the thumbs-up to take off. No big ocean waves could have been as exhilarating as riding on skateboards while Jace drove eighty miles an hour down a dirt road.

Blake Shelton's "Boys 'Round Here" came on the radio and he turned up the volume. He rolled down the window, letting the hot air blow past him as he pushed the gas pedal to the floor.

Seventy miles an hour, the dust kicking up behind the truck just like the song said. At seventy-five, he checked the rearview and imagined that Lila was back there wearing a pair of cutoff denim shorts, cowboy boots, and a tank top that hugged her body like a glove. Her jet-black ponytail was flying out behind her, and that tall, well-toned curvy body kept balance on the imaginary skateboard every bit as well as it had back then.

At eighty, he tapped the brakes enough to make a sliding right-hand turn from the highway to the lane back to the ranch house. The house was a blur when he blew past it and the speedometer said he was going ninety miles an hour when he braked and came to a long greasy stop in front of the barn doors. Gravel pinged against the sheet metal and dust settled on everything inside his truck's crew cab. He sucked in a lungful of it but it did nothing to slow down his racing heart, thumping hard enough to bust a rib. Gripping the steering wheel so tightly that his forearms ached, he checked the rearview mirror. The vision of Lila was gone, leaving only a cloud of dust in its wake.

You're not eighteen, Brody Dawson. The voice in his head even had the same tone and inflection as his mother's did. *You're a responsible rancher, not a kid who drives like a maniac with the music blaring loud enough they can hear it in Amarillo.*

Blame it on Lila. She brought out the wild side in me *back before I had to handle all the ranchin' business,* he argued, and felt a sudden rush of shame because he hadn't stood up for her in those days. Then he had time and opportunities; now he barely had time for a glass of tea with all the sticky situations of Hope Springs falling on his shoulders.

His phone pinged with another text: *Sundance is in a mud bog out on the north forty. Need help. Bring rope. Where the hell are you?*

Just as he was about to get moving, his grandmother stepped out of the barn and made her way to his truck, shielding her green eyes against the hot afternoon sun. Gray haired and barely tall enough to reach Brody's shoulder, she might look like a sweet little grandmother to strangers, but looks were definitely deceiving when it came to Hope Dalley. She had a backbone of steel and nobody messed with her.

"Did someone die? I heard you driving like a bat set loose from the bowels of hell. I bet you wore a year's worth of rubber off them tires the way you skidded to a stop."

"Everything is fine, but Sundance is in a mud lolly, so I've got to get some rope and go help Jace," Brody said.

"Damned old bull. He got bad blood from his father when it comes to breakin' out of pens, but he's a damn fine breeder so we have to deal with his ornery ways," Hope said. "I'll go with you and help."

"We can get it done, Granny. What are you doin' out here in this hot sun anyway?"

"Bossin' the boys about how to stack the hay. I can't just sit around in an air-conditioned house and do nothin'. I'd die of boredom," she said.

"Long as you're supervisin' and not stackin', that's fine, but I'd rather see you in the house with Kasey and the kids," he said.

"I'm not ready to be put out to pasture yet, boy. Kasey don't need my help. She has the toughest job on the ranch, taking care of those three kids as well as all the household stuff and the book work. That's a hell of a lot more exhausting and tougher than stacking hay. And she's doin' a fine job of it. Now go take care of that blasted bull." She waved him away.

Fun and excitement were over. It was time to man up and not expect to relive the glory days when Lila had lived in Happy and everything had been fun and exciting.

* * *

When it rained, the pond on their north forty would hold water for a few days and then slowly evaporate, leaving a muddy mess. Sundance, their prize breeding bull, loved water, but this time he'd waded out into nothing but mud.

He was bawling like a baby and thrashing around when Brody parked the truck. "How long has he been there?" he asked his brother, Jace, who was covered head to toe in mud.

"Too damn long. He's so stressed that we'll have to keep him in the barn for a week. We got cows to breed and he won't be worth a damn until he's settled down."

"Since you're already a mess, how about I lasso him and pull, and you keep pushing," Brody suggested.

Brody grabbed a rope from the back of his truck and landed it around the bull's neck on the first swing. "Got him. Now push!"

Jace put his shoulder into the bull's hindquarter.

Brody felt every muscle in his body knot as he tightened the rope. "Son of a bitch weighs a ton."

Jace pushed but the bull barely moved. "Two tons from the feel of it. He's moving a little bit. Pull harder!"

Brody wrapped the rope around his gloved hand another time and hauled back, leaning so far that Sundance wasn't even in the picture. All he could see was sky and big fluffy clouds that reminded him of lying in the grass with Lila beside him on a Sunday afternoon many years ago. She said that one big white cloud was the shape of a bull's horns and he'd said it looked more like two snow cones stuck together.

One minute he was smiling at the memory and the next he was flat on his back with no wind in his lungs and that crazy bull was pulling him along like a rag doll. He quickly untangled the rope from his hand and let go, sucked in enough air to get some relief, and threw a hand over his eyes to shade them from the blistering hot sun.

Sundance kept moving until he was under the shade of a big oak tree and then he threw back his head and bawled. Jace flopped down on the ground beside Brody and groaned. "If he wasn't such a damn good bull, I'd shoot that sumbitch right between the eyes and turn him into steaks and hamburgers."

"Meat would be too tough and rangy to eat—the old bastard," Brody said. "He can stay in the barn a few days to get settled down and by then we'll get a fence built so he doesn't wander back here again."

"My poor body feels like it's eighty years old after all that pushin'," Jace gasped.

Brody groaned as he sat up. "I'll take care of gettin' him back to the barn. You can go on to the house and get cleaned up."

"Thanks." Jace rolled onto his feet. "I'll help get him tied to the truck. He's so tired that he shouldn't give you too much trouble."

"You just best be out of the shower when I get there," Brody warned.

"Will do. Hey, I heard that you stopped at the café for lemonade. Lila changed any?"

Brody stood up slowly. "Who told you that?"

Jace took the first steps toward the oak tree where Sundance was grazing. "Gracie called the café lookin' for Paul, and Molly told her that you were flirting with Lila."

"I was *not* flirting," Brody protested.

"Yeah, right." Jace laughed. "Remember wind surfing and sneakin' into old Henry Thomas's barn on Saturday nights? You always flirted with Lila. I bet all that old stuff about Henry disappearing right before they left town will shoot to the surface now that she's back. Did she say anything about him?"

Brody fell into step beside Jace. "The great Happy, Texas, mystery of Henry Thomas's disappearance didn't come up. I wonder why folks are even still talking about that. It wasn't like he was anyone's best friend. He stayed out on the ranch most of the time and didn't even go to church with his mother."

Jace poked him on the shoulder. "I know but Lila and her mother left and that same week, Henry disappeared. It was all folks talked about for years, and every so often, the gossip starts again. Man, it never was the same here after Lila left. She was so much fun. What's she been doin' since she left?"

"Actually, we didn't talk about much of anything."

"Too damn bad." Jace grabbed the rope around Sundance's massive neck and tied him to the back of Brody's truck. "If he gives you any trouble, he's going to be dog food in the morning. We've got his son, Cassidy, that we can always start using as our prime breeder," Jace said. "See you at home, brother."

Brody kept a watch on Sundance from his side mirror as he drove from the pasture toward the barn. He had to stop thinking about Lila, but it wouldn't be easy. Seeing her standing there in those tight jeans with the waitress apron slung around her well-rounded hips brought back feelings that he thought he'd finally gotten over. Her full lips begged to be kissed and those big brown eyes full of mischief all the time made him feel alive, like he had back in the days when they were meeting in secret out in Henry's old barn—and in her bedroom late at night. That afternoon the perfect woman was right there within arm's reach and there wasn't a damn thing he could do about it. He inhaled deeply and let it out slowly, regret washing over him about that last night she'd been in Happy.

But Brody was not that crazy kid anymore. He was a ranch owner with responsibilities. She was a teacher, for God's sake, so she'd changed too.

"Lord, I've missed those days... and her," he muttered.

Chapter Two

Brody inched along at a snail's pace so the tired critter didn't have to do anything but a slow walk. It had been a long day already but Brody would have to wash the bull down, then feed and water him before he could go to the house and stand under a cold shower himself. But he was glad for the time alone so he could collect his thoughts and give himself a severe lecture about Lila.

The business of sorting things out was a lot easier said than done. It was impossible to shake that picture of her big brown eyes going soft when they were so close together in the café. He jumped and hit the gas when his phone vibrated in his hip pocket. He quickly removed his foot from the pedal and gently tapped the brakes to stop. Checking the side mirror, he could see that Sundance was all right.

He worked the phone out of his dirty jeans pocket, checked the ID, and tossed it onto the seat. After five rings it stopped but only for a few seconds before starting again. He slapped the steering wheel and answered the damn phone. If he didn't, she'd try a half dozen times and then she'd call Kasey to get into the ranch truck to check on him.

Turning the ranch over to him hadn't meant that she'd let go of the reins completely—not by a long shot.

"Hello, Granny."

"Where are you now?"

"I'm taking Sundance to the barn to clean him up," Brody answered.

"Why didn't you tell me Lila Harris was back in town?" she demanded. "I heard you've been at the café flirtin' with her."

Brody rolled his blue eyes toward the sky and then quickly blinked when the bright sun nearly blinded him. "I was not flirting. I was just making conversation. With all I've got on my plate, when would I have time to flirt with anyone? I barely have time to sleep."

"That girl is a bad influence, Brody. I hope that café sells real quick and she goes back to whatever rock she crawled out from under. You'd do well to stay away from her," Hope said.

"Doin' a little judgin' there, are you, Granny? Reckon you'd better go to church twice this next week."

"No, simply statin' facts." Her tone raised an octave or two. "And don't you sass me."

"Did your gossip sources tell you that she's a teacher now and she's only here for the summer?" Brody asked.

Hope's quick intake of breath told him that she was not pleased. "Are you takin' up for the likes of her? I thought you'd turned out to be a better man than that."

"I'm statin' facts. And I'm almost to the barn with this critter, so I'd better say good-bye. See you at supper?"

"Yes, you will and we will talk more about this, so don't think the conversation is over."

Without a good-bye, the phone went dark and he tossed it back onto the seat. He parked the truck in front of the horse barn and got out. When he tugged on the rope to get Sundance started toward the barn doors, the bull balked. He yanked again and Sundance promptly sat down, threw back his head, and glared at him.

"So you don't want to stay in the barn. I wouldn't either. It's hotter in there than it is out here," Brody said. "How about we put you in the corral for a couple or three days until you get over nearly going into a full-fledged stroke?"

Sundance lowered his massive head and took a step. Brody got back in the truck and moved around the barn to the attached corral. This time when he undid the rope, Sundance followed him like a puppy on a leash into the corral.

"I'll get the water hose goin' and get you cleaned off and cooled down. Then we'll fill the tank and bust open a bale of hay for you," Brody said as he shut the gate and locked it. He whipped off his cowboy hat, pulled out a bandana, and wiped the sweat from his brow. When he'd finished, he settled his hat toward the back of his head and stuffed the bandana back in his hip pocket.

Normally, old Sundance had a little mean streak in him but that day he didn't even flinch when Brody hosed him down. "It don't take much of that wallowin' in the mud to wear a guy out, does it? You never knew Lila Harris before she left, but she's a force like you are. Full of spit and vinegar, and God help anyone who ever gets in her way. But underneath all that bluster, she's got a soft heart of the purest gold. I was such a fool not to stick up for her and tell everyone in town to go straight to hell. I damn sure should have kept my word the last night she was in town, Sundance." He dropped the hose into the watering trough to fill it.

He stared at the water for a long time, lost in the thoughts of what he'd do if he could have a second chance with Lila. Finally he shook his head and exhaled loudly. No use wishin' for what couldn't happen. Nowadays he flat out didn't have time for women—not even Lila. He had a ranch to run and too many people who depended on him for any kind of romance.

While the trough filled, Brody went inside the barn and hefted a bag of feed onto his shoulders. Carrying it out to the corral, he shook his head toward Sundance. "You got it easy, old guy. You just breed the cows and then forget them. But me, I've never been able to get Lila out of my mind. Her coming back to Happy is most likely my punishment for being a cocky little shit who didn't know the best thing in the world when she was standing right in front of him."

He dumped the feed while Sundance drank his fill of water. The bull snorted and moved to the feed trough.

"That's all you got to say? Some therapist you are," Brody said as he looped the hose into a circle and hung it on the rack on the back side of the barn. "You think about what I told you and next time I come out here I expect more than a snotty old snort."

* * *

"Got him in the barn?" Jace yelled from the porch.

Brody was too tired to hop over the fence, so he went through the gate. "He sat flat down and refused to move. Evidently he didn't like the idea of the barn, so I put him in the corral, washed him down, and fed him. I hope one of those beers is for me."

Jace held out a can, but Brody got sidetracked when Kasey's two older kids, five-year-old Rustin and three-year-old Emma, ran across the yard to wrap their arms around his legs. Rustin was all Dawson with his dark hair and blue eyes, but Emma was the image of her red-haired mother, down to the spunky attitude.

"Uncle Brody, where have you been? Uncle Jace got here a long time ago." Emma was small for her age and her deep, gravelly voice sure did not match her looks and size.

He picked her up and swung her around. "That crazy Sundance got stuck in a mud hole and we had to get him out."

She squirmed. "Put me down. You stink. Did you get in the muddle puddle with Sundance?"

"Yes, I did." He set her on the lawn and she ran off in pursuit of a big yellow butterfly. So much like her mother, Emma had stolen his heart from the first time he'd held her in his arms. Someday he wanted two or three daughters and that many sons—when he found a woman to share his life with.

Rustin tilted his head back and stared into Brody's face. "Someday, I'm going to be a cowboy like you and Uncle Jace and I'm going to stink too."

Brody ruffled the little boy's dark hair and smiled. "Don't get into too big of a hurry, buddy. Be a little kid as long as you can. This adult stuff isn't easy."

"Okay, Uncle Brody, but when I'm a cowboy, I'm going to be good help." He took off toward the jungle gym in the corner of the yard.

Brody sat down on the top step and took the beer from Jace's hand. "Look at those kids. All that energy at the end of the day makes me jealous."

"We were like that when we were their age." Jace finished off his beer and crumpled the can in one hand. "Guess our next job is to fix the fence near the springs so Sundance can't get out. Wonder why he don't wade in the water there?"

"It would freeze his balls off." Brody tipped up the can and swallowed several times before he set it back down.

"Just a heads-up that Granny is in the house with Kasey, and she's not happy," Jace said flatly.

"I got a phone call, so I'm not surprised. Who'd have thought that Lila comin' back to Happy would cause this much crap?" Brody held a mouthful of the icy liquid a couple of seconds before he swallowed.

Jace went on. "Granny is on the warpath. She says it's my job to keep you away from the café and Lila. That a leopard does not change its spots and Lila is going to lead you straight to hell."

Brody grabbed the can and finished off the last two swallows of beer. "What makes Granny think you or anyone else can keep me away from Lila or that she's going to hell?"

Jace's gray eyes twinkled. "She'll get over it. To tell the truth, for some fun like we all had in high school, I'd go with you, not try to keep you away from her. We could always depend on her to come up with something crazy."

The door swung open and Kasey stepped out on the

porch with her third child, Silas, slung on her hip. She slipped between them and set Silas on the lawn. The little blond-haired fellow toddled out to the yard and promptly fell on his butt. Brody was instantly on his feet and hurried over to help him.

"Steady now, Silas," Brody said. "You ain't quite ready to run just yet. One step at a time."

Silas gave him a big grin and toddled off in the direction of the other kids. Brody slumped down on the step, resting his back against a porch post. "He sure does look like Adam."

"I know." Kasey choked up.

Brody patted her on the shoulder. "Sorry."

"Hey," she said, "we can't stop talking about him. Memories are all I have, even if they do make me sad. Silas is like Adam and I love that."

A little bit of anger still ate at Brody when he thought about Adam being killed during a military mission. There were evil people in the world who deserved to die—Adam didn't. He'd had a wife and two kids and Kasey had been pregnant with Silas. Sometimes fate was a bitch.

"So I hear Lila is back in town." She suddenly stood up. "Emma Grace, don't you dare hit your brother with that stick."

"He hit me," Emma said.

"Did not!" Rustin declared. "I was just spinnin' around and she got in the way."

"Then you stop spinnin' around." Kasey sighed as she sat back down. "Heads-up, Brody. Granny is making biscuits and cussin'. I'm supposed to watch you like a hawk circling the sky lookin' for breakfast—her exact words. She says Mama is goin' to pitch a hissy if you get involved with that girl again." Most Dawson women were tall and thin, but Kasey was short and curvy and the only one in the family in three generations with curly red hair.

"Again?" Brody asked.

"Hey, the whole family knew you were sneakin' around with her when y'all were in high school but they thought you'd get over it," Kasey said.

"I can't believe they didn't say anything." Brody shook his head slowly in disbelief.

"Mama figured if she said anything you'd set your heels like Daddy did."

Jace opened another beer. "And back then everyone figured you'd go to college and find someone else, that it was just a passing thing."

"We'll never know what it was." Brody frowned. "I've got to get a shower before supper."

"Well, I'm supposed to watch you so..."

Silas stumbled and fell again. Brody was on his feet the moment the little guy's hands hit the grass. "Easy, cowboy." He picked the toddler up and righted him. The moment he let go, Silas raised his hands in an attempt to catch a bright orange butterfly.

Brody returned to the porch and eased down on the porch step. "Does that mean you're going to stand outside the bathroom door while I shower, sis?"

"Hell no! But get ready for some opposition—not from me. God knows I liked Lila. I admired her. But Granny and Mama?" Kasey wiped her brow in a dramatic gesture.

"Later tonight, I'll get out the binoculars and follow him, Kasey. We can take turns and write down in a little book all about where he's been. Let's see—seven-thirty p.m., went to check on Sundance. Eight-thirty p.m., came back to the house and had a beer," Jace teased.

Brody shot a dirty look toward him. "You going to the Silver Spur with me to keep me out of trouble? Because that's where I'm going after supper, and if Lila happens to be there, I intend to dance with her," Brody said.

Kasey raised her hand. "I'd go with you if they'd let me bring three kids with me. I heard that you stopped in at the café and talked to her. Is she still as pretty as she was in high school?"

"Oh yeah," Brody sighed.

"Well, you'd better not let Granny see you with that look on your face at just the mention of her name," Kasey said.

"Granny, nothing. Wait until Mama hears that Lila is in town." Jace rolled his eyes.

"Sweet Lord! I remember those nights when you didn't come home until thirty seconds before curfew. Mama would rant and rave about you probably being somewhere with Lila Harris," Kasey said.

"He probably was and I was most likely with him." Jace grinned.

Brody ran a hand down his face. "This is worse than being in junior high all over again."

"Ain't that the truth," Kasey said. "I feel your pain, brother. I'll run interference for you as often as I can. Sometimes life throws stuff at us that's pretty damn hard to endure."

Brody patted her on the shoulder. She'd been strong at Adam's funeral, but day after day without him had to be lonely as hell. "I'm going to take a shower soon as I can force my old bones to stand up."

"Old my butt," Kasey laughed. "You've got a long way to go before you can claim senior citizen's rights. Back to the Lila thing. You'll have to suffer the wrath of Mama and Granny if you don't stay away from the café. They're in cahoots to get you and Jace both married and settled, and believe me Lila Harris is not in the picture they're painting for either of you. They want a sweet little ranchin' woman who will pop a kid out once a year and who attends church at least twice a week and it wouldn't hurt if she had wings and a shiny halo."

Jace's gray eyes popped wide open. "Hey, now! That's not even funny. I'm not ready for a wife or kids. Right now I just want to be your kids' favorite uncle. Thinkin' of marriage gives me hives," Jace said. "Granny ain't out kickin' the bushes for a wife for me, is she?"

"She was actin' strange," Kasey answered.

"How so?" Jace asked.

"Well, first she was cussin' about Lila. Then next thing I knew, she was askin' about Henry Thomas."

"Really? Why?" Brody rushed out to remove a handful of petunia blossoms from Silas's hand. "They might be pretty, buddy, but they'd taste awful." He turned him around and showed him a blue jay in the tree. "If you can catch that bird, you can eat every bit of him."

"Brody!" Kasey fussed.

"Well, he can." Brody grinned. "Now what about Henry?"

"Granny got a faraway look on her face and next thing I know she's wipin' away tears on her apron tail. Then she went back to cussin' about Lila was the cause of every bad thing that ever happened in Happy. Hell's bells! I think she even blamed her for all the businesses on Main Street closing down," she said.

"It was a tough time everywhere, but none of it was Lila's fault," Jace said seriously. "We lost Gramps and Daddy. Henry disappeared and Lila left town. In her mind, it's all rolled into one big ball. Blaming Lila for all of it would be easy."

"Seems like Lila's coming back to town sure stirred up a lot of old memories," Brody said.

"I can't imagine why Henry's disappearance was such a big deal. He told his sister he was leaving. His mama had died, so he wasn't needed on the ranch next door. I guess it's the not knowing where he went or what happened to him that worries the gossipin' folks." Kasey lowered her voice. "And we all know that Granny and her church buddies keep the rumor mill going."

"Oh, yes, we do and the gossip vines have been about to dry up lately. This should make them happy. Maybe you ought to flirt with Lila just to give 'em something to talk about." Jace nudged Brody in the ribs with his elbow.

Brody put a hand on his shoulder and shoved him. "Why don't you help me out and do something crazy so they'll have something to talk about?"

"Wouldn't take the spotlight off you for anything." Jace popped him on the shoulder in a friendly brotherly slap. "Hey, Kasey, what's for supper? If our old-man brother will go take his shower, we might get to eat before it gets cold."

"Barbecued chicken and rice. I made two chocolate pies for dessert and it'll be ready in"—Kasey checked her watch—"fifteen minutes."

Brody's head bobbed once. "That'll give me enough time for a fast shower. Emma told me that I stink."

"She's an outspoken one. Reminds me of another little red-haired girl named Kasey," Jace said.

His sister's and brother's voices faded as Brody headed inside. When he and his siblings had all moved into the house a couple of months before, Kasey took the south wing for her and the children and Jace and Brody each chose a room on the north side. Granny Hope still had a bedroom in that side of the house, but she'd moved her furniture out to the house that the foreman had vacated when he moved away. Located about a quarter mile behind the house, it was where she spent a lot of her time these days.

Brody stripped out of his clothes in his bedroom and padded barefoot to the bathroom. Letting the cool water beat down on his back, he remembered a time when he and Lila had sat under the falls at Hope Springs. The water had flowed down on her dark hair, plastering it to her naked back, and they'd made wild, passionate teenage love right there in the cold water.

He sighed and put away the memories, and after he'd dried off, he remembered to splash on a little cologne so that Emma would be happy with him. He dressed in fresh jeans and a snowy white T-shirt and made it to the table just as Kasey and Jace put the last of the food out.

Slinging an arm around his grandmother's shoulders, he leaned down and kissed her on the forehead. "I hope you made plenty of biscuits. Ain't none better than yours."

"Not even Molly's down at the Happy Café?" She walked away from him.

"Can't compare." He smiled. Usually a hug, a kiss, and a compliment worked, but the frown on her face said that it was going to take a while for her to cool down.

"You smell good now," Emma said.

"Well, thank you." Brody dropped a kiss on her red curls. "I wouldn't want to be all stinky when I read to you tonight."

Emma sighed dramatically. "It's not your turn. It's Uncle Jace's turn to read me the bedtime story."

Good Lord, had he lost his touch with all the female population?

"And mine tomorrow night," Kasey laughed. "Looks like you got all cleaned up for nothing."

"If I can't read to the princess, then I'll read to the boys," Brody said.

"No, it's my turn to do that." Hope set the hot biscuits on the table and motioned for them all to take their places.

Brody slid into the chair to Hope's right. "Then I'll just go on to the Silver Spur."

"You can say grace, Brody," Hope declared as she sat down at the head seat. Sure, she'd given the running of the ranch over to Brody and Jace but there were some things she didn't relinquish and the head chair was one of them.

Jace thanked God for the food, family, and life and then said, "Amen."

"I like it when Uncle Brody says the blessin'." Rustin handed his plate to his mother. "He don't have to talk forever like Uncle Jace."

"Your uncle Brody needs to talk to Jesus more and get God's opinion on women and bars," Hope fussed. "I'm not callin' names but he knows exactly who I'm referring to. When it comes time for him to settle down, he needs a good churchgoin' woman who knows how to run a ranch and can cook and—"

"And has angel wings and a halo?" Brody quickly finished for her.

Her green eyes squinted into slits and her mouth puckered so tight that it brought on a new set of wrinkles. "Someday I'm going to enjoy saying that I told you so. Don't come runnin' to me whinin' like a baby when you make the wrong choice, because I ain't goin' to feel a bit sorry for you. Are you goin' out with him, Jace?"

Jace put a chicken leg and a thigh on his plate and passed the platter to Brody. "No, ma'am. I got other plans tonight but they don't have anything to do with one of them angel women, Granny."

"I like angels," Emma said.

"I like cowboys. If cowboys go to bars, then I want to go." Rustin bit into a biscuit.

"Me too." Emma nodded. "Can I wear my boots, Mama?"

"Girls can't go to bars, right, Granny?" Rustin frowned at his sister.

Kasey shook a finger toward the kids. "Neither of you is going to a bar. When you're thirty, you can go with your uncle Brody to the Silver Spur and not before. Now hand me your plate, Emma."

"Thirty?" Brody asked.

Kasey's finger turned toward him. "When you have a daughter, you can decide when your little girl can go to a honky-tonk."

"Forty," Jace said quickly. "And only then if I go with her."

"Amen!" Brody agreed.

"Well, you'd better get to lookin' for someone who can live with your sorry asses because if your daughter is forty, then y'all will be sixty-eight and seventy. And that's sayin' you can find a woman in the next year." Hope slathered a biscuit with butter and laid it on the side of her plate.

"Granny said a bad word," Rustin singsonged.

"And when you're twenty-one you can say that word." Kasey finished helping him with his plate. "For now, you concentrate on eating a good supper and then you can have chocolate pie."

"And ice cream?" Emma asked.

"If you promise to never set foot in a nasty old bar," Hope said with another sidelong glance toward Brody.

"Okay." Emma grinned.

"I'll just have pie if that's the way it is," Brody said. "Or maybe I'll go by the café before it closes and have a banana split."

"I can buy that place and burn it down to keep you out of it," Hope said. "Don't test me, Brody Dawson. Besides, you've got a work load too heavy to be gallivantin' to town every day."

"Oh, Granny, we all know that inside that tough exterior is a heart full of love and sweetness." Brody reached over and laid a hand on her shoulder. "We all love you."

"To the moon and back," Emma said quickly.

"I love you the purplest." Rustin nodded.

"What?" Jace asked.

"It's a book that I read to him last week about a mother who loves her kids in colors," Brody explained. "I think we all love Granny Hope the purplest."

"Oh, hush, all of you." Hope smiled. "Eat your supper before it gets cold."

Chapter Three

Jace had thought that he might go to the bar with Brody that night, but then Paul called. He and the guys were getting together at Fred's house for a poker game and needed a couple more guys to sit in. It didn't take much to talk Brody into going with him rather than going to the bar that Friday night.

But family came first and Jace had to read the kids their bedtime stories. That gave Brody a whole hour after supper with nothing to do but think of Lila.

He paced back and forth across the porch, checked the time over and over, and finally forced himself to sit down on the steps to wait. Patience was not written in the bright stars and the moon that night. Pretty soon he was back on his feet and walking around to the back side of the house. Maybe a walk to Hope Springs, the watering hole at the back of the ranch, would clear his mind. He headed that way and then heard a coyote howling over toward the adjoining ranch, the Texas Star—Henry Thomas's old place. If the varmint was thinking of attacking one of his calves, he'd put it running.

When Brody reached the barbed-wire fence separating the two ranches, the coyote had found a friend because he could hear two distinct coyote voices. Brody leaned on a post for a moment and wondered where Henry had gone when he left the place. He had a sister who lived somewhere over in the eastern part of the state and now leased out the whole section of land to Paul McKay, but the house hadn't been lived in since Henry left more than a decade ago.

He set his hand firmly on the top of the wood post and jumped over it. Paul was his friend and Kasey's father-in-law. He wouldn't mind if the Dawsons walked across his land to the old hay barn where the kids used to hang out. It was only about a quarter mile from the fence and with Brody's long strides, he got there in a few minutes.

Sitting down on a bale of hay, he let his eyes adapt to the semidarkness in the big, old weathered barn. He'd kissed Lila while she was sitting in the seat of the old green John Deere tractor parked right over there. He could visualize her perched on the seat. She wore cutoff jeans so short that the pockets hung down below the frayed out bottoms, and her long legs looked as if they went on forever. Barefoot, a gleam in her eye as the sun set, and those bright red lips begging to be kissed. Later, she'd told him that it was her first kiss ever.

The last time he'd kissed her was at the barn door just before they went their separate ways on a starlit night just over a dozen years ago. That was the night he'd asked her on a real date—their first date—dinner and a movie in Amarillo. He'd promised that he'd pick her up at six-thirty. The thought of living in a big place terrified her. Huntingdon, Pennsylvania, was by no means a big city, but compared to Happy, population less than seven hundred, the place seemed huge with almost eight thousand people. He didn't tell his brother or his family that he was going out with Lila—didn't see any use in starting a war right there in Happy.

A huge white cat startled him when it jumped into his lap and headbutted him until he started petting her long fur. In a few minutes she jumped down and disappeared into the hay, leaving him alone.

He'd left Lila alone that night. He just couldn't face the tears he knew would be coming—combined with the fit his parents and Granny would pitch when they found out he'd gone on a real date with the notorious Lila Harris. So when his buddies invited him to the Silver Spur, he'd taken the chicken's way out.

With fake IDs they'd had a few beers and danced with a lot of girls. He'd been a jerk and was absolutely miserable all night. Nothing, not illegal beers or other girls, would ease the pain of what he'd done to his best friend and secret girlfriend. He'd tossed and turned until morning and rushed to the café to see her before she and her mother left town. He'd known that he'd screwed up really badly and was prepared to tell her that not seeing her again forever was worse than seeing her cry. That he was hurting every bit as much as she was and to beg her to call him when she got to Pennsylvania.

He'd gotten there just as they were getting into the van. He tapped on the window but she wouldn't roll it down. Instead she'd looked straight ahead while tears rolled down her cheeks and left wet circles on her T-shirt. He'd never forgotten her mother's words that morning before she got into the vehicle and drove away.

"I've told her for years that you were just toying with her, that you'd always feel like you were better than her and that she was in for heartache. You finally proved me right, Brody."

It wasn't going to be easy to shake the memories or the yearning he still felt for Lila.

He checked the time and started toward the fence at a slower pace. When he had his hand on the post, ready to jump, he heard something in the distance that sounded like a motorcycle, but he didn't know anyone in Happy who owned one. He glanced over his shoulder and saw nothing.

"Most likely an old truck about to bite the dust," he muttered as he lengthened his stride. Jace said they were leaving at eight and he had only fifteen minutes. They usually played in the tack room at Henry's old barn but sometimes Fred insisted they come to his house. Brody had to admit that the snacks were usually better at Fred's place than they were when they met at the barn.

* * *

Lila finished unpacking, took a shower, and quickly found she was too restless to stay in the small apartment her mother had built behind the café.

It was at least an hour until dusk and she'd been inside all day. Swiping her keys from the hook by the front door, she went out to the garage and revved up her motorcycle.

Feet still on the ground, she tucked her black hair

under the helmet, popped the face mask down, and then walked the bike backward out of the garage, leaving the door open. The sun was sinking slowly out where land and sky met in the flat land of the Texas panhandle when she roared out to the cemetery. She went straight to her father's tombstone, dismounted, and was busy pulling weeds when her phone rang.

"Hi, Mama," she said.

"How'd the first day go?" Daisy asked.

"It went fine. And fast. I'm sitting in front of Daddy's grave right now. Decided I needed some fresh air, so I rode my bike out here," she said.

"What are you doing in the cemetery at dark?" Daisy asked.

"Texas is an hour behind Pennsylvania, remember? It's not even eight o'clock yet, so I can still see without turning on the bike's lights."

"I worry about you on that thing. I wish you'd sell it," Daisy said. "Just last week I read about a girl who was killed because she hit a pothole and went flying through the air. I know what those roads are like in Happy and—"

"Mama, quit worryin'," Lila interrupted. "I'm careful and I wear a helmet." She changed the subject. "Would you believe that everyone is trying to figure out what happened to Henry Thomas? You'd think they'd be talking about Molly and Georgia, right?"

"Molly is still there and no one believes she'll really leave. Georgia was last week's topic when she retired and moved," Daisy said.

"But she worked here and leased this place for more than a dozen years," Lila said. "And there's very little talk about the café bein' for sale. But nearly everyone who comes in mentions Henry. What was so great about him anyway? I don't hardly even remember him except that he came in the café a few times and always ordered jalapeños on his burgers. I wonder if they even realized that you and I left."

"We didn't just fall off the face of the earth like Henry did. That makes him their go-to topic when all the other gossip has gotten old like Georgia leaving Happy and moving to Florida. I'm surprised that you aren't the center of the rumors right now," Daisy said. "Comin' into town with a Harley. Flirting with Brody Dawson."

"I'm not flirting with him and tonight is the first time I've taken the bike out," Lila protested.

"Okay, okay, have it your way. Has anyone even asked about buyin' the café?"

"Not yet. Word will get out that the place is for sale and I did put a sign in the window. We may have to go with a Realtor." She braced her back on the tombstone.

"We might have to do that. I need to get back there for a visit," Daisy said. "I haven't been to your daddy's grave in all these years and..." There was a long pause. "Sometimes I wish I'd never left."

"Why?" Lila asked.

"Your aunt Tina and I aren't getting any younger and I don't want to spend my elderly years in this cold climate," Daisy said. "And yet I'm not so sure I want to live in Happy again, either. I guess as long as the café was mine, I kept a connection to your dad, even though he never did know I'd bought the old building and put in an apartment and a café. I don't know, I'm rambling."

"I understand. I'm undecided about going back to

Florida. I might start looking around at other places," Lila said.

"I thought you were happier there than you'd been in Memphis or in Little Rock."

Lila shut her eyes tightly but all she could see was Brody in that tight, sweaty T-shirt. Her therapist said that she kept moving to hunt for happiness but she had to find it inside herself first. Maybe it wasn't Brody that drew her back to Happy but the whole big picture where she had to prove to everyone that she was no longer that wild kid who was constantly in trouble. When she did that, she could move on.

"Lila?" Daisy raised her voice.

"I was thinkin'," she said quickly. "I was happy in Memphis and in Little Rock and I do love teaching in Panama City Beach. Maybe I've just got a travelin' bug that begins to bite me after a couple of years."

"Or maybe Happy is the only place that feels like home for both of us."

"I kind of doubt that, but who knows? We'll see what happens this summer. I'm off for a little country ride and then I'm going home to read a boring book until I fall asleep," Lila said.

"Promise me you will be careful on that thing. I hated it when your daddy rode one and even more when he put you in front of him and took you all over the county," Daisy said.

"I promise." She took a long, deep breath. "Good night, Mama."

As Lila hung up, she caught a movement in her peripheral vision. A black cat with a white blaze on his face was sitting on top of a tombstone and staring right at her.

"Here, kitty, kitty," she called to him.

He didn't budge. She held out her hand and called out to him again. Finally, she got up slowly and started walking that way. "You're a pretty boy. Where do you live?"

When she was close enough, she reached out to pet him but like a lightning streak he jumped down and in seconds he'd disappeared, knocking over a fresh wreath of daisies in his hurry. She straightened the flowers, made sure the metal tripod was secure in the ground, and then noticed the name on the tombstone—Weston Dalley. Birth and death dates recorded right there. Brody's grandpa had died June 1, twelve years ago. On the other side of the granite tombstone was Hope Dalley, birthday engraved but no death date.

"I know how much you loved him, Brody. I'm so sorry that you lost him." She went back to her father's grave and laid a hand on his tombstone. "I miss you, Daddy. I miss those afternoons when you took me for a ride down through the canyon, so this ride is for you."

Helmet on and a kiss blown toward the skies in hopes that her father would know that she was thinking of him, she headed off to the east. Her idea was that she would ride through the canyon, but when she got to the lane leading back to Henry's ranch, she slowed to a crawl and turned. The white picket fence around the yard shined in the moonlight. The long, low house felt empty even from that distance, but then it probably hadn't been lived in for years. Molly said that Henry's sister left it as it was in hopes that he'd come home someday.

The old barn drew her in. Heeding her mother's warnings, she drove slowly, keeping her eyes open for potholes. Scraggly weeds grew between fresh tire tracks left by trucks. She parked the bike close to the side door, which squeaked when she opened it just as it had done years ago.

Sitting on a bale of hay, she imagined a big green tractor between her and the door. That's where she'd gotten her first kiss and it had been from Brody. It had plumb set her insides on fire and every one after that had had the same effect.

A big, white cat made its way from the stacked hay toward her, rubbing around her legs and purring until she picked it up and held it close to her chest. Two cats in one night—one wary of her, the other wanting to be loved. Was this one of her mother's omens? And if so, should she pay attention to the cemetery cat or the one that liked her?

She inhaled deeply and let it out slowly. She sniffed again and then one more time. The cat smelled just like Stetson, the cologne that Brody used to wear back in high school. She glanced around the barn but didn't see anyone—most likely another kid used the same kind of cologne and had been out here earlier waiting for his girlfriend.

The cat hopped down and disappeared into the dark shadows, leaving Lila alone. She brushed the white hair from her dark T-shirt and jeans and inhaled again. The smell still lingered, so someone had been there. It couldn't have been Brody, because at thirty, he'd be taking his women to something a little more upscale than an old barn.

Chapter Four

So where have you been?" Jace asked.

"Out for a walk. Don't have many free evenings when nothing is hollerin' at me to come take care of it," Brody answered.

"Amen to that, brother. We've worked on these two ranches our whole lives but owning one is a lot different. It's a twenty-four-seven job." Jace started toward his truck.

Brody followed him. "You're sure enough testifyin' but I'm grateful to Granny for this. If we worked our whole lives and saved every penny, we couldn't buy something like Hope Springs."

"Or Prairie Rose." Jace nodded. "Fred and the guys are already itchin' to take our money. How much you got to lose?"

"Not more'n ten dollars but at a cap of a quarter we shouldn't lose too much," Brody chuckled.

Fred met them at the door and ushered them into the dining room. They took their places around the table and Paul shuffled. "So what do you think about Lila bein' back in town? Y'all goin' to get things started where you left off?"

"Lord almighty, this boy has so much on his platter that he ain't got time for women," Fred said. "He's got a ranch to run, kids to help his sister raise, and a granny to take care of."

"He's always got time for women, especially Lila." Paul winked dramatically.

"What makes Lila so special?" Jace asked as he arranged his cards.

Brody sorted through the hand he'd been dealt and bit his tongue to keep from giving them a list half a mile long.

"I'm not sure but there's sparks all over the place whenever she's around him." Paul nodded toward Brody.

"We here to talk women or play poker?" Fred asked.

"At our age we can do both. That woman on the television says it's multitasking." Paul reached for a cookie from a full platter in the middle of the table. "How'd you get your wife to let you have all these when all the other women are takin' stuff to my house for that social thing them women do every month?"

"I didn't ask," Fred answered. "I just emptied the cookie jar into a plastic bag and hid them until she was gone. Got some cold beers and soda pop in the 'fridge when y'all get thirsty. And there's a bag of pretzels if you want something salty."

Brody laid a card down and held up a finger. Paul slid one across to him.

"You gettin' serious about playin' or just wantin' us to hush about Lila?" Fred asked.

Brody nodded. "Maybe a little of both."

"If I were in your boots, I'd damn sure move in a hurry." Paul threw away three cards and motioned for more. "Young cowboys around here are going to come sniffin' around that café real soon when they hear that somethin' that pretty is workin' there."

"Why don't you hush? You're worse than an old woman at meddlin' in people's business," Fred fussed at him.

"Have some pretzels and beer and don't tell me what to do," Paul shot back.

Jace chuckled. "You reckon when we get old, we're goin' to be like these two, Brody? And I thought there was a couple more guys who would be here."

"Old!" Fred gasped. "We're like fine wine. We get better and see things clearer with age. Y'all young whippersnappers would do good if you were half as smart as us when you get to be sixty."

"Just us four. The others all had stuff to do," Paul said.

Brody looked at his terrible hand and thought of the hand life had dealt him. Grandfather and father both passing away the same summer that Lila had left. Going straight to work on the ranches rather than going to college like he'd planned. Now like Fred said, helping Kasey raise three kids, helping Jace organize and run Hope Springs. He loved the work but sometimes the weight of it all was pretty damn heavy. But a picture of Lila flashing through his mind brought a ray of light the likes of which he hadn't even realized was possible.

Still, after that last night and twelve years' worth of

water under the bridge, there was probably no way she'd ever want to start anything new with him. He'd blown his chance and the bridge had burned, leaving them on opposite sides of a deep gully.

"Brody!" Paul raised his voice.

He laid all his cards but one on the table, keeping the queen of hearts. "Guess I need a wheelbarrow full," he said.

Paul slid several cards across the table. "Not too lucky tonight, are you?"

"It can change," Brody said.

"Never too late to change or to start over," Fred said.

"You gettin' all philosophical on us, Fred?" Jace threw down two cards.

"Just callin' it like I see it." He shoved a quarter out to the middle of the table.

"I'll see your two bits and raise you four," Paul said.

Brody's hand had improved enough that he wouldn't lose too heavily on the first go-round. His mind kept wandering back to Lila. He'd rather be sitting in the hayloft with her than playing poker with Fred, Paul, and Jace but he didn't have that option. He glanced down at the queen of hearts and smiled.

"He must be about to take all our money," Paul said.

"Nah, he's thinkin' about a woman. Poker don't put a grin like that on a man's face," Fred argued.

Jace pushed three quarters out to the middle of the table. "I'll raise your four bits and add two more to it."

Brody laid his cards on the table. "Y'all got me. I'm out."

"Can't believe a Dawson has a bad luck streak," Paul said.

"We're playin' poker, not talkin' women, remember?" Jace teased.

Brody punched him on the arm. "You're as much an old woman as these two are."

Fred laid out a full house and raked in the quarters. "I'll have enough to buy a hamburger at the Happy Café if my luck holds out."

A vision of Lila in those tight jeans flashed through Brody's mind and he bit back a groan.

* * *

Lila hadn't awakened that Saturday morning with dancing on her mind, but when the café closed, she'd turned on the radio and danced through the top five country songs with the mop as a partner. She hadn't been out to an old country bar in years but the music brought back memories of the time when she and Brody managed to get into the Silver Spur with fake IDs. They'd drank beer and danced until thirty minutes before curfew, then drove like bats set loose from Hades to get home in time.

She was dressed in skinny jeans, boots, and a sleeveless Western shirt after she'd applied makeup and curled her hair. She'd worked hard for the past years to subdue that wild inner child, but tonight she was turning it loose and letting it come out to play. She listened to a Blake Shelton CD on the way to the Silver Spur and wiggled her shoulders to the beat. The words to his song would be her theme song for the night. She'd leave when the place shut down or when they ran completely out of cold beer.

The parking lot was pretty full when she arrived. That

meant that she would have plenty of guys to dance with. Lila held her breath as she walked through the fog of cigarette smoke and ignored the whistles of several cowboys who'd already drank too much. She had her money out to pay the cover charge but the bouncer waved her on in.

"Ladies' night every first Saturday. Free cover charge and beers are two dollars until ten o'clock. Enjoy," he said.

"Thank you." She shoved the money back into her small purse and went straight toward the bar.

The dance floor was full of line dancers and the sound of their boots hitting the wooden floor was music to her ears. She hiked a hip on a bar stool and ordered a beer.

A tall, blond cowboy with pretty blue eyes claimed the place beside her within seconds. "How about I buy you a drink? I'm Rick, short for Derrick, and you're Angel, right?"

"No, I'm Lila, short for Delilah, which is about as far from Angel as you can get. But that's a pretty good pickup line, Rick," she answered. "I've already got a drink ordered but thank you."

The line dancers made a beeline for the bar as the next song started. When the first guitar strands of "If You're Gonna Play in Texas" began, Rick held out his hand and she put hers in it. He led her to the middle of the floor and wrapped his arms around her. She was grateful that they were the same height and his nose wasn't resting between her breasts. He was smooth on the dance floor and dancing with him was fun.

The band's singer stepped up to the mic. "We have a request for 'Sideways' by Darryl Worley. This isn't the Rendezvous Club like he sings about but it's definitely time to get a little sideways in the Silver Spur for most of you folks and there's plenty of fiddle in this one."

The blond cowboy was pretty smooth on his feet and Lila was enjoying the dance until a petite redhead tapped her on the shoulder. "Mind if I have a turn at this cowboy?"

Lila stepped back and someone grabbed her hand, spun her around in a swing dance, and then brought her back to his chest. Her heart knocked against her chest so hard that she thought it would fly out of her chest when she looked into those cerulean blue Dawson eyes.

"Brody?" Of course it was Brody. No one else created such turmoil in her body, soul, and mind.

"Lila." He smiled.

"I thought you were too busy for a night out or maybe I should say two nights since you played poker with Fred and Paul last night. I sure didn't expect to see you here tonight."

"How'd you know that I was at Fred's playin' poker?" he asked.

"Rumors are nourished and fed at the café." She grinned. "Paul and Fred came in for their usual afternoon snack and gossip session. I don't know how they get anything done on their ranches."

"They've each got a good foreman and lots of hired help. And I probably shouldn't take two nights off in a row but I heard that you might be here tonight."

"Oh, really?" She raised both dark brows.

"The café isn't the only place that gossip flourishes." He smiled. "Molly was fussin' about you and it got back to Kasey."

She should walk away and not look back but she was

enjoying being close to him too much to do that. "I don't imagine your granny and your mama will appreciate that," she finally said.

"Right now I'm not real concerned about what anybody thinks." He drew her closer and buried his face in her hair.

Every nerve in her body was aware that she was in his arms and all her hormones kicked into double time, begging her to drag him out to the truck and fog the windows. When the song ended, another line dance started. He kept her hand in his and led her back to the bar, where they claimed the last couple of stools at the very end. He held up two fingers and pointed to the Coors bottle the guy beside him held. The bartender nodded and brought two ice-cold longnecks to them.

"Talk to me," he said.

"About?"

"You. Why didn't you call me after you moved?" he said.

"My heart was shattered, Brody. Why did you stand me up that night?" She couldn't tell him that she'd called the ranch but when his mother answered, she'd hung up.

"I didn't want to see you cry again, so when the guys asked me to go with them, I went. And..." He paused, leaving a big empty space hanging over their heads.

"You didn't want to be seen in public with me without a crowd around us, right?"

He nodded. "I'm sorry. I wish I could go back and redo that night, Lila. But there was another reason."

"And that is?"

"I didn't want you to see me cry," he said. "I really do wish I could get a redo."

"Sometimes it's too late to do what you should have been doing all along, Brody."

It had taken a lot of therapy for her to realize that Brody had been a complete jerk. That the way he treated her wasn't her fault and that she had been worthy of a decent relationship even if they were just teenagers.

"I tried to sweet-talk a phone number out of Molly and Georgia both. I still can't believe that she retired and moved so far away. She and Molly were an institution at the café. I knew they'd have some way to get in touch with your mom but they wouldn't budge. Then I sent a letter to you, thinking they would forward it to your new address but it came back stamped with 'refused' in big red letters."

"Mama was tired of watching me get hurt. She knew we'd been sneaking around and that I was…that I'd had a big crush on you for years." She couldn't make herself say that she'd been in love with him. "Then when you finally asked me out for real, you stood me up. If a letter had come, she would have burned it." She lowered her voice. "And your folks thought I was a bad influence on you and everyone else. I just wanted you to like me, Brody, but that ship has sailed and I burned the bridge between me and you. It's too late for us."

"Then we'll have to build a new ship and a new bridge." He ran a rough hand down her cheekbone. "You're still as beautiful as I remember and it's never too late." He parroted Fred's words from the night before. Or was it Paul who'd said that? Either way, it was good advice.

Sitting so close that his arm grazed hers when he took a drink of his beer, looking like sex on a stick, smelling exactly like that white cat in Henry's barn—the wild child inside her wanted to come out and play so badly. But she wasn't that girl who'd fall all over herself for a little attention from Brody Dawson. When she'd started college at Penn State, she'd become the girl who studied hard, got good grades, and graduated with honors. According to her therapist, she'd been out to show everyone that she'd amount to something.

Brody opened his mouth to say something but a young woman who was probably right out of high school pushed her way between them and motioned toward the bartender. Evidently he knew what she drank because he grabbed two mugs and began to fill them with beer. While she waited, she turned her face toward Brody and flashed a brilliant smile. "Hey, there. Want to dance?"

"Not tonight. I'm with this lady right here."

"This old gal"—she eyed Lila up and down—"is way below your league."

"No, thanks," he said. "And don't talk about my... my..."

"Your mother?" the woman giggled.

Lila would bet that her ID was fake and she wasn't a day over eighteen. The joke about her age wasn't what lit a fire under her anger—it was that nasty little remark about her being way below his league.

"I'm not his mother, darlin'," Lila said.

"Sister, mother, friend, neighbor. It don't matter." She worked a quarter from her skintight jeans and laid it on the counter in front of Lila. "Here you go. Go call the senior citizens' van to take you home."

"What did you just say to me?" Lila's temper flared

as she tucked a leg behind the woman's knee and gave a slight kick. The girl crumpled to the floor in a heap.

"You bitch," she said as she tried to regain her footing.

Lila hopped off the stool and pulled her up. Then she leaned in close to her ear and whispered, "If you want to play with the big dogs, you'd best get your rabies shots."

"I was just teasin' and havin' a little fun. My friends dared me to get him to dance with me," she whimpered.

"Be careful who you insult next time you want to have a little fun," Lila said.

"God, I've missed you," Brody laughed as the girl limped away. "She thought she was tough."

"She's just a kid out with her friends." Lila could remember acting just like that more than once, but it hadn't been her girlfriends she'd wanted to impress—it'd been Brody Dawson.

"I guess we've all been young and stupid. Did you ever think about all the good times we had before you moved away? Want another beer?"

She shook her head and put a hand over the top of the beer so the bartender could see. "Sure I thought of you. I taught in a high school in Memphis where I was the junior class sponsor. That meant I had to attend the prom as a chaperone. I thought of you that night and how handsome you looked in your tux when you escorted Gloria Tanner into the room. Hmmm." She tapped her chin with a finger.

"I told you back then that I wanted to take you but...," Brody stammered.

"It's water under that bridge that I burned down." She slung her purse over her shoulder and slid off the bar stool.

"Don't go. I'm sorry, Lila, for everything," Brody said.

"When I come back home, I'm still the wild child and you're Brody Dawson, the most popular cowboy in Happy, Texas," she said. "You were the quarterback of the football team, the high-point shooter in all the basketball games, class president, and voted most likely to succeed. If they'd had a tough cowboy title, you would have won it too."

"We are the cowboys," he reminded her. "Do you remember everything about everyone?"

"Of course. I remember dancing with you one time right here when we snuck in with fake IDs. You didn't mind holding me close in a bar but you wouldn't even sit with me in church. What does that tell you?" She wanted to dance with him again so badly that she could feel his arms around her, but wild horses or a Texas tornado couldn't drag her back out onto the floor.

"Stay until I finish my beer and I'll walk you out to your truck. I'm about ready to call it a night too. Just five more minutes, please?"

She fought with herself for a moment before she sat back down on the stool.

"So you're a teacher now?" he said.

"Yup. High school English."

He took a long draw from the bottle. "Where do you teach?"

"Taught in Memphis and, believe me, in the neighborhood where I taught, the fourteen-year-old girls were as tough as nails. Then I taught in an inner-city school in Little Rock that was even rougher and the past two years I've been in an upscale place in Panama City, Florida."

"I can't imagine you in a classroom," he said.

"Where did you imagine I'd be in twelve years? Living in a run-down trailer park with six or seven kids and a drunk for a husband?"

"No, you were too smart for that. I just figured you'd be a lawyer or maybe the mayor of Philadelphia or something really big and important. Not that a teacher isn't a fine job. So you never got married, right?"

"Your beer is done. To answer the question, though—I told you in the café I wasn't married."

"Yes, you did but that's not what I'm askin'. You aren't married now but have you been at some time?"

She shook her head. "My therapist says I have commitment issues."

It was the truth and Brody was the one who'd caused those issues.

"You?" she asked.

"Nope, my sister says the same thing about me and commitment. She's probably right."

Lila slid off the stool. "How's Kasey? Adam's death must have hit her hard."

"She's trying to move on but it's not easy. Three great kids help but she misses Adam a lot." Brody threw a few bills on the bar and followed her.

"Tell her hi for me. See you around." Outside, she inhaled the clean night air and wished that she could get him out of her mind and heart as swiftly as leaving a bar full of the smell of sweat and beer.

"You're two different people. One is the smart teacher. The other one is the girl who left and they're fightin' with each other," he said.

"You got it. And the winner takes all." She walked faster.

He matched his long strides with hers. "Which is?"

"The prize." She stopped abruptly. "Don't feel like you have to walk me to my vehicle. I'm a big girl and I've been takin' care of myself for years."

"You've always been able to take care of yourself, Lila, but I want to walk with you." His hand went to her lower back.

The intense heat would probably leave a print on her back that would look like a bright red tattoo for days, but she didn't argue or shrug it away.

When they reached her bright red truck, he whistled under his teeth. "Nice vehicle."

She dug around in her purse and found the keys. "I left the motorcycle at home."

"Oh, really?" His expression said that he didn't believe her.

"Yep, I didn't want to arrive with helmet head."

"Are you serious?"

"Why would you be so surprised? I am, after all, the resident bad child of Happy, Texas. I'm surprised there's not a picture of me beside the city limits sign warning everyone to steer clear of Lila Harris. If you rub shoulders with her, you get an instant ticket to hell. Do not pass go. Do not collect two hundred dollars. Just get on your poker and get ready for the ride."

"Motorcycles are dangerous. You shouldn't—"

She laid a finger over his lips. "I stayed on a bull for eight seconds and climbed to the top of the water tower. You didn't fuss at me about those things because, wait, you were right there with me. Well, darlin', buy a Harley and we'll terrorize Happy before we have to use that quarter and call for the senior citizens' bus. Good night, Brody."

With a hand on each side, he pinned her against the truck door. She put both hands on his chest with intentions of pushing him away, but she made the mistake of looking into his eyes. Lashes slowly closed to rest on his cheekbones and she barely had time to moisten her lips before she was swept away by a scorching hot kiss.

She should push him back but instead, her arms went around his neck and she touched his bottom lip with her tongue. He groaned and opened his mouth, deepening the kiss into fiery hot passion. She would have been there until daylight, but he finally stepped back, picked up her hand, and kissed her palm twice.

"One kiss for the Lila I remember, the other for the woman she's become. Both are very special." Then he turned and disappeared into the darkness.

With weak knees, she hit the button to unlock her bright red truck and crawled into the driver's seat, leaned her head back, and sighed. Her whole body tingled and every single frayed hormone was crying out to call him and tell him to meet her at the springs. But instead she started the engine and drove south toward Happy at five miles under the speed limit.

She pulled into the garage and got on her cycle, rode it out to Henry's ranch, and parked it at the barbed-wire fence separating Hope Springs from Texas Star. Jumping a fence was like riding a bicycle—once done, it was second nature to do it again, even after a dozen years. She put a hand on a wooden post and gave a hop, cleared the top strand, and came down on Brody's property.

Hot! Damn hot! If hell is seven times hotter than this, the devil might already be cooling off in Hope Springs, she thought as she made her way from the fence to the cold spring that bubbled down over a tiny little waterfall into a pool. The water came from an underground spring that flowed all year and no matter how hot the weather was the water was never warm.

She jogged a quarter mile back to the springs, where she jerked her boots and socks off and waded out into the icy water until it reached her knees, not caring if her jeans got wet. That didn't help the place where his hand had been on her back. It was still too warm, so she went back to the grassy shore, shucked out of every stitch of clothing, and dove into the icy water.

"Oh. My. God!" She gasped when she surfaced. "I forgot how cold this is even in the summer. Are you happy, my inner wild child? I'm a thirty-year-old woman out here trespassing and skinny-dippin'."

Somewhere down deep inside her soul she heard a very loud, *Hell, yeah, I am.*

Chapter Five

On Sunday morning, Lila awoke to the sound of rattling pots and pans in the kitchen. She covered her head with a pillow. "This is summer. I'm not supposed to be working. June, July, and August are the number one reason people go into the teaching field. This place makes me crazy. I'm talking to myself. I need a pet." She threw the pillow at the wall.

Molly was rolling out dough for morning biscuits by the time Lila showered and made it to the kitchen. She frowned and shook the wooden rolling pin at her. "You won't ever live down that wild kid reputation by going to the bars. You *will* be in Sunday night church services this evening. You can sit with me. We can't go to morning services what with having to run this business but God will be there tonight as well as this morning."

"You aren't my boss," Lila said.

"Oh, yes, I am, especially on the Sundays after I hear that you were seen talkin' to Brody Dawson at the Silver Spur of all places. You don't need to be hangin' around with him. Your mama told me that he plumb broke your heart the night before y'all left town," Molly said.

"Maybe he's different now that he's grown up."

"Why are you takin' up for him?" Molly stopped what she was doing and cocked her head to one side.

"I don't know but—"

"No buts." Molly shook her head. "If things are right, then there are no buts."

"Don't stomp a hole in that soapbox." Lila filled both coffeemakers.

"Don't sass me. I can still walk out that door, and if I do, you'll have to close down this place. Then it won't ever sell. Nobody will buy a café that's been shut down for months," Molly declared.

Lila threw up her hands defensively. "Yes, ma'am. I won't sass you again, Miss Molly."

"That's better. Now let's get to work."

* * *

Brody only caught a sentence here and there of the Sunday morning sermon. With Emma on one side of him and Rustin on the other, he spent the time switching between handing Rustin crayons so that he could work in his cowboy coloring book and peeling off stickers for Emma to plaster in her book.

His heart went out to Kasey, who was sitting on the other side of Emma. Adam should be the one helping with the two older children and making Kasey smile every evening when he came home from work. Only when she looked at her kids did her eyes light up—the rest of the time she was still struggling with her loss.

He wondered what it would be like if things had worked out between him and Lila right out of high school, and then he'd lost her to an accident that no one could even talk about. His chest tightened and the pain was so sudden that it brought tears to his eyes. If nothing more than a thought could bring on that much hurt, his poor little sister was doing good to crawl out of bed every morning.

He glanced over his shoulder to see if Lila might be back there somewhere, then reminded himself that she was at the café. If she attended Sunday services at all, it would be that evening. If the family wasn't gathering at his mother's for dinner, he would have gone to the café just to be sure that Lila was okay. But he'd promised Emma that he would sit beside her, and a man was only as good as his word, whether it was to a three-year-old girl or a ninety-year-old cowboy.

Guess you learned that lesson the hard way, didn't you? that irritating voice in his head said. *If you'd kept your word, maybe you and Lila would have stayed in touch all these years.*

Yes, I did. He nodded. *And after the misery I've lived with for years over that, I've tried to never go back on my word again.*

There were few parking spots left at the café when he drove past it after church. He tapped the brakes and slowed down, but all he could see in the windows were people sitting at tables and in booths. He could picture Lila practically jogging between customers as she took orders, served them, and kept everyone's drinks filled. Her black ponytail would be flipping from side to side. She'd be smiling at Fred and Paul's banter. And those tight jeans would stretch over her butt, and her T-shirt would hug her breasts.

When he got to his mother's house, he untucked his shirt, more to cover the bulge behind his zipper than for comfort. He removed his hat at the front door and hung it on a hook beside Jace's on a hall tree in the foyer. He could hear three distinct women's voices in the kitchen—his mother, Valerie; Granny Hope; and his sister, Kasey. Jace was in the living room surrounded by three kids all begging him to go outside with them. Brody slipped down the hallway to his old bedroom and slumped down in a rocking chair.

"Hey." Kasey poked her head in the door a few minutes later. "Dinner is on the table. Rustin said he thought he saw you coming this way. Everything okay?"

Brody shook his head. "No, but there's no one to blame but me."

"Want to talk about it?"

He pushed out of the rocking chair and draped an arm around her shoulders. "Short version. I really hurt Lila the night before she left town. We had a date, a real one where I was going to take her to dinner and to the movies."

Kasey whistled through her teeth. "Did Granny and Mama know about it?"

He shook his head. "Nobody did but me and Lila. I stood her up and when I tried to apologize the next day, right as she was leaving, she wouldn't talk to me."

Kasey stepped back and popped him on the bicep. "I

wouldn't have talked to you either. I might have shot you. You liked her a lot. Why would you do that?"

He grabbed his arm and winced. "Damn, Kasey, that smarted. To answer your question, I couldn't bear to see her cry."

"That's not a good reason or even a good excuse," Kasey said. "She was probably floating on cloud nine and then you didn't show up. God, Brody, that's terrible."

"I blew it with her and now all these years later..." He hung his head and let the sentence hang.

"Maybe she'll forgive you if you show her that you really care," Kasey said as she started walking again. "But just between me and you, I wouldn't."

Emma patted the chair beside her when they reached the dining room. "Right here, Uncle Brody."

Jace said grace and then it got loud. Plates, platters, and bowls were passed. Brody cut Emma's meat into small pieces while he listened to her talk about butterflies and kittens.

"So what's on your agenda for the rest of the afternoon, Brody?" his mother asked.

"I'm going out to check on Sundance, to make sure that he hasn't broken through the fence again. I was gone two nights and that wild critter is like a kid. He has to have constant supervision. Then I'm going to Sunday night services," he said.

The room went uncomfortably quiet for several seconds; then Rustin slapped a hand on either side of his face. "Why would you do that? Church is boring."

"Rustin!" Kasey gasped.

"It is." Emma nodded.

"Is it because Lila might be at church tonight?" Valerie

passed the green beans to him, and he sent them on to Jace without taking any.

"You got to eat your beans or you don't get any cake, and Nana made a pecan pie too." Rustin tucked his chin down on his chest and looked across the table at Brody.

Brody motioned to Jace and the bowl came back to him. "I sure wouldn't want to miss out on Mama's pie."

"You didn't answer me," Valerie said.

"Could be," he said. "But if she's not, I know how to knock on her door."

Hope rolled her eyes and Valerie shot a dirty look his way.

Brody fixed his eyes on the green beans. He wasn't arguing or fighting with either one of them but his mind was made up. He was going to church and hopefully Lila would be there.

"Guess I'm going to church tonight," Hope said.

"Me too." Kasey nodded.

"I wouldn't miss this for all the dirt in Texas." Jace grinned.

"What's going on here?" Brody asked.

"We want to see if the clouds part. You haven't been to Sunday night services since your grandpa died. You usually only go on Sunday morning," Hope answered.

"He didn't go to Sunday morning," Brody said defensively. "So I waited and went with him to night services. Besides, I always liked to hear him sing."

"Well, if y'all are going, then I am too," Valerie said.

Brody shoveled green beans into his mouth. They might get more than they bargained for, but hey, it was their decision.

* * *

The buzz in the packed café at lunch that day was that the old grocery store out on the edge of town had burned to the ground that morning while church was going on. A tornado had ripped off the back part of the roof ten years ago and the building had gone to ruin since then.

"Where were you this morning about ten o'clock?" Fred whispered when Lila set his plate of chicken and dumplings on the table.

"Right here helping Molly make those dumplings," Lila answered with a smile.

"Does seem strange," Fred's wife said. "We ain't had trouble since you left and you come back and it starts all over again. Maybe you don't have to do anything at all. Could be that trouble follows you around like a puppy dog."

"Well, I'll be gone at the end of summer and nothing bad will ever happen in Happy from that day forth. Maybe if you find a buyer for this café, I'll be gone even sooner. Y'all enjoy your dinner and holler if you need anything," Lila said.

"Order up!" Molly yelled from the kitchen.

When Lila reached for the plate on the shelf, Molly turned around from the stove and smiled. "Blamin' you for this mornin's fire, are they?"

"How'd you know?"

"I figured it would happen when I heard the fire engine going and heard that the old grocery store burned to the ground. The volunteer firemen have been tryin' to get the owner to let them burn it for years."

"Why didn't he?" she asked.

"Have no idea, but it's good riddance to bad rubbish. That thing was an eyesore. I wouldn't be surprised if the owner set the fire himself. When the store went belly-up, he moved off to San Antonio. The property has been for sale so long that the Realtor's sign has faded until you can't see who to call for information." Molly went back to filling orders. "Don't let them rile you. Tell 'em all to go straight to hell ridin' on a rusty poker."

"That's bad for business."

"Where else they goin' to eat without driving fifteen to thirty minutes?" Molly laughed.

The café cleared out a little by one-thirty, but there were still a few sipping glass after glass of sweet tea or coffee and discussing the fire. At two-thirty, Molly started cleaning the kitchen and putting the last of the dirty dishes in the two commercial-sized dishwashers. There was no one in the place at three when Lila locked the doors and started sweeping the floors.

Molly waved from the door into the kitchen. "I'm going home for my Sunday afternoon nap. I'll pick you up right here at six-thirty for evening services. I like to get there a little early and visit with my friends before the singin' starts at seven."

Lila leaned on the broom. "I'm not going to church."

"Yes, you are. Churchgoin' women do not set fires," Molly declared. "See you at six-thirty. And wear a dress."

"Okay," Lila sighed. "But I'll drive myself and be there at a quarter to seven."

"Promise? It won't hurt you and you'll see a lot of your old friends."

And all those old friends probably think I burned down

a building just for kicks. The only thing I ever set fire to was a tire Jace Dawson got out of the ranch trash pile. And it was in the middle of Main Street where it couldn't hurt a thing. It stirred up smoke and a big stink, but it didn't destroy property.

"I'll be there. Have a good nap," Lila said.

She got everything ready to open again the next morning and carried a tall glass of water with a slice of lemon in it to a table. She kicked off her boots, sat down, and propped her feet on a chair. Tomorrow she intended to drag out her sneakers with a nice thick, cushy sole. Running the café was a seven, six, six job—seven days a week from six in the morning until six in the evening, except Sunday when they closed at three.

Her eyes grew heavy, so she picked up her water in one hand and the boots in the other and padded through the kitchen. She made sure all the doors were locked before she went to the apartment and stretched out on the sofa.

A ping on her cell phone awoke her two hours later. She checked the text, saw that it was from Molly reminding her about church, and shut her eyes for another few minutes. Then she realized that she had twenty minutes to get dressed and get to the church or she might be running the café single-handed tomorrow. She sat up so fast that the room did a couple of fast spins.

She jerked her shirt over her head and was yanking her jeans down as she rushed to her bedroom. No time for a shower. She applied fresh deodorant and shook her hair out of the ponytail, slipped into a cute little knee-length orange sundress, and cussed loud enough to blister the paint when she had to search for both sandals in the bin of shoes she hadn't unpacked yet. In the garage, she eyed the motorcycle but the rumor mill would have a feast with the story of her riding to church with her skirt blown up, showing off a pair of red bikini underbritches.

She did take a moment when she reached the church to flip down the visor mirror of her truck and apply bright red lipstick and a touch of mascara and run a brush through her hair. Then she rushed into the church and located Molly, who frowned, tapped her watch, and gave her a you-were-testing-my-patience look before she pointed at the third pew from the front. Now wasn't that just the big old red cherry on top of a hot caramel sundae? Lila would have been much happier claiming a corner on the backseat where she could escape quickly after the last prayer.

"I overslept and had to rush," she whispered.

"Next time set an alarm. Them fancy phones y'all carry can do everything, including telling you bedtime stories, so there's never an excuse to be late for anything," Molly said out of the corner of her mouth.

The preacher took his place behind the pulpit and cleared his throat, and silence filled the little church. "I'm glad to see Lila Harris with us tonight and to hear that she's helping out at the Happy Café. Now, if you'll all open your hymn books to page three hundred, we'll sing together before the sermon."

The hymn ended and the preacher made a few comments about hell being seven times hotter than the Texas heat wave. That brought out a few chuckles, and Lila was sure if she turned around, she'd see more than one person using those cardboard fans to ward off such fire and brimstone.

"And now I will ask Brody Dawson to give the benediction," the preacher said.

Lila's heart stopped, then raced ahead, beating twice as hard as it ever had. From his voice, it was plain that he was only a couple of pews behind her, but she couldn't hear a word he said for the pounding in her ears. Her cheeks turned fire-engine red as she remembered the kiss from the night before.

Any second the skies were going to go dark and lightning was going to split through the roof and zap her dead for thinking about the heat she'd felt when Brody kissed her. She glanced out the window to see nothing but big, fluffy white clouds and the sun slowly sinking toward the horizon. Evidently God had given her a pass since she hadn't been in a church since she left Happy and he was just glad to see her sitting in a pew.

She heard Molly loudly say, "Amen!" so she knew when to raise her head and open her eyes.

Molly smiled as she stood to her feet. "Didn't hurt too bad, did it?"

"What?" Lila asked.

Molly bumped shoulders with her. "Coming to church."

"Hey, Lila," a feminine voice said at her elbow. "You haven't changed a bit."

"Kasey? It's great to see you, and, darlin', you look the same as you did in junior high school. Are these your kids?" She smiled.

"Yep, these three belong to me. This is Rustin." Kasey pointed toward a little dark-haired boy with blue eyes. "This is Emma, and this critter here on my hip is Silas."

"You've got a beautiful family. Emma is the image of

you at that age. Bring the kids to the café sometime and I'll treat them to an ice cream sundae and we'll catch up."

"Yes!" Rustin pumped his fist in the air. "Can we go tomorrow, Mama?"

"Maybe later in the week. Tomorrow all three of you're spending the day with your nana." She winked at Lila. "That's Adam's mother. You remember Gracie McKay, right? And we will take you up on that offer, Lila. Maybe later in the week?"

"Any day that's good for you. I look forward to it," she answered.

"Does the invitation extend to me too?" Brody's warm breath tickled her neck as he stepped out into the center aisle.

"Only kids under twelve get free ice cream. You might not be older than that mentally but your size gives away your age." Lila hoped that her voice didn't sound as high and squeaky to everyone else as it did in her own ears.

Kasey giggled and nudged Brody on the shoulder. "You've met your match, brother. You've got to pay for your ice cream."

"Is that right, Lila?" His eyes bored into hers.

Neither of them blinked for several seconds and then she smiled. "Yes, it is right. Free ice cream comes at a great price. You'd have to rob a bank to get that much money."

Suddenly, a tiny little hand slipped into hers and she looked down to see Emma smiling at her. "I like ice cream," the little girl said. "And you're pretty. Can I be your friend?"

"I would like that very much and you're very pretty

too." Lila ignored all the people around her and stooped to Emma's level. "What is your favorite kind of ice cream?"

"Strawberry," Emma said seriously.

"Then I'll be sure that we have lots of that kind when you come to visit me sometime this week."

Emma nodded. "And will you read me a story?"

"That's what good friends do, isn't it?" Lila answered. "But I don't have any books that I can read to you, so maybe you'd better bring your favorite one with you that day."

" 'I will bring ABC. C is for camel. C. C. C,' " Emma quoted.

"Dr. Seuss?" Lila glanced over toward Kasey.

"Her favorite, but...," Kasey said.

Lila stood back up. "I would love to read to the kids. Please pack a couple of books to bring along. Most any evening is good for me. Just give me a call."

"Thank you." Kasey smiled.

Lila shook hands with the preacher and was ten feet away from her truck when she realized that Brody was parked next to her. Standing there, with his arms crossed over his chest, wearing a white pearl-snap shirt and creased jeans, he flat out took her breath away. By the time she reached her truck, he'd dropped his arms to his side and opened her door.

"You look very pretty tonight," he said.

"Thanks."

"I'll see you sometime tomorrow at the café if I can sneak away for a few minutes or if I have to come into town to the feed store."

"For real or will you change your mind?"

"Not this time, darlin'," he said as he shut the door.

Lila sat in the hot truck, sweat rolling down into her bra, heart pounding and her thoughts running around in circles for a long time before she finally switched on the air-conditioning. Being angry at him when he was hundreds of miles away and when he wasn't standing so close that she could have touched him was a whole different ball game.

Chapter Six

Lila danced around the café with the broom to Gretchen Wilson's "Redneck Woman." The singer asked for a big hell, yeah, from the redneck girls like her and the broom turned into a microphone. From then on, Lila lip-synced the rest of the song and then hit the replay button on her phone so she could get the message out there to the whole empty café.

The beat was still pounding in her ears as she two-stepped the broom back to the kitchen, where she kept it in one hand and loaded a tray with ice cream toppings with the other. In a few minutes, Kasey and the kids were coming for an ice cream party and she'd looked forward to the evening all week.

She carried the tray to the dining room and set it on a table that she'd covered with a red and white checkered cloth. She wanted it to be a real party for the kids and for Kasey.

It had been a crazy week. On Monday, Brody had come into the café, had a glass of lemonade, and didn't even get to drink it before he got a call from the ranch about fencing. On Wednesday he dropped by again but didn't even get to sit down before Jace phoned saying that they needed six more rolls of barbed wire, so he turned around and left. On Thursday a florist brought a single red rose with a pretty white ribbon around it. The note said: *Welcome home. Brody.* Molly was fit to be tied when she put the rose in a pint jar.

"I'm tellin' you that you're on the road to heartache," Molly fussed.

"All over a single rose?" Lila asked.

"Just that much will bring Hope and Valerie out gunnin' for you," Molly had said.

"I'm not a kid anymore. I'll take them on," she'd answered.

He didn't come around at all on Friday but Kasey had called that morning to see if she and the kids could come to the café for ice cream about six-thirty that evening. Lila had been so excited all day, just thinking about reading to the kids. She went back to the kitchen and placed five crystal boat dishes on a tray. The last time they'd been used was probably for her sixteenth birthday but they'd only needed two that night—one for her and one for her mother. She heard doors slamming and hurried back to the kitchen to bring out four flavors of ice cream. She hummed all the way back into the dining room.

The door flew open and Emma's short little legs were a blur as she ran across the floor to meet her, but Rustin stood back close to Brody's side. Lila stopped so fast that the cartons of ice cream started to slide and it took some fancy footwork to keep them steady. Even blinking a dozen times didn't magically turn Brody into Kasey.

"Hey, Lila. Kasey got one of her migraines about thirty minutes ago." He lowered his voice. "I can't stand to see Emma disappointed. So I hope you don't mind getting me instead?"

For the first time in many years, Lila was totally speechless. He looked like he was afraid she was going to kick him out of the café. And she wanted to set the tray on the table, hug him, and assure him that it was fine.

"Thank you for bringing them and of course it's all right. I couldn't disappoint that precious child either." Her voice finally came out hollow and slightly breathless. "Emma says her favorite is strawberry. What's yours, Rustin?"

"Chocolate." He crawled up in a chair, pulled a napkin free of the dispenser, and tucked it into the neck of his T-shirt. "We already had our baths and Mama said not to get all messy."

Rustin's dark hair still had a few droplets of water hanging on it. Emma's braids were damp and Silas's blond curls kinked all over his head. She could never deny the kids, or herself either for that matter, the party—even if Brody was there.

"I bet Silas likes chocolate with whipped cream on top, right?" Lila reached for the baby and he didn't even hesitate before holding out his little arms.

"He loves anything chocolate." Brody's arm brushed across hers in the transfer. The tension, sparks, and heat were so steamy that it was a pure miracle the ice cream didn't melt.

"I'll get a booster for Emma and a high chair for Silas," Brody said.

"Bananas!" Emma peered over the top of the table.

"Whipped cream and cherries. Yummy." Rustin rubbed his tummy. "This is the bestest party ever."

Emma poked a finger in his shoulder. "Lila is my friend, not yours."

"I'll be everyone's friend." Lila settled Silas into the high chair that Brody brought from the far end of the café.

"Everyone's? Does that include the ones that are too old for free ice cream?" Brody set the booster in a chair and then helped Emma into it.

"Depends on lots of things," she answered.

"I don't need a booster anymore," Rustin said. "I'm a big kid and someday I'm going to stink just like Uncle Brody."

Lila locked eyes with Brody. The toughest cowboy in the whole state of Texas was blushing.

"Sometimes Uncle Brody stinks," Emma whispered, and her little nose twitched. "You don't stink. You smell good, like Mama's perfume when she's gettin' all pretty. Uncle Brody took a bath, so he don't stink no more, either."

"Man, she talks plain," Lila said.

"Since the day she said her first word. She has to keep pace with Rustin." Brody chuckled. "But she's right. You do smell really good. And this cowboy refuses to let us feed him anymore." He pulled a bib from his hip pocket and fastened it around the baby's neck. "Can I help with anything, Miss Lila?"

"I'll scoop and you can put on the toppings," she answered. "Let's start with Silas."

The baby pointed to the container of chocolate as soon as she opened it.

"He's gotten real definite in what he likes and doesn't. Anything that has orange flavor isn't his thing," Brody said.

"Must run in the family." She dipped out a big round scoop of ice cream and put it in one of the fancy dishes.

Their eyes met over the table.

"I still don't," he whispered. "Surprised that you remembered that detail."

"Like I told you." She tapped her forehead with a forefinger. "I remember everything."

"Banana?" she asked.

The baby nodded several times.

"Whipped cream?"

He shook his head.

"Guess he really does know what he likes."

"Uncle Brody don't like whipped cream neither and he don't eat the white stuff on chocolate pie," Rustin said. "Mama says that Silas is just like him but I don't think he'll stink as bad as I will when I'm a cowboy. I get to haul hay when I'm ten and I'd like a banana and whipped cream and two cherries on top and some of that chocolate syrup."

"And I just want plain old strawberry. And a banana to eat all by itself," Emma said. "These dishes sure are fancy."

"My mama used them for special times." Lila filled the dishes and slid them across the table for Brody to do the rest.

"So tonight is special?" Brody asked.

"Anytime I can spend an hour with three kids falls into that category. What can I get for you?" she asked.

"I thought free ice cream was only for kids under twelve," he drawled.

"Rules change when the place is officially closed." If someone had told her a month ago that she'd be spending a Friday evening with Brody and three kids in her café, she'd have thought they were certifiably insane.

"Double dip of vanilla with caramel topping and a layer of nuts over that," he said. "Next to pumpkin pie, this is my favorite dessert."

She dug down deep into the container and heaped each scoop.

"What are you having?" he asked as he poured caramel on the top of his ice cream.

"One of each," she answered as she fixed her sundae. "With whipped cream and nuts and a cherry for each flavor."

Rustin grabbed his forehead. "Too much. Too cold."

Lila felt the same way. Too much Brody but not too cold. Much too hot. She rushed over to the counter and filled a pitcher with tap water, and took it back to the table with a stack of unbreakable glasses.

Filling a glass half full, she handed it to the child. "Drink this and it will get better real quick."

He tipped it up and swallowed several times before he set it down. "That's magic water." He grinned.

"I want magic," Emma declared.

"She can't let Rustin get a step ahead of her," Brody said in a low voice.

His whisper was every bit as sexy as his deep Texas

drawl. If a doctor could invent a pill to take care of that crazy infatuation called first love, he could sell it for a fortune and retire with enough money to buy a remote island.

Lila poured water into a glass and gave it to Emma. Brody reached into the diaper bag and brought out a sippy cup and handed it to her. She was careful not to touch his fingertips but that didn't keep the electricity between them from sparking. When was that doctor going to get busy and create those pills?

* * *

Brody kicked back in a booth where he could see Lila reading the second book to the kids. She was even more adorable sitting on the floor covered in kids than she'd been with that dollop of chocolate stuck to her lip a few minutes before. He'd wanted to lick it away with a kiss but—there always seemed to be a lot of buts in his roller coaster of relationships with Lila.

Rustin sat on one side, and Emma and Silas had both managed to crawl into her lap. Were all the men in the states where she'd lived total idiots?

His phone vibrated in his back pocket. His sister's picture appeared on the screen and he hit the button to answer. "We're on the second story, so we'll be home soon. Are you feeling better?"

"Are the kids behaving? Better yet, are you?" Kasey asked.

"We're all having a great time. They'll be full of sugar and want to tell you about it as soon as we get home," he said.

"Good. I'm going to lie right here on the sofa until you get here."

"Need anything?"

"Not a thing," Kasey said. "Tell Lila thank you."

He stole long glances at Lila. Those could be their three kids in her lap if he'd done the right thing that last night like he should have.

Silas crawled out of Lila's lap and toddled over to where Brody was sitting and raised his arms. Brody got out of the booth and took the little guy into his arms. Someday he was going to have a house full of kids just like these three. Kids who would snuggle down into his chest like this and a wife who was willing to sit on the floor and read to them like Lila did.

"I think it's getting close to bedtime for this little guy. We should be going. Rustin and Emma?"

"Thank you." Rustin threw his arms around Lila's neck. "I like it that you can be my friend too. When I'm a big cowboy, I'm going to dance with you."

"I'm going to remind you of that when you're a big cowboy." Lila grinned.

Brody was jealous of his nephew for putting that twinkle in her eyes. Granny Hope said that you can't fool kids or dogs. But Brody Dawson was living proof that idiot cowboys were a different matter.

Emma yawned. "Me and you can paint fingernails and chase butterflies."

"I'd like that." Lila hugged her. "Maybe next time your mama will feel better and can come with y'all."

Emma laid her head on Lila's shoulder. "You will sit by me at the rodeo."

"We've taken enough of Miss Lila's time, kids."

Brody offered his free hand to help Lila get to her feet.

To his surprise, she didn't shake her head but put her hand in his. "Thank you for bringing them. It's been a lovely evening."

Rustin craned his neck back to look up at her. "It's not a rodeo. It's a bull riding and Uncle Brody and Uncle Jace are going to ride in it. I'm goin' to win the sheep ridin'."

"I bet you will," Lila said. "Do you have sheep out on Hope Springs?"

"No, but Uncle Brody and Uncle Jace made me a ridin' thing that they pull the ropes and it tries to buck me off. I'll be ready," Rustin answered.

Brody threw the diaper bag over his shoulder and headed for the door. "Well, we have to get out of here or your mama will send all the hired hands out to look for us."

"So you're ridin'? When?" Lila asked.

"Tomorrow night but it's not a big thing. Just a bunch of us local guys havin' some fun and the admission fees all go to a family between here and Tulia who lost their home in a fire last week."

"And you clearly don't want me sittin' with Emma," she said.

"I don't care where you sit," he said. "If you do want to go, it's five dollars at the gate and there will be a few vendors selling stuff."

Lila took a step forward into his space. "Still don't want to be seen in public with me, do you?"

"I won't even be in the stands. I'll either be riding or helping out with the chutes," he argued. "And I'd say that the rose I sent would let everyone know that I didn't care what they thought."

"Thank you for the rose, but, Brody, this isn't my home. I'm just passing through for a few weeks to help my mama sell this place." She caught his gaze and refused to blink.

"You're very welcome, and..."

"No ifs, ands, or buts. That's the way it is," she said.

"I see. Well, thanks for having us." His tone turned cold.

Emma tugged the leg of Brody's jeans. "Are you fighting with my friend?"

"No, darlin'." Lila stooped down to her level. "We are havin' a big-people discussion, not a fight. You enjoy the rodeo and maybe in a couple of years you'll be in the mutton ride."

Emma puffed out her chest. "I will ride a bull."

"And I bet you'll be really good at it, Emma." Lila stood up. "Y'all sleep tight and have sweet dreams."

"Thanks for the ice cream." Brody hurried the kids out to the van and got them situated.

"I love Lila," Emma said.

"Me too. I'm goin' to dance with her," Rustin said. "You won't care, will you, Uncle Brody?"

"Why would you ask that?"

"Because Uncle Jace says you got to ask a cowboy for his okay before you dance with his woman," Rustin answered.

Brody looked back over the seat. "What makes you think that she's my woman?"

"If she ain't, then what's wrong with you?" Rustin threw up his hands in exasperation. "We love her and Mama says she's a good person."

"You're five years old, boy, not fifteen," Brody chuckled.

Rustin crossed his arms over his chest. "Well, do I have to ask if I can dance with her or not?"

"When you get to be a big cowboy, we'll talk about it then," Brody told him.

"Shhh, Silas is sleepin'." Emma shushed them.

He was about to start the engine when he heard a tap on the window. Turning, he saw that Lila was standing there in the shadows, looking like an angel. He hit the button to roll down the window.

"I wanted to thank you for that beautiful rose. I didn't thank you properly. I would have called but I don't have your number," she said.

"Are red roses still your favorite?" He removed an ink pen from the visor and reached for her hand.

Without a moment's hesitation, she stuck it out and he wrote his number down on her palm. "Call me anytime, night or day."

"Yes, red roses are my favorite. Probably always will be. Well, I'd better get back inside. I enjoyed the kids this evening. Thanks for bringing them." She turned around and went back to the café.

"I'll buy her roses," Rustin said.

"Me too," Emma said. "I'll buy more than you will."

"Will not!"

"Will too."

"That's enough or you'll both wake Silas." He started the engine and Vince Gill's voice came on the radio singing "Feels Like Love." Brody could relate to every single word, especially when the lyrics said that it felt like love wanted a second chance.

Kasey met them at the door when they got home. Her

eyes were still bleary and her face said that the pain wasn't completely gone but she had a smile on her face. "Did y'all have a good time?"

"Lila is goin' to be my girlfriend when I grow up," Rustin said.

"She's my friend and you can't have her," Emma declared.

"And you?" Kasey asked, glancing at her brother.

"It was good ice cream but I like your pumpkin pie better," he said. "How's the headache now?"

"Functional now that I had a couple of hours to lie down with an ice pack. Thanks for taking them. Would you please put Silas in his crib for me?"

Brody carried Silas to the bedroom and gently laid him in the crib. He removed the boy's sandals and handed them to Kasey.

"I bet he doesn't even wake up when I change his diaper and clothing," Kasey said.

"I'll do that while you get the other kids into bed."

"She rattles you, don't she?" Kasey whispered.

"Little bit," Brody said.

"Lila is going to sit with me at the rodeo," Emma said from the doorway.

"Well, that sounds like fun. Let's get you into bed and you can tell me which two books Lila read to you." Kasey took her hand and led her across the hallway.

Rustin had toothpaste on his lips when he came from the bathroom. He peeled out of his clothes and tossed them on a chair. "Mama says I have to wear a T-shirt to sleep but Uncle Jace sleeps naked. Do you have to wear a shirt, too, or do you get to sleep without no clothes?"

Brody chuckled. "We'll talk about that later on too."

Rustin sighed. "I got a lot of growin' to do."

"Yes, you do." Brody finished with Silas and tucked Rustin into bed. "But don't get in too big of a hurry, son. Once you're a big man, you can't go back and be a little one again."

"But bein' a big one looks like so much more fun." Rustin yawned.

"Not all the time." Brody kissed him on the forehead. "Good night, little cowboy."

"Night, Uncle Brody."

Back in the kitchen, he found Kasey with a cup of coffee in her hands.

"You sure you're all right? You don't usually drink caffeine this late."

"It helps with the headache. I don't get them often anymore but today is the anniversary of the first time that Adam kissed me. I guess I thought too much about losing him."

He opened his arms. "I'm so sorry that you have to go through this, sis."

She set the cup on the cabinet and walked into his embrace. "It helps to be here at home with y'all. The kids have grandparents and relatives. It's just that letting go is so hard. Now, what's this about Lila sitting with us at the bull riding?"

He raked both hands through his hair. "I sent her a rose this week, but she made it clear she's not sticking around Happy for the long haul. Why start something that will just cause both of us to get hurt again?"

"Do you have any idea what I'd give to have Adam sitting beside me at that bull riding? I'd use every bit of my strength to talk him into getting out of the army and staying in Happy and going into the ranchin' business with his dad. I'd do anything to keep him with me, even live in a tent under a pecan tree with no indoor plumbing. You've got an opportunity here, brother, that might not come your way again." She laid her head on his shoulder and sobbed.

His heart broke for her and at the same time for Lila. He couldn't bear to see her hurt again, and if she went to sit with Emma...well, it could be a damn disaster. Little Emma was already going to be sad when Lila left. Getting even closer to the woman would make it tougher.

Who are you preachin' at? Emma or yourself? that aggravating voice in his head asked.

Kasey took a few steps back and carried her coffee to the table. "The whole time I was growing up, Lila was my idol because she was such a daredevil. I didn't want to be like her. I wanted to be her. And for your information, that crap about her burning down the old grocery store is just that—a load of crap. The fire department said someone probably threw a cigarette out because they could see a trail from the road to the building."

"I didn't think that she burned down anything. I'm going out for a ride to clear my mind."

"Get over her, Brody, or man up and do something about the way you feel." Kasey swiped a kitchen towel across her eyes.

His brow furrowed so tight that a pain shot through his head. "I got over Lila Harris years ago."

"Yeah, right," Kasey said. "Like I got over losing Adam."

"I'm not having this conversation with you, sis." He

snapped his mouth shut and left her in the kitchen with a cup of coffee and a headache.

* * *

Brody peeled the T-shirt over his head and grabbed his last clean pearl-snapped one from the closet. In no time he was back in his truck, heading north to the Silver Spur and hoping that it was jumping with noise and excitement—anything to take his mind off the picture in his mind of Lila sitting on the floor reading to three little kids.

Two miles out of town he took his foot off the gas and tapped the brakes. He pulled off to the side of the road and sat there for several minutes before he turned around and went back home. He drove straight to the corral where Sundance was kept and sat down on the ground, bracing his back against a fence post. The bull eyed him from across the corral but stayed his distance.

"I've messed up again, old boy," Brody said. "It was all goin' good until the kids mentioned the bull riding. I've been going by every day so that she can see I'm keeping my word when I tell her that I'll see her tomorrow. Lila is so different from other women that I think fate or God or destiny is hitting me in the head with a two-by-four and yet I keep thinking about my responsibility for this ranch. I have to make it grow. I have to leave it bigger than it was when it was put in my hands. Lila doesn't need a man who is already married to a ranch. I work most days from daylight to past dark. She deserves someone better than that."

Sundance bawled once at the moon and stuck his head into the water trough.

"That all you got to say? Well, this ranch pays for your comforts, so you can listen to me," Brody said. "I don't like this feeling, so I'm going home. Thanks for the therapy session."

The bull snorted and turned his back on Brody.

Chapter Seven

Lila stopped by the rodeo's concession stand and bought a big dill pickle, an order of nachos, and a bottle of root beer. The bottle went into her purse and the pickle in the side of the cardboard container with the nachos. That way she could make it to the top of the stands without dropping anything. She was halfway when she saw the Dawson family all sitting with the grand matriarch, Hope Dalley, down at the other end of the rough wooden bleachers. She kept going until she was at the very top and sat down on the end of the empty row.

Dust boiled in the arena as the first cowboy lasted all of three seconds on a big bruiser of a bull. The clowns in all their bright, outlandish costumes hurried out to lure the bull away from him so the cowboy could get up, take a bow to the folks in the stand, and swagger back to the chutes.

A chip covered with cheese and jalapeños was halfway to her mouth when she saw Brody's tall figure disappear down into the chute. The chip fell from her hands, splattering on the toes of her boots, but she didn't even look down. Her breath caught in her chest, tightening it into a dull ache.

When she decided to attend the bull riding, the last thing she expected was such an explosion of emotions rattling around in her heart and soul.

"Devil Dog is a tough bull to ride, and Daniel has only been riding six months, so let's give him another big hand." The announcer's booming voice filled the place. "Better luck next time, Daniel. You've got the makings of a fine bull rider. And now coming out of chute two is Brody Dawson riding Barbed Wire, a young bull destined for great things. Brody is no stranger to riding bulls. He's been doing it since he was in high school. He is the co-owner now of Hope Springs Ranch right here in Happy, Texas. He's testing the rope and getting his hat set just right and..." The announcer paused and all noise stopped. Then he yelled, "The chute is open!"

Yelling and whistling began the minute that the bull came out with both hind feet in the air. Barbed Wire twisted around until his head was practically touching his tail and then he whipped back around, almost putting his big wide horns on the ground. Two seconds down, six to go when Lila clasped her hands together so tightly that they hurt.

Brody kept one hand in the air but his straw hat flew off after the first two seconds and the bull stomped it into the dirt. Four seconds, halfway through the ride. Lila wanted to shut her eyes but she couldn't.

Six seconds into the ride, Brody went flying over the top of Barbed Wire's head and landed on his side. She jumped to her feet so fast that the rest of her nachos went flying everywhere. *Please, God, let him get up.*

He quickly scrambled to his feet and she plopped down with a thud. Then she realized that the bull was right behind him. She was back on her feet, mouth open but no words came out. The noise in the stands sounded as if it were a mile away. The bull got closer and closer. Lila's racing pulse thumped in her ears, blotting out the whoops and hollers from the crowd cheering him on. Then Brody slapped one hand down on the top fence rail and cleared it in a graceful jump. She let out the pent-up air in her lungs in a long whoosh.

One of the clowns grabbed Brody's hat and made a big show of popping it back into some kind of shape. Another one stole it from him and ran toward the fence. On the way the third one snatched it and took it straight to Brody, who settled it on his head and took a bow to his screaming fans.

With her heart doing double time and the only one in the whole stands still on her feet, she lost sight of him as he rounded the arena and headed toward the chutes. The announcer was introducing the next rider when she finally slumped back down into her seat. The next rider came out and it was an exciting eight seconds, but it didn't produce nearly the adrenaline rush of Brody's ride.

* * *

When Brody reached the chutes, Jace handed him a cold beer. He rubbed it across his forehead before he washed the dirt from between his teeth with a long swallow. "That Barbed Wire is one mean hunk of bull."

"But he could help a rider rack up the points. He's pure evil," Jace said.

"So when is it your turn?" Brody asked.

"Last one on the docket. They're saving the best until last," Jace teased. "Lila is in the stands."

"When did she get here?" Brody located his family. There was Emma in her pink cowboy hat and Rustin pointing at the clowns but no Lila. His eyes swept the stands a section at a time until he located her at the very top.

"She saw you ride, if that's what you're askin'." Jace grinned. "Now she knows you aren't perfect."

"She's known that for years," Brody said.

"Yeah, right." Jace air slapped Brody on the arm. "All I've heard since this morning from Rustin and Emma is Lila's name. I heard about the ice cream and the reading but mostly they talked about how they wished she lived on the ranch with them."

"She was really good with the kids last night." Brody nodded.

Jace nodded. "I'd better warn you. Granny was not happy about you taking the kids to the café. She didn't mind if Kasey did, but not you."

"I'm thirty years old and both Granny and Mama can mind their own business and let me take care of mine," Brody growled.

"I hear you and so do they, but they don't believe it like I do. Granny told Kasey that the two of you were going to have a long talk," Jace told him.

"Please tell me you're kiddin'," Brody moaned.

"Wish I was but she said she was coming to our house tonight right after the riding. You might want to offer to do a second ride so you'll have an excuse to soak the soreness out of your muscles until she gets bored and goes on to her house," Jace said.

"I'll give you a hundred dollars for your ride. You can say that you decided to get into your clown gear and help the guys out," Brody said.

Jace laughed. "If you got hurt, she'd sit beside your hospital bed all night. You've always been her favorite."

Brody swiped sweat from his forehead with his palm. "I'd thought about going to sit with the family after my ride, but I think I'll stay down here and help with the chutes. And I'm not her favorite. I was just the firstborn, so she's had a little longer to smother me."

"No gripe from me. I'll let you be the favorite because you have to endure the consequences. And you're welcome for the warning, brother."

Brody clamped a hand on his brother's shoulder. "Thanks."

Jace handed him a second can of beer. "Anytime. We learned a long time ago when it comes to Granny's meddling that we have to stick together."

Brody found an old metal folding chair behind a chute and popped it open. He sat down and propped his boots on the rails of the chute where Barbed Wire was still penned up.

"Don't you snort around at me. You won that battle, but this isn't the last time we'll cross paths this summer, and next time I'll win." Brody raised his can toward the bull.

He could see Lila at the top of the stands all alone.

She was sipping on either a bottle of pop or a beer. When she finished, she got to her feet and started down toward the concession stand. A couple of cowboys stopped her, their body language saying clearly that they were hitting on her and hers leaving no doubt that they'd been refused. She waited in line at the concession and exchanged a few words with a couple of women, using her hands as she talked to them like she'd done back in high school. He remembered telling her once that if he tied her hands behind her back she wouldn't be able to say a word.

She bought something at the concession stand and then headed off toward the gate. He pushed out of the chair and leaned on a rail so he could watch her disappear into the darkness.

* * *

Lila set the nachos on the passenger seat in her truck beside two cans of cat food. She'd thought she'd pass plumb out when Brody hit the dirt, but the next two riders, though exciting, didn't affect her like those six seconds had when she'd watched Brody try to hang on to the rope. When her heart finally slowed down, it was time to go on the mission that she'd planned after the bull ride. One would involve being a Good Samaritan and giving a black and white cat a good home. The other would mean she was blowing the bottom out of that commandment about stealing because she wasn't going home without a cat.

She drove to the cemetery and parked in front of her father's grave. "Daddy, I want something to talk to and to cuddle with me while I watch television at night. If you've got any connections with a cat whisperer up there—" She tilted her head back to get a better view of the full moon and stars. "You might tell that homeless critter to show his face or else I'm going out to Henry's old barn and I'm stealing that big white cat. You going to keep me on the straight and narrow or let me fall back into my wild ways?"

She got out of the truck, pulled the tab from the top of the can, set it on the ground, and propped a hip on her father's tombstone. Eating a few of the nachos while she waited, she saw the black and white cat slink out from behind a floral wreath not far away. He sniffed the air and warily made his way to the cat food. Careful not to make a fast move and scare him off, she set the nachos to the side and, speaking in a calm voice, took a step toward the cat.

When she was two feet away, he took one more bite and was nothing more than a blur as he took off into the darkness. She slapped her thigh. "I tried to do it the right way, so I don't think I should be punished for stealing. Besides, Paul might not even know that cat is in his barn. I might be doing him a favor."

Carrying her food back to the truck, she frowned at the stars. She started the engine and drove straight to Henry's old barn. She parked the truck and made her way across the floor—nachos and cat food in a wooden crate in her arms.

"I'm here to get a cat and I'm not leaving without one," she muttered as she sat down on a hay bale, opened the can of food, and dumped it into an old pie pan she'd brought from the café.

She chewed on nachos as she waited. The white cat came out first but it wasn't long before she was surrounded by four kittens. Two black ones, a white one, and a yellow one with four white feet. Lila captured one of the black ones by the scruff of the neck. It clawed and growled, slinging its paws all the way to the crate. In the commotion, the mama cat and two of the other kittens skittered off to hide behind a bale of hay. But the fearless white kitten kept right on eating.

"And you will keep Mr. Feisty here from whining because he has no one to play with." She scooped it up and put it in the crate with the black one and they howled out their anger together. "You'll have a good home and lots of food and I'll pet you every single day. Hawks won't swoop down and carry you away, so stop your bellyachin'."

The big mama cat came back out after a bit and rubbed around her legs. "Good thing those babies came out with you. I'd feel terrible if I took you away from them when they were too young. Are you thanking me for giving them a good home? Well, you're welcome. Now I have something to talk to other than a broom, so thank you, mama cat, for letting me adopt two of your babies."

She put her nacho trash on the top of the crate, and carried the whole thing to the truck, where she set it on the passenger seat. She had driven down to Tulia right after work and bought litter, a pan to put it in, and a dozen cans of cat food. The kittens were going to love their new home once they got used to it. And she'd be willing to bet that Paul would be glad to get rid of the kittens. But to be on the safe side and not get into trouble with that business of thou shalt not steal, she would ask him the next time he came into the café.

Her phone rang as she turned the key to start the engine and she dug around in her purse until she found it. "Hello, Mama. I wasn't expecting a call from you tonight."

"You're in Texas and for the first time in years, I'm homesick. Where are you right now?"

"Out at Henry Thomas's old barn stealing kittens. Paul McKay leases this place and I don't reckon he'll mind. He probably doesn't even know how many there are," she answered.

Daisy gasped. "I was afraid when you crossed the Texas border you'd get crazy."

"It's just kittens. I didn't set fire to anything or borrow a tractor or..."

"Delilah Harris." Daisy's voice went all whispery like it did when Lila was in trouble.

"Would you rather I adopted two children?"

"I definitely would not!" Daisy's voice jacked up an octave. "It's an omen that I got homesick today. Fate is telling me that you need me. I should take the café off the market and move back to Texas."

"I'm doing all right now that I've got something to talk to that breathes and even meows once in a while," Lila said. "Hey, I even went to church last Sunday and Molly says I have to go tomorrow. She's keeping me pretty straight and very busy. So be sure you want to make a drastic move before you talk to Aunt Tina. And remember, Mama, it's hotter'n hell in Texas in the summertime."

"You can't tell me anything about the panhandle of Texas that I don't already know. But it's either sweatin' in

Texas or suffering through butt-deep snow here in Pennsylvania. I can get cool with air-conditioning in Texas."

"But that danged old northern cold can cut right to the bone, can't it?" Lila said.

"Promise me you won't steal anything else."

"I promise, but I'm not giving my word about skinny-dippin' out at Hope Springs."

"Sweet angels in heaven!" Daisy shrieked. "I was right. Texas brings out that wild streak in you."

"Yep, the minute I crossed the line I got the urge to steal something, go skinny-dippin', and make out with Brody Dawson in Henry Thomas's old barn. Blame it on Texas," she laughed.

"I'm not having this conversation with you. Tell me about those cats."

"One is pure white with a little yellow spot on its head and the other is black as sin. Want to help me name them?"

"I do not," Daisy said emphatically. "I'm not going to contribute to your crime spree."

Lila laughed harder that time. "If they throw me in jail for thievery, will you bail me out?"

"No, but I will feed the kittens for you until you serve your time. I'll be glad when you're back in Florida this fall. Now good night," Daisy said.

"Good night, Mama."

* * *

Granny Hope showed up in the kitchen before Brody took the first bite of the chocolate cake he'd put on his plate. She cut out a slab of cake that came close to being too big for the dessert plate and brought the gallon jug of milk with her to the table.

"We need to talk," she said to Brody.

"About?"

"You already know but I'll say it out loud. Lila Harris."

"You talk and I'll listen," he said.

"Have you ever heard the history of Hope Springs?"

"I can recite it to you."

She lowered her chin and looked at him from under arched gray eyebrows. "Don't be a smartass. It don't hurt you to hear a little of this again. You know that I was the fourth-generation owner of Hope Springs. I've been pleased with the way you're doin' things since I turned the place over to you. You and Jace are doin' a great job."

He nodded as respectfully as possible and bit back a yawn.

Hope stopped long enough to take a few bites of cake and drink half a glass of milk. "Since you know the story about my great-grandparents helping get this area settled, I'll skip that part. At the same time Hope Springs was coming into its own as a reputable ranch, the Dawsons were doing really well with their ranches on down the road toward the canyon."

Brody poured another glass of milk. A history lesson was better than a scolding, but so far she had not mentioned Lila, so that might still be on the agenda.

"The rest of what I'm going to say is in confidence. That means it doesn't go any farther than this kitchen. Agree?"

He nodded. She had his full attention.

"The ranch had a reputation to uphold by then. So as the only heir, I had a lot to learn and a tremendous amount of responsibility upon my shoulders. It was a big place by then and I couldn't let my folks down."

Brody had never seen his grandmother flustered. She took the bull by the horns, spit in its face, and dared it to come after her. But that night her eyes kept shifting from one corner of the kitchen to the other.

"It's not easy letting go of the control. I was so tired of making decisions that I thought it would be good to step back and turn it all over to you boys. But I was wrong. I miss the work and all of it," she said.

Scenarios played through Brody's mind at warp speed. In the foremost one his grandmother was about to change her mind about the ranch.

"I feel like a duck in a desert. No water in sight and I can't swim in sand."

He patted her arm. "Sometimes I feel like that, too, and that's when I call you and ask for your advice. You're always going to be needed, Granny. We're all taking baby steps in this whole transfer and we're glad that you decided to stay in Cooter's place so you're nearby. I'm not sure Kasey could handle the load without you to help."

"Thank you, darlin' boy, but that's not the point I'm trying to make. I'm not sure that I can put it into words, and I'm past seventy years old. Your grandpa has been gone a dozen years and without work from daylight to past dark, I'm lonely."

"Granny, do you have a boyfriend?" Brody whispered.

"Good God, no!" she gasped. "I'm tryin' to put my feelin's into words and explain to you how I felt tonight at that bull riding. But in order to do it, I have to say some things I've never told anyone."

"I'm listening." He covered both her hands with his and squeezed gently.

"I was twenty years old the year that Dad hired a new foreman. He came from over near Clovis, New Mexico, and his name was Weston Dalley."

"Grandpa, right?" Brody asked.

"That's right. Wes was twenty-five, a good man and a fine manager. My dad loved him like the son he'd never had." Her eyes misted slightly.

"And so did you evidently," Brody said.

She took a deep breath and let it out slowly, "I did love your grandpa. Don't ever doubt that for a minute. But..." She paused.

"But?" Gramps had been Brody's idol. He didn't want there to be a *but* anywhere in his life or in his relationship with Granny.

"But he was not my first love." She met his gaze and her eyes floated in tears. "Wes was a good man."

She didn't have to convince Brody of that. Wes Dalley was well respected in the whole area and he loved his entire family. In Brody's eyes he was more than just a good man—he could walk on water.

"I've never told anyone this before and I expect you to keep it to yourself."

Brody swallowed hard and nodded in agreement.

"I had an argument with the man I loved. Over Wes. In a fit of anger, this other guy joined the service and I turned to Wes for comfort. We were married six months later, and Daddy built the north wing onto the house for us to live in. Mama had come down with her illness by then and someone needed to be here all the time. We had your mother that next year."

"And the first love?" he asked.

"He spent more than twenty years in the service, came back to Happy to take care of his parents, and then left when they died," she said. "The point of this whole story is to tell you that I had a responsibility to the ranch. My first love hated ranching. He was a dreamer with no roots. I did the right thing by marrying your grandfather."

"Do I hear another *but*?" Brody asked.

Her eyes met his. "I always wondered what my life would have been like with him, and there was a little part of my heart that Wes never had because of him. Now remember that when I go on to the rest of my story."

"Lila?" Brody yawned.

Hope inhaled deeply and let it out in a gush. "Always in a hurry. It comes from all that instant gratification you kids have with technology. I knew when you were born I was going to leave Hope Springs to you when you were old enough to take the reins."

"What about Jace? Right now you've given it to both of us."

"But when he gets ready to settle down or if Valerie decides to step down from runnin' the ranch, he will inherit Prairie Rose and this one will be yours alone. Lila Harris is your first love, right?"

"Can I answer? You told me to be quiet."

"Just nod."

He did.

"I saw her at the bull riding tonight. She sat at the top of the stands all alone. I watched her actions without her even knowing it. Emma talks about her all the time and Rustin thinks she flat out hung the moon. I hear that Silas went right to her when y'all went for ice cream last night."

He nodded again.

"I stand by my reasoning back when you and Lila were teenagers. She was wild and I could see that you would mess up your life if you got involved with her at eighteen."

"And?" Brody asked.

"I could feel what she was experiencing tonight. Neither Wes nor my first love rode bulls but when you came out of the chute, I was experiencing that rush that I used to get when I was sneaking off to see—" She stopped before she said his name.

"Sneaking?" Brody's eyes widened.

"Dad didn't think he was good enough for me. Like I said, he was a dreamer, not a rancher, and I had a lot of responsibility toward Hope Springs. Back to what I was trying to say—she had eyes for no one else tonight and almost fainted when the bull was chasing you. She left before the rides were finished. I know that feeling that she had, and I expect your heart reacts the same way when you're around her, right?"

Another nod.

"Then it's time to see if there's enough left for another chance or to get over her," Hope said.

"Was it worth losing your first love for this place?" Brody asked.

"At this point in life, I can say yes, it was," she answered. "If I'd done what my heart wanted instead of what my mind knew was the right course, you wouldn't be sitting here having this conversation with me."

A long, heavy pause hung over the room like dust at the rodeo arena.

"You're thirty years old and so is Lila. You have a chance that I never had. You cannot re-create the past. It's gone and done with. Decisions made. Consequences paid. But if you see something in that woman, then you have the opportunity to see if there is a future there," she said.

Brody almost fell out of his chair. "You aren't against me seeing her?"

"You're a grown man and you had a lot of responsibility laid on your shoulders when your grandpa and daddy both died that summer. I'm proud of you, Brody."

"You didn't answer my question," he said.

Hope inhaled and pulled her hands free. "Always in a hurry. That's your decision. Lila is a responsible woman with a pretty good head on her shoulders from what I've found out since she came back to Happy. I knew that wild girl but I don't know the woman Lila. Take my advice and either get her out of your system while she is here or else do something about the attraction. It's time for you to have a child so Hope Springs can live on through another generation. This summer needs to tell the story of who the mother of that child will be."

"Again, Jace?" he asked.

"I told you. He will inherit your folks' place when Valerie steps down like I did, probably in the next couple of years at the most, and he will sign Hope Springs over to you and move back down the road to Prairie Rose," Hope said. "And that is the confidential part."

"And Kasey?"

"We'll cross that bridge when the time comes. Now it's well past my bedtime and you need to get a shower. You've got dirt in your hair and behind your ears."

"Yes, ma'am." He grinned.

She covered a yawn with her hand. "Good talk, as you kids say today."

"It was and thank you, Granny," he said.

"But," she whispered, "let Jace think I gave you a hard time. It keeps up my image."

"You got it. I'll take care of the cleanup here and see you in the morning," he said.

"Bright and early. Ranchin' starts with daylight and ends when there's not enough light to see anymore."

"Amen." Brody rose to his feet and kissed his grandmother on the forehead. "Sweet dreams."

Hope stopped at the door and turned around. "Your mama has never forgiven Lila's mama for trying to get between her and Mitch Dawson when they were in high school, so you might not get off so easy with her. But that's not my business so you're on your own there."

Chapter Eight

Lila hated the church social, where everyone who had ever preached at the church, had ever attended, or who had even lived in Happy was invited back for a reunion of sorts. More than once in her younger years she'd faked sickness in an attempt to get out of going but it never worked. Molly insisted that they were going to close the café just like always and go to morning services and then to the social.

"No buts about it," Molly said seriously as they prepared for the breakfast run that morning. "Your mama started the tradition when she managed this place and we ain't changed it."

"I'm not going. I've got two kittens I have to take care of today. They're in new surroundings and I need to spend time with them," Lila said.

"You'll be home all evening to do that." Molly slid another pan of chicken and dressing into the oven to warm.

"You can tell them cats bedtime stories and rock them to sleep."

"Okay," Lila sighed. "I'll rush back to my apartment and get a shower right after we close."

"Good! Glad that the spiritual light finally showed through into your soul." Molly slapped a thick slice of ham on the grill for the next breakfast order.

Molly was a tyrant. Lila loved her and appreciated her staying on at the café until she could get the place sold, but good grief, Molly was the same to her as Hope was to Brody. They both had a grandmother figure who was doing their dead level best to make their lives miserable.

"If I didn't love you like my own kid, I wouldn't tell you what to do. You can ride with me."

* * *

It was less than a mile to the church and Molly parked as close to the back door as she could so she could unload the food. The kitchen was empty but four tables were laden with covered dishes. Space had been left at the end of the first table for Molly's four large pans. When they were situated to suit her, she pointed toward the door leading from there to the sanctuary.

"You go on in and get settled. I'll be there soon as I make a stop in the restroom."

Lila nodded and headed toward the sound of "I'll Fly Away." Well, now, that was a fitting song to hear since she would have rather been appreciating the handiwork of God while riding her bike down in the canyon rather than in a packed church that morning. Flying away to anywhere sounded better than sitting on a hard oak pew.

She found the song in the hymnal and sang the last verse along with everyone else. The choir director stepped aside and the preacher took his place behind the pulpit. Feet shuffled, folks whispered to children to settle down, a few old men cleared their throats, and a couple of Amens floated out over the church.

The preacher had just read the scripture when Molly took her place beside Lila. "Good timin'. I won't miss the sermon." Molly set her purse and Lila's on the floor. "I brought your purse. You left it in the kitchen."

"Thank you," she whispered.

The preacher said something about sin being in many forms and then hesitated. It was during that pregnant pause that the phone in her purse started playing an old tune, "Heaven's Just a Sin Away." She'd turned the volume as high as it would go earlier that day because she expected a call from her mother. In the quiet church, it sounded like it was coming from a concert stage.

Some folks tried to part the back of her hair with dirty looks; others giggled. She blushed scarlet and grabbed her purse, plopped it down on the seat between her and Molly, and started digging for the phone. It stopped before she could get a grip on it and she set the purse on the floor again.

"Like I said..." The preacher's booming voice reached to the back of the room. But then Lila's phone started again, as if trying to help him prove the point. She grabbed the purse and, thinking she had both handles, jumped up to get out of the building. Blushing crimson, she stepped out into the center aisle, hit the lopsided purse on the edge of the pew, and sent everything in it flying everywhere. She dropped to her knees and started gathering it all up, snatching the phone first, but it slipped from her hands and skittered under the pew right beside her.

Valerie Dawson's high heel hit the thing and sent it back another pew. Lila was ready to crawl in that direction when Brody left his seat, knelt in front of her, and helped her get everything put back in place. Her face burned like fire with embarrassment when Rustin crawled out from under a pew and handed the phone to Brody. It had stopped ringing but every eye in the entire congregation was on them. Some would even have kinks in their necks tomorrow from trying to see around other folks. The buzz of whispers filled the place as Brody handed it to her.

"As I was saying," the preacher cleared his throat, "sin comes in many forms."

"Guess he don't recognize your music or he'd know you were agreeing with him," Brody whispered as he extended a hand to help her and made sure she was seated before he returned to his own pew.

The preacher went into a long-winded explanation about sin and Lila sent a text to her mother: *Church. Annual social.*

She immediately got one back: *OMG! So sorry!*

"Why in the world do you have that song on your phone?" Molly said out the side of her mouth.

"Mama always liked it," she answered.

"Well, thank God she didn't call during benediction," Molly said.

Lila should have set her foot down and refused to go to church that morning. This whole thing was one big omen telling her that she did not belong here. She'd smooth things over with Brody to ease the anxiety in her heart and then she wasn't doing one thing but working and talking to her cats. No more church, not even if Molly did quit.

The little church was so full there wasn't room to cuss a cat without getting a mouthful of hair. Paul McKay's wife, Gracie, a short, round woman with a bouffant hairdo and enough perfume to douse down the whole church, was on the other side of Molly and then there was her husband and another couple beyond that.

Lila felt someone staring at her, so she took a quick look over her shoulder and right into Brody's sexy blue eyes. He winked slyly and she started to whip around but caught Valerie Dawson glaring at her. After the morning she'd had, she wasn't going to let that woman intimidate her, so she slowly slid one eyelid shut. Valerie's jerky body language said that she was totally offended.

Tall, dark haired, and slim built, Valerie had always had a no-nonsense way about her that reminded Lila of those old tintype photographs—the ones where the woman looks like she could cut steel with her eyes and would shoot first and ask questions later. Lila straightened her back and smiled. Valerie's cold eyes piercing her head like a bullet didn't matter. She'd lived through the embarrassment and Brody had helped her right out in public, even though they hadn't parted on good terms. And now that she'd had time to settle down, she thought the whole episode was humorous. She couldn't wait to tell her mother about it.

The sermon seemed to last an eternity. She bit back a sigh when the preacher finally asked Paul to deliver the benediction. There was a little more room on the pew when he stood to his feet, bowed his head, and gave thanks for everything from the beautiful day to the folks who'd come from afar to attend the social. Lila began to think that the whole congregation was going to die of starvation before Paul wound down and said, "Amen."

But finally he got around to thanking God for the food they were about to eat in the kitchen and for the hands that had prepared it and said the magic word that made everyone in the church pop to their feet.

"Hey." Gracie McKay reached out a hand toward Lila the second they were standing. "So is it true? You going to sell the café since Georgia retired? We are going to miss Molly so much in the Ladies' Circle here at the church," Gracie said.

"Yes, ma'am, the Happy Café is for sale. If you know anyone who might be interested, just give them the phone number." Lila nodded.

"Well, good luck, darlin'. Much as we love havin' a café in town, folks around here ain't got two pennies to rub together and those who ain't from here don't want to be," Gracie said.

"Ain't it the truth," Molly agreed. "Let's sneak out the back door and go straight to the kitchen. That way we don't have to stand in line. I'll shake the preacher's hand before we leave."

Lila followed the two older women out of the sanctuary and down a short hallway to the kitchen. When they arrived, the place was already bustling with women taking covers off the dishes and getting things ready for the dinner.

Molly grabbed her arm and led her to the far end of the tables. "You can help Valerie cut cakes and pies and get them ready to serve."

God hates me for sure. She should have listened to

the sermon and she dang sure should not have winked at Valerie Dawson. This was her punishment for both infractions right there in the church.

"I'd rather help with the chicken and dressing and roast," Lila said.

"Nonsense!" Molly protested. "Gracie and I have taken care of this job for years. You go on and help out with desserts." Molly lowered her voice to a whisper. "Face your enemies head-on. Don't run from them."

"She's not my enemy," Lila protested.

"Yeah, right."

Gracie nudged Lila on the arm as she passed by her. "You know what they say about the social?"

"What?" Lila asked.

"That if you ever help serve at one, you'll be serving at them until you die," she answered.

Lila sighed and went to the other end of the food line.

Valerie handed her a knife. "You can cut the pecan pies. Make them into six slices each," she said with ice dripping from her tone.

Was the woman certifiably goofy, handing her a knife? Evidently she did not value her life one bit.

She leaned in close to Lila and whispered, "I don't like this any better than you do but we will be civil while we are in church. Understood?"

"Mrs. Dawson, this is such a treat to get to work with you. I haven't got to see you since I've been back in town," Lila said in a voice made of pure sugar. "We can use this time to catch up. So how are things on Prairie Rose? I was so sorry to hear about Mitch's passing."

"Sarcasm will get you nowhere with me," Valerie said from the corner of a pasted-on smile.

"And threatening me won't get you anywhere," Lila said.

"I hear that you aren't stickin' around after the summer?"

"One never knows what might happen by the end of August," Lila answered.

Brody pushed through the back door and yelled from across the room, "Miz Molly, I'm here to carry tables out under the shade trees. How many do you think we'll need?"

"Eight," Gracie yelled. "We used ten last year and two weren't used. Old folks like to sit in the cool to eat, so we've already got two extra ready in here."

Brody's biceps strained against his plaid shirt when he had a folding table under each arm but he stopped dead when he saw his mother and Lila side by side.

"Great to see you here, Lila," he said from across the room.

"Thank you," she muttered.

"Guess I'd best get busy or Molly will fire me." He grinned.

"She's pretty tough on the hired help." Lila smiled back as she eyeballed the three exits. One at the back, one at the side, and the last one through the kitchen. Any one of them would provide a good escape as soon as dinner was over.

* * *

Jace met Brody midway across the church lawn and relieved him of one of the tables. "What happened with Granny last night?"

"It didn't go like I figured it would."

"Really?" Jace's dark brows shot up.

"Nope. She was pretty calm and she didn't threaten to disown me. She says I'm thirty years old and it's time for me to settle down but whoever I want to do that with is my decision. She did say that Mama would have a different notion because Lila's mother tried to get between Dad and Mama when they were dating. And I'm supposed to tell you that she came down on me real hard so she won't lose face, so that's confidential."

"Small towns!" Jace said. "I love Happy but there's a part of me that wishes it was so big that everyone didn't know everyone else."

"And who they did and where it was." Brody nodded seriously. "Mama and Lila are in there working together."

Jace's eyes widened and he sat down hard on a chair. "How in the devil did that happen?"

Brody shrugged. "I don't think either of them would ask to cut cakes and pies together. Molly probably has something to do with it."

"Holy hell! They both have knives?" Jace asked.

Brody nodded and sat down beside his brother. "There's a chill in the room that ain't got a thing to do with the air-conditioning."

Kasey pushed a baby stroller in between them and slung an arm over each of their shoulders. "Have y'all seen Rustin? If I don't watch him, he'll get a plate full of desserts and nothing else."

Emma came running and tugged on Kasey's hand. "Mama, Rustin is with Grandpa Paul and I'm hungry to death."

Brody stooped down to Emma's level to hug her.

"Then we'd better get on over to the door and get in line if you're that hungry. What are you going to eat today?"

"Chocolate cake and cookies." She beamed. "And so is Rustin."

"And chicken?" Brody stood up.

She frowned and nodded at the same time. "No Russell sprouts. They are nasty."

"I agree." Brody took her hand and started toward the building where the people were starting to line up.

"Mama and Lila were cutting cakes together," Jace whispered to his sister.

"Sweet Jesus!" Kasey looked over her shoulder at Brody.

His wide shoulders raised slightly. "Mama needs to get over it."

"Y'all need to go first." Paul took the stroller from Kasey and led them all to the front of the line. "And don't worry, Kasey. I'll see to it that Rustin eats more than chocolate. Oh, and did Gracie tell you guys?" He handed the stroller back to her. "Y'all are taking care of the bouncy house right after we eat. You might need one more person to help out, though."

"Why's that?" Jace asked.

"Not me." Kasey shook her head. "I've got my hands full with my own brood."

"I'll watch after Rustin," Paul offered. "I bet Valerie will take care of Silas so you can take care of Emma."

"Grandpa, don't make me eat those old nasty green beans that's got white stuff in them." Rustin wrinkled his nose.

"I won't if you'll eat all your fried chicken and potato salad." Paul grinned at Kasey.

"I'll even eat baked beans," Rustin said seriously.

Molly threw open the double doors into the fellowship hall and folks flowed inside, laughing, talking, and getting into a line behind the Dawsons.

"Lila!" Emma yelled so loud that everyone in the place turned around and silence filled the room. "Mama, I want Lila to help me. She won't make me eat Russell sprouts."

Brody's mouth went dry at the sight of her crossing the room. Her hips swayed, swishing that skirt about her legs. Her eyes were all soft and dreamy as she zeroed in on Emma.

"I'd love to help," Lila said, and slipped in between the stroller and Brody. "What does Emma want for dinner?"

"No Brussels sprouts," Brody whispered.

"I understood that much." Lila smiled.

She filled a plate for Emma and let her pick out the table where she wanted to sit and was back around the table by the time Brody reached the dessert end of the tables.

"Pecan pie, right?" she said, and heard someone say her name right behind her.

"What?"

"Brody said that he and Jace need a third person to help with the bouncy house. I just volunteered you." Molly set a pumpkin pie on the dessert table. "She loves kids."

"Thanks, Lila." Brody flashed a smile her way. "And yes, ma'am, I do want a slice of Mama's pecan pie."

Closed inside a bouncy house with Lila—now that's what Brody called a stroke of fate. He felt as if he were floating on air as he carried his plate to the table where Kasey and the rest of the family were sitting.

* * *

Lila cornered Molly as she headed back to the kitchen. "Why did you do that? You fuss every time his name is even mentioned and now you're putting me right with him?"

"If I didn't, folks would think y'all was carryin' on in secret, especially after the looks that was goin' on between the two of you in church this mornin'. This way they'll know there is nothing between you," Molly whispered. "Go on and fix your plate since you're going to help out with the kids." Molly gave her a quick hug. "I told your mama I'd watch out for you and I know what I'm doin'."

Lila had planned to sit in the kitchen when she'd gotten her food but Brody had come back to get a plate of hot rolls for the folks at his table. "We've got an empty chair at our table. Emma would love it if you'd come sit with us."

"No!" Molly hissed at her elbow. "That's going too far."

"I'd be glad to. Save me a seat and I'll be right there," Lila said.

"You're going to be the death of me," Molly groaned.

"Don't die this week. My black dress is a little snug."

She inhaled deeply and made her knees take her across the floor to sit with the Dawson family. Kasey was smiling. Jace and Hope were both leaning forward to look at Valerie.

Emma waved and yelled out, "My friend Lila! Look, Mama. She's goin' to sit with me."

"Hello, Emma," Lila said as she sank into the chair that Brody held for her.

Then he sat down right beside her. "Lila is going to help us in the bouncy house."

"I saved you this seat," Emma said.

"Well, thank you." Lila's knee brushed against Brody's under the table. "So sorry, Brody."

"No problem." He grinned.

Yes, there was a problem. Every time she was around him, that inner wild child begged to be released. She'd started to feel like a person with multiple personalities.

"So, Emma, are you ready to play in the bouncy house?" Lila hoped her cheeks weren't as red as they felt. Or if they were, that everyone at the table thought it was from working near the hot kitchen.

"Yes, and the pool too. My bathing suit is in Silas's bag," Emma answered.

"About twenty minutes in each one and then one of the games inside the church and we're goin' home to get our naps," Kasey said.

Emma stuck out her lower lip. "I want to stay with Lila all day."

"Naps are wonderful." She leaned down close to Emma's ear and whispered, "And I'm going home when you do so I can have a nap too," Lila said.

"Thank you!" Kasey sighed from across the table.

"What else is new? I don't remember bouncy houses and kiddy pools when I was a kid and coming to these things. I don't even remember having anything when I was a teenager," Lila said.

"I know." Kasey shrugged. "They didn't have anything to entertain us when we were kids, did they? All we got was lectures if we whined."

"Uncle Brody." Emma tugged on his arm. "Did I eat enough mean beans?"

Brody scooped up the last spoonful of green beans and ate them for her. "Looks to me like they're all gone."

"Look, Mommy, I made a happy plate." Emma beamed.

"Good job," Kasey said, and turned back to Lila. "Has anyone shown an interest in buying the cafe?"

"Not yet but it's only been on the market a couple of weeks."

"Be a shame if it closed. Not much left of the town as it is," Hope said.

Lila was shocked that Hope was talking to her and daggers were not shooting from her eyes. She ate a small bite of the pecan pie. "Oh. My. Goodness. This is amazing. What's your secret?"

"A little bit of cream cheese between the crust and filling keeps it from getting soggy." Valerie's eyes went to Brody. There was definitely a heavy dose of pride there. "It's Brody's favorite."

"Yes, it is," Brody said. "And Kasey's pumpkin pie comes in second."

Emma tugged on her arm. "Are you going to get in the pool with me?"

Lila's attention went to Emma. "I didn't bring my bathing suit, but I am going to get into the bouncy house with you. I'll sit in the corner and you can bounce all the way to me."

Emma pumped her fist in the air. "Yay!"

"Hey, Brody." Kasey grinned. "I forgot to tell you. Gracie said that we're getting a new pianist at the church. She's moving here from Abilene to teach junior high English at the end of summer and she's already contacted the preacher about transferring her church membership. You should think about asking her out."

He shook his head emphatically. "No thank you."

Valerie's eyes cut across the table like a machete through warm butter. "I know her family very well. They live in Canyon and are in the Angus Association with me. You'll remember her if you think about it. Tara McDowell—she's a good woman."

"Not interested, Mama," Brody said. "Jace can ask her out."

"Don't throw me under the bus," Jace protested.

Valerie turned her gaze on her younger son. "She might be the very thing to settle you down. I'm going to invite her to supper on Friday night and you will be there."

"Can't. I have a date," Jace protested.

"With whom?" Valerie asked.

"You don't know her. I don't bring a woman home unless it's serious."

"You're both too late," Hope said. "I heard that the preacher himself has already been out with her a couple of times."

"Well, you could beat the other guy's time." Lila looked around Emma toward Brody.

"No, I will take the higher road and not interfere with true love. Jace can work on taking her away from the preacher." Brody sighed and then a wide grin spread across his face.

"Is your heart shattered in a thousand pieces too?" Kasey looked down the table toward Jace.

"Humpty Dumpty could never put it together again," Jace joked.

"You're all horrible," Valerie snapped.

"Hey, Paul, I hear you got some kittens out in Henry's barn." Kasey changed the subject before it went into a full-fledged argument. "Emma's wanted one for a long time. Got one I could have?"

"Go get whatever you can catch. Gracie is going to make me take a couple more mama cats out there this afternoon. Someone dumped them on us and they're about to pop. If you can't find one you like right now, there will be more in six weeks," Paul said. "You want one, too, Rustin?"

"No, Grandpa Paul. I want a puppy. It can be an old mutt and I'm askin' Santa for one if I don't get it before Christmas," Rustin answered.

"Gracie already told Lila to go out there and get however many she wanted too. Why don't y'all take that big white mama cat that's in the barn and whatever kittens she didn't already take?" Paul said.

"I want a baby cat, not a mama cat," Emma declared.

"Then that's what you should have." Brody gave her a sideways hug. "Hey, Paul, have you got your hay all cut and in the barn?"

"Yep, got the second cutting done this week. Why?"

"I'd like to hire the kids you had workin' for you. Reckon you could send them over to my place tomorrow?"

"Be glad to." Paul nodded. "They were wonderin' where they could find some more work."

Fred stopped by and laid a hand on Brody's shoulder. "Did that prize heifer of yours ever throw that calf?"

"Not yet but she's been keepin' me awake," Brody answered. "I sure don't want to lose her and didn't mean for her to even get bred this year."

"So that's why you've got dark circles under your eyes. I thought it might be you was worryin' about something else." Fred winked and chuckled. "Let me know when that calf is born. I'd sure like to see the critter. Maybe it'll be one of Sundance's boys and turn out to be good breeder stock."

"Don't know what bull got in with her but the way Sundance can jump a fence, I wouldn't be surprised," Brody said.

"Y'all ready to get that fun house goin' for the younguns?" Jace finished off the last bite of food on his plate.

"Yes," Emma squealed. "Me and Lila are going to have fun."

"Yes, we are, sweet girl. Kasey, is it all right if I take her with me now?" Lila asked.

"Of course. I'll come get her in about twenty minutes. She'll be ready for the kiddy pool by then."

"Glad you got that job." Fred squeezed Brody's shoulder. "With my arthritis, I'd be moanin' for a week if I had to crawl inside that bouncy house thing."

"We might be groanin' after today," Lila said.

"Oh, so you're goin' to help him?" Fred raised an eyebrow.

"Yes, she is," Emma piped up.

"Okay, let's get the show on the road." Jace led the way outside.

Emma tucked her hand into Lila's and chattered all the way out to the children's area. "Do you like my granny Hope?"

Lila wasn't sure how to answer that question. It was loaded like a double-barreled shotgun. Finally she said, "Of course. She's a lovely lady."

"I like her too. She reads to me like you do and makes the voices." Emma skipped along beside her. That kid was brilliant. The teachers were going to absolutely love working with her when she got to school.

"Here we are." Brody unzipped the house and stepped back to let Lila and Emma in first.

"You've got a bouncy house and the kiddy pools for the little kids. What about the older kids?" Lila crawled inside with Emma right behind her.

"There's Ping-Pong and games going on in the Sunday school rooms," he answered.

"No poker, though," Jace teased.

"You remembered." Lila smiled.

"Oh, yeah," Brody said. "You wiped all us boys out over there under that old lonesome scrub oak tree that summer after our sophomore year."

"I'd just finished the eighth grade and thought I was a better poker player than anyone, especially a girl. By the time we went home that day, I was just glad we weren't playing strip poker," Jace said. "I'd have lost my socks and everything else. As it was, I lost my lunch money for a whole week. Had to eat in the lunch room."

"Poor baby. Did you lose your lunch money too?" she asked Brody.

"I lost a big chunk of my pride." He crawled inside behind Emma and Lila. "Jace, you see to it they take off their shoes and know the rules. No shoving or hitting or spitting or fighting. I'll sit in one of the supervisor's corners and Lila can sit in the other."

Within ten minutes the noise was deafening and Lila couldn't stop laughing at the antics of the kids. Give them something to jump up and down on and they were happy critters. Too bad adults weren't as easily pleased. Half an hour later, Kasey took Emma out of the crowd and in a little more than an hour the rest of the children had had their fill and had one by one run off to play in the kiddy pool or to go inside to one of the rooms where popcorn was being served while an animated movie played.

"Break time," Brody said from his corner. "Let's call it a day and go get something cold to drink. It's hot in this place even with the fan running."

"You don't have to twist my arm."

Lila tried to get to her feet but tumbled right over onto Brody. He wrapped his arms around her but still they wound up tangled together like a basketful of baby kittens. Pushing away from him only made her roll toward him more.

When she finally got a grip on his broad chest and was able to sit up, her first thought was that adult toy stores needed to sell these houses. Then two strong hands gripped her around the waist and drew her toward him like she weighed no more than Emma. One second she was floating; the next she was sitting firmly in Brody's lap.

She started to thank him but his dark lashes fluttered closed and his lips came down on hers. The kiss started off sweet and tender, then the embers turned into a blaze and the heat came close to melting the bouncy house into nothing but a pile of plastic right there on the church parking lot.

Her arms went around his neck and her fingers tangled into his dark hair as she pressed closer and closer to him. The entire world disappeared and they were in a special vacuum created just for them. Desire for more than scalding hot kisses filled her body. Then she realized where she was, who she was with, and what was going on. Thank God they were still zipped inside the bouncy house and no one saw them.

She pulled away quickly.

"You're still that famous wild child." He grinned.

"But it's time for me to be something else," she whispered. "I need a glass of cold water or lemonade. I'll see you inside."

"We should really talk," he said.

"About what? This is Happy, Texas, where nothing ever changes, not even when it wants to," she said as she crawled out of the house.

Chapter Nine

Slow days in the café were much worse than busy ones. Time dragged and the tips for the whole day wouldn't buy an Orange Julius at the mall in Amarillo. But that was Wednesdays—always had been and most likely always would be—especially on rainy days. Molly left six o'clock sharp. It was time to lock up the place and go on back to the cats but Lila was sitting in a booth finishing the last bites of a grilled cheese sandwich when Kasey darted inside out of the drizzling rain.

"Oh my gosh. It's closing time for you, isn't it? I thought I had half an hour, but I guess I lost track of time." Kasey threw back the hood on her shirt and nodded toward the clock on the wall above the cash register.

"No problem. Come on in. What can I get you? The grill and grease are still hot," Lila said.

"I wanted a burger basket and a glass of lemonade but..."

"Have a seat and it'll be right out," Lila said. "Where are the kids?"

"Mama wanted them for the day and she's taken them to Bible school tonight. My brothers drove down to Plainview to talk to a man about the fall cattle sale on the ranch," she said. "First time in weeks that I've had a day to myself."

"What'd you do?" Lila called out as she flipped a patty on the grill and dumped a bunch of fries into the grease.

"Errands that have been piling up. What I wanted to do was spend the whole day at the spa. Adam gave me a gift certificate for my birthday the first year we were married to that fancy place and I've always wanted to go back. Believe me, he got lucky that night." She smiled.

"I can't imagine how tough losing him would be. Everything on the burger?" Lila asked.

"Mustard and no onions. I'm not sure I'll ever get over it. Crazy talking about food and him at the same time," Kasey said. "I can say his name now without crying, so I guess that's progress."

"I can't even imagine the shock," Lila said seriously.

"It's like an earthquake. You know it's possible, even in Texas, but you never expect it to happen in your area. Then it does and it upsets everything in your life. But it doesn't end there. There's the after-tremors that keep shaking things up. I got used to him being away pretty often. I keep thinking that in two days or two weeks, he'll be back and things will be fine, but then reality hits, and it hurts all over again." Kasey's eyes went all misty but she kept the tears back.

Lila could relate to that better than Kasey realized. There was the shock of leaving Happy and settling into a new place. Her mother and aunt started working at the new café they bought and Lila and Daisy moved into the apartment above the business. She'd thought that the loneliness would kill her. Then she went to college and found out that being away from her mother and relatives was even worse.

There were days when she'd walk down the street, see a guy ahead of her and think for a split second that it was Brody Dawson—that he'd come to take her home. Then there were all the nights that she dreamed about him and woke up with a wet pillow from crying. Oh, yes, she could certainly feel what Kasey was saying.

Lila threw the burger together, shook the fries from the basket, and put them into two separate baskets. "You said lemonade, right?"

"I got my own and refilled your tea glass. Hope that's all right," Kasey said.

Lila sat down at a table and propped her feet on an empty chair. "Ever want a second job, I'll hire you as a waitress."

"Don't think I can fit another job into my schedule. Thank you for doing this. Other than church dinners, I can't remember the last time I sat down by myself and had a burger," Kasey said. "Can I ask you a personal question?"

"Shoot," Lila said.

"What was it like when you moved away?"

Lila swallowed hard. Putting emotions into mere words was near impossible. She'd left part of her heart behind in Happy, Texas, and found out that it was impossible to get it back anywhere else.

"Different," Lila finally whispered. "And a little intimidating. I knew who I was in Happy but . . ." She paused. "It's hard to explain. No one knew me or anything about Happy, Texas. I was just another waitress in my aunt and mama's café and then I was just another student at the college. I felt like a real fish out of water until I reinvented myself."

"I know exactly what you mean." Kasey tucked a strand of red hair behind her ear. "I became a different person. I was an army wife, not Brody and Jace's kid sister. I had responsibilities even before I had a family. New friends with the same lifestyle I had and we all stuck together when our guys were out on a mission. We worried together, shopped together, babysat each other's kids, and then Adam was gone and I had to start adjusting to something different again. I'm sorry for unloading on you like this."

Lila reached across the booth and patted Kasey on the shoulder. "Don't be. I can so relate to what you're saying. I didn't lose a husband but when I got to a different state I was a new person. It took me a while to know that girl. I felt like a shell, a walking, talking person who smiled and did what she was supposed to but had no heart."

"And now we are back and we are the same as when we left. You're in this café and I'm living on a ranch with my brothers. It's like there's two women fighting inside me and I'm not sure which one I want to win," Kasey said.

Lila couldn't have stated it any better than Kasey did. That's exactly what she was fighting against these days. The two attitudes inside her were so very different. But when it all burned down to ashes, it was actually kind of simple. One had a beating heart in her chest and the other one was a walking, talking shell.

"One is the wild child and the other is a responsible schoolteacher," Lila said softly.

"You got it. Only with me, one is still an army wife who organizes lawn picnics and car pools and then there's this kid sister who's trying to be as smart and as tough as her two older brothers. Which one will conquer?"

"You ever hear the story of the old rancher and the coyote?"

Kasey shook her head.

"Coyote had ribs showing and was plainly starving, so the old rancher tossed out some scraps for the poor thing. Coyote came back the next night and the next and the rancher didn't want him there because it was time for spring calves to be born and coyotes can't be trusted. So he asked a friend what he should do."

"And?" Kasey squirted ketchup on her fries.

"Friend said, 'Stop feeding him if you don't want him around.' I expect it's the same with us. With me, if I want to be the respectable schoolteacher, I have to stop feeding the desire to be the wild child."

"But what if we want to be both? I love the ranch and living around family but I'm tired of them all bossing me around like I'm still a teenager," Kasey said.

Lila frowned. "Is that possible?"

"Don't know but I intend to find out. And it'll take some severe putting my foot down with my brothers and my mother," Kasey said.

Was it possible to pick what she wanted from both personalities? She was mentally making a list of what she'd keep and what she'd trash when she realized that Kasey was staring at her.

"Sorry, I got lost in my thoughts," Lila said. "Will you let me know how that turns out?"

"You bet. I owe you that for keeping the café open and cooking for me." Kasey nodded. "I admired you so much when you were in high school. Lord, I wanted to grow up and be just like you."

"Really?"

"Oh, yeah. You had it together."

"Oh, honey, I didn't have jack squat together." Lila shook her head. "Still don't."

Someone in Happy had believed in her after all. Kasey might have been five years younger, but knowing how Kasey felt put something indescribable into Lila's heart.

Kasey stuck her fingers in her ears in a dramatic gesture. "Don't ruin my memory. Let me keep it."

"Sure thing." Lila smiled.

The fingers came out and Kasey finished off her burger. "This has really been the best part of my day. Most of my friends left Happy. Let's be honest, if you're not a rancher or, in your case, own a café, there's not much here to come back to. It's nice to sit and talk to someone who knows the way things are, and yet..."

Lila took Kasey's glass to the fountain for a refill. "And yet what?"

"It's more of a feeling than it is something that can be put into words. I guess I just need to stop overthinking things and stop feeding that particular coyote. Can you put that in a to-go cup? I've got to get to the church or Mother will start calling every thirty seconds. And tally up how much I owe you."

"It's on the house. We'll call it payment for a therapy session," Lila said.

"Thank you," Kasey said. "Sometime we'll have to take a swim in Hope Springs and call it a spa day."

Lila handed her the cup and followed her to the door. "I'd like that."

Kasey stopped at the door and turned around. "You're welcome anytime on the ranch, Lila. Come have a glass of tea with me or, better yet, we'll have a cold beer."

"That is so sweet. I might do that sometime." She flipped the sign around from OPEN to CLOSED, locked up, and turned off the lights. She had an invitation to Hope Springs without breaking the law by jumping the fence where a NO TRESPASSING sign was posted.

She crossed the kitchen and went through the storage room into her apartment. The kittens were playing a cat game of hide and scare each other around the coffee table. She removed her shoes and stretched out on the sofa. The conversation with Kasey had been both wonderful and yet strange at the same time. She was Brody's sister and the two people inside of her were different than Lila's two but the feelings were the same.

"Kind of like y'all are as different as night and day," she muttered at the cats. "Black and white and yet both of you are still kittens."

Would this summer be the turning point in her life? The meeting point of that wild girl and the responsible one? She stared at her surroundings and got to her feet. Pacing from the living room, through the kitchen, and back down the hall, she tried to get a handle on all the emotions.

She grabbed a long-sleeved chambray shirt on her way

past her bedroom and in a few minutes she was roaring out of town on her motorcycle. She turned to the east at the first opportunity and had gone only part of a mile when she saw a white truck in her rearview. It got closer and closer and then started to pass her before she realized that it was Brody. When he was right beside her, she flipped up the face shield and winked at him. Then she sped out ahead of him.

He stayed right behind her all the way to the T in the road, where there was a stop sign. She turned on the left blinker. The highway would take her right down into the Palo Duro Canyon and then up on the other side not far from Claude. From there she'd ride to Amarillo and then south to Happy.

Brody didn't stop at the sign but pulled right out in front of her and skidded to a stop. He jumped out of the truck and swaggered back to where she'd stopped. "You weren't kiddin' about havin' a bike. That's a pretty piece of machinery. But..."

"But what?" She jerked her helmet off and shook out her black hair.

He took two steps forward, bookcased her cheeks with his calloused hands, and then his lips were on hers in a hungry, fierce kiss. She dropped her helmet on the ground and wrapped her arms around his neck. His tongue teased its way past her lips to make love to her mouth. The sun's heat was nothing to the fire in the kiss that came close to melting the paint off his white truck as well as the stop sign.

He took a step back and she almost fell off the bike before she could catch her breath. "I missed you, Lila."

"You missed the wild Lila. You barely know the

responsible Lila." She picked her helmet from the ground and slapped it back on her head. "Now if you'll get out of my way, I'm going to Amarillo."

"Good God! Not down the canyon? You could get killed on those turns and curves."

"If I do, your mama will dance a jig on the church altar. You want to go with me?" She patted the seat behind her.

"No, thank you."

"I watched you ride that mean bull, so I know there's some daredevil left in you. I guess you're too macho to ride behind a woman. I suppose you could ride on the handlebars."

He crossed his arms over his chest. "I'm not sixteen anymore."

"Too bad," she said as she took off in a blur around the truck. She glanced in the rearview mirror to see him slap his thigh with his hat.

* * *

Brody got back into his truck and gripped the steering wheel so tightly that his hands ached. That woman had always twisted his insides in knots and time had done nothing to change that. He turned the truck around and drove toward the ranch. He felt like he'd been doing that for years—leaving her and going to the ranch. It didn't feel right but he had no idea how to fix it.

Not even the kids chasing lightning bugs out in the yard put a smile on his face when he parked next to the yard fence, got out, and slammed the truck door. He stomped toward the porch where Jace and Kasey were sitting and went straight into the house without a word. Getting out the bottle of Jack Daniel's from the cabinet, he set his mouth in a firm line, and poured a double shot in a water glass.

Kasey followed right behind him. "What's got your britches in a twist? You don't get that bottle down unless you're mad, sad, or a mixture of both."

He took a sip, letting the smoky flavor sit on his tongue a second before the warmth shot down his throat. It didn't replace or erase Lila's kisses. "Nothing that you'd understand."

"We might understand if you'd explain. Use your words, brother. What's her name? Lila Harris?" Jace joined them with the three kids trailing right behind him.

"Is Lila comin' to see me?" Emma crawled into a kitchen chair. "I want cake and milk."

"You've had enough sweets for one evening. Peanut butter sandwiches are what y'all are havin' for night snacks," Kasey said. "I saw Lila this evening. She kept the café open late and made me a burger and fries. We had a wonderful visit."

Brody tossed back the rest of the shot. "What did you talk about?"

"Your name didn't come up, believe me." Kasey put the bottle back in the cabinet. "We talked girl stuff that guys aren't interested in."

Brody settled Silas into his high chair, then helped Emma get into her booster seat.

Jace headed toward the counter to help make sandwiches. "So, am I right? Lila?"

Brody shrugged. "I'm going for a walk to clear my head."

"If you find Lila, can she read me a bedtime story?" Emma asked.

"Girls!" Rustin rolled his eyes.

"Boys!" Emma huffed.

He could hear Jace's laughter all the way out into the yard but it did not lighten his mood one bit. With no place in mind, his long strides and anger soon took him toward Hope Springs. The sound of bubbling water calmed him before he ever sat down under the drooping branches of a weeping willow tree.

A splash out there in the water took his attention slightly upstream from where he was sitting. There was no doubt that it was Lila even if her back was toward him. Moonlight lit her up, showing jet-black hair flowing over white skin, water rippling around her in big, wide circles.

He blinked twice and then a third time but every time he opened his eyes, she was still there. Then a flicker of white caught his eyes and he realized he was looking at a T-shirt lying not four feet from him. Thrown beside it were jeans and shoes, along with a white bra and a skimpy pair of underpants.

He stretched out his long legs, crossed them at the ankles, and drank in his fill of her. The water covered most of her body, but he didn't need to see her to know what she looked like or even how she'd feel in his arms if he were out there below the rocky water falls with her. Those things had been burned into his mind for years and years.

She finally turned around and sank down farther into the water. "What are you doin' here?"

"Hot night brought on thoughts of cool water," he answered. "I would've brought a bottle of Jack Daniel's if I'd known you were here."

"How long have you been there?"

"Long enough to know that you're skinny-dippin'. I thought you were going to the canyon."

"Changed my mind." She moved to the shallow edge and hurriedly sat down so that she was still covered.

He kicked off his boots and tossed his plaid shirt and white T-shirt over with her clothing before he waded out toward her.

"What changed your mind?" He gasped when the water reached his knees.

"Needed cooling off after that kiss." Lila never beat around the bush or played games. She dealt in black and white, not shades of gray.

"Well, this will for sure cool a person off." He sat down beside her in the shallow edge and quickly ducked his whole body under the water. "I haven't done this since..."

"Since when?" she asked.

Use your words, Jace had said, but when it came to Lila there were no words. Only raw emotions and hot passion, both of which were the lifeline to his heart.

"I think you remember as well as I do. After all, you have the memory of an elephant, right?" With very little motion, he was glued to her side. "I'm just now realizing it was our body heat that kept us from freezing to death."

"Why, Brody Dawson, have you gotten too old for sex in cold water?"

"Probably, but five minutes under that willow tree would cure the problem in a hurry," he answered.

"If that willow tree could talk, it could tell some tales, but we can't go back," she said. "And even if we could, I'm not sure I want to."

"No, but we can go forward," Brody told her.

"I'm not so sure that's a good idea, either," she said. "There would always be the shadow of the past hovering nearby."

He moved his foot slowly down the side of her leg. "That might make for an interesting relationship."

She moved her leg away from him. "What brought you out here anyway?"

"Thinkin' about you and worryin' that you'd get hurt in the canyon. When you left that summer, I'd sit under the willow tree and imagine you like this in the water on hot evenings. I'd go to Henry's barn in the wintertime and wrap up in that old quilt we liked."

"Oh!" she gasped.

"What?"

"I'm going to name my white cat Cora. It just came to me when you said something about that old quilt."

He'd been baring his soul to her. Using his words. And she was thinking about naming a stupid cat? What was wrong with this picture?

"That's a definite change of subject. And what's this about cats?"

"I got two from Henry's old barn. I'm naming the white one Cora from that old movie we saw. *Quigley Down Under*. Remember Crazy Cora?"

Suddenly it all made sense. They'd snuck into Henry's house one time, just the two of them, and put the old movie into the DVD player. She'd wrapped a quilt that had been draped on the back of a rocking chair around both of them. He'd wanted to have sex right there on the sofa but she wouldn't. Said it wasn't right. Borrowing his house to watch a movie and his quilt to stay warm was one thing and a few kisses were okay, but nothing past that.

"The black one is Duke," she said.

"For John Wayne?"

"No, for the character in *The Notebook.* Did you ever see that one?"

"Only movie that ever made me cry," he said.

"I didn't know that tough cowboys ever cried." She stretched.

He sucked in air when part of her breasts showed in the moonlight. Even though the water was cold, he was getting hard. "I believe that Hope Springs might be the fountain of youth. Looking at you in this light—God, Lila, I want you so bad but I want more than a fling."

She leaned over and cupped his chin in her hands. "I'm not even going to answer that, Brody. It's getting late. I should be going. Shut your eyes."

"I've seen you naked, Lila. I'm sitting close enough that I can feel a lot of your bare skin right now." He covered her hand with his and brought it to his lips to kiss each knuckle.

"Tonight you're going to shut your eyes and promise me that you won't open them until I tell you that I'm dressed," she said.

"Whatever you say," he said. "Can I have a good night kiss?"

She leaned over and gave him a quick kiss. "Good night, Brody. Now shut your eyes."

He pulled her closer and tangled his hands in her wet hair, pulling her to his body for a real kiss so hot and passionate that it left them both panting. He pulled away, his eyes still closed. "*Now* you can get dressed."

He waited a few seconds before he opened his eyes. If possible, Lila was even more beautiful than she'd been when she was younger. Shapely legs and a small waist above the curve of rounded hips. She disappeared under the willow tree branches and when she reappeared, she was fully clothed.

"Your turn." She raised her voice. "I'm being a good girl and not taking your clothes with me. I should because you opened your eyes."

"Seems only fittin' that I get a little glimpse of you since you got a full-frontal nude shot of me when I got into the water," he said. "Did you like what you saw?"

"Did you?" she threw back at him.

"Oh, honey," he groaned.

"Liking the way you look was never my problem," she said. "Be seein' you around, I'm sure."

She disappeared into the night and he got out of the water, let the warm night air dry his body before he got dressed, and whistled all the way back to the house.

Chapter Ten

Four days.

She'd had four days to talk to the cats about the skinny-dipping event, to relive every word and feeling that she'd experienced sitting next to Brody with nothing but water between their naked bodies. For the next three days—Thursday, Friday, and Saturday—she'd watched for him every single moment of the day. And that night she'd thought he might be at church but he wasn't.

After services, she'd driven out to the cemetery and laid a wildflower bouquet wrapped with a bright red ribbon in front of her father's tombstone. She removed her sandals, sat cross-legged on the grass, and ran her fingers over the engraving: BILLY HARRIS, 1962–1999.

"Happy Father's Day, Daddy." She wiped a tear from her cheek.

She felt a presence before she got a whiff of Brody's shaving lotion, but before she could turn around he'd sat down beside her. They were as close as they'd been when they were skinny-dipping out at Hope Springs. His bare skin wasn't touching hers but the heat still flowed through his jeans and plaid shirt just as well as if it had been.

Brody took her hand in his and rested it on his knee. "I've missed seeing you, but we've been so busy on the ranch that I couldn't even get away for an hour. Thought I could make it to church tonight but Sundance got out of his pen again. Sometimes I'm ready to let Jace turn him into dog food. I finally got things finished and remembered that it was Father's Day. I didn't bring flowers but I had to come see Dad and Gramps."

"It's been years since I got to visit my dad on his special day," Lila said softly.

"I remember when he died in that oil rig accident. We were in the seventh grade and it was the first time any of us had lost a parent. I didn't know what to say to you." Brody's sincere voice reached deep into her heart, making her forget the angst over the past four days. It had been like that when they were in high school. She was constantly watching for him, disappointed when he wasn't around, and then when he was, everything was all right.

"You hugged me at the dinner they had at the church after the funeral. You didn't say a word but that hug meant the world to me right then," she said. "You must have been totally devastated to lose both your grandpa and your dad the same summer."

"It was the toughest year of my life," Brody said. "You left and then I lost them. Mama wanted me to go on to college that fall, but I couldn't leave her and Granny both with big ranches to take care of. We had a foreman on both Prairie Rose and Hope Springs but..." He shrugged.

Lila waited a few seconds while he collected his thoughts. He swallowed hard several times before he said, "Even more than being tough, it was the loneliness that was horrible. I threw myself into the work and that was that."

Lila nodded. "I did the same with college. Turned my DNA completely around and became more like Mama."

He drew his brows down. "How's that?"

"Mama was the stable one. Daddy was the fun parent. Probably because he was gone a lot of the time and we all wanted everything to be happy when he was home. When we moved, I made a complete switch and went from the fun Lila to a more serious girl. Looking back, it was a form of coping and escapism, I guess."

Brody gently squeezed her hand. "Funny how that works, isn't it?"

"I still miss him." She swallowed hard and a lonely tear found its way down her cheek.

He let go of one hand and gently brushed it away. "I'm sorry if I brought back sad memories."

Her mind flashed back to that day. She had come home from school and found her mother sitting on the sofa crying with her Sunday school friends surrounding her. There was already food everywhere, more than two people could use in a month. She knew before Daisy even stretched out her arms what had happened. She dropped to her knees and put her hands over her ears. If no one said the words, then it wouldn't be true.

He took her hand back in his and made lazy circles on her palm with his thumb. "And right after that, y'all moved to the back of the café. My family was there on the first Sunday to eat dinner and you were helping by serving the drinks. It was the first time I ever really noticed how pretty you are."

"I hated it," she whispered. "It was like we left Daddy behind in that trailer. I knew he was dead but his spirit lived and we didn't move it to the new place with us. He was back there with strangers. I used to sneak out at night and go sit in the backyard and pretend that he came outside to talk to me."

"I'm so sorry," Brody said.

She stared at the tombstone and visualized her father sitting beside her in those old metal lawn chairs in their postage-stamp-sized backyard. Sometimes they didn't talk at all but if she had a problem concerning anything, from snotty girls to pre-algebra, they'd discuss it.

"Then we left him again when Mama made us move. I didn't want to leave Happy. I even offered to not go to college and to help her run the café if she wouldn't make me leave. It took a long time for me to forgive her." Lila's voice sounded hollow even to her own ears. "Her only sister was out there in Pennsylvania and she wanted to get me out of this atmosphere and for me to go to college. She was afraid I'd never get an education if we stayed here. She was probably right."

He dropped her hands, wrapped both arms around her, and pulled her close to his chest. With an ear pressed right next to his heart, she could feel the steady rhythm of the beat—not just hear it, but actually feel him doing his best to ease the pain they both felt in remembering.

"This is always an emotional time of year for me too," Brody whispered hoarsely.

Lila nodded and then repositioned the side of her face

so that she could hear his heart again. "It was a bad summer for both of us, wasn't it?"

"You leaving broke my heart, Lila."

"Sure didn't seem like it at the time." She leaned back and their gazes met in the few inches separating their faces.

"Men don't cry. Cowboys don't cry. Boys don't cry."

"And that has to do with what?"

He gulped a couple of times. "I wanted to be with you that last night but I couldn't bear to see you in tears again. When you told me you were moving away—well, like I said, boys don't cry and I would have carried on like a little girl."

"But I did cry, remember? When Mama said that we were moving in a week, I cried until my face hurt and your shirt was wet." She looked even deeper into his eyes.

He nodded. "So did I when I got home but I couldn't go through it again. So I went out with the guys and was miserable all night. I was going to apologize to you the next day but you wouldn't roll down the window. Not that I blame you one bit."

"I thought I would die just looking at you in the rearview mirror," she said.

He buried his face in her hair. "I sat down behind the café, put my head in my hands, and thought the worst thing ever had happened. Then..." He hesitated again.

She wrapped both arms around his neck and hugged him tightly. If she'd lost her mother and Aunt Tina that summer in addition to leaving Brody behind, she might have truly stopped breathing. How Brody had survived was a mystery.

She had shared things with him that evening that she'd kept closed off from the therapist she'd started seeing last winter in Florida. Raw things that brought about pain and yet, there she was sitting in a cemetery telling Brody about them.

"Have you forgiven and forgotten?" he whispered.

"Who? You or Mama?"

"First, your mother." He inhaled deeply. "I love the smell of your hair."

"Forgiven." She nodded. "She was only doing what she thought was best for me and she let me finish school here with my class. She'd wanted to be near her sister for a long time."

Lila loved Aunt Tina and all her kids and grandkids. Thanksgiving and sometimes Christmas was fun at her house, but Huntingdon, Pennsylvania, would never be home, not like Happy, Texas. Not even if they moved her father's body out there and she could visit him every week.

"And your dad's family?" Brody asked.

"Dad was a foster child from the time he was about two years old. Thrown about from place to place until he was eighteen and then he went to work in the oil fields. He didn't talk about his life but he did say that all those drunk driving tickets he hadn't paid was the best luck he'd ever had."

"How could unpaid tickets be lucky?" Brody asked.

"They put him in front of the judge, who said that he had a choice of six months in jail or he could join the service. He chose the army and got stationed over in Lawton, Oklahoma. A guy invited him to go home with him one weekend and it turned out the fellow was from Tulia. He was dating my aunt Tina and they introduced Dad to my mother. He and Mama married when he got out of the service and he moved here so he could work in the oil wells again. My aunt Tina didn't marry that soldier but she did marry an oil man and moved back east the next year after Mama and Daddy married."

"I can't imagine going through those tough years without my dad. Thinking about losing him even now makes me so sad," Brody said. "I should go and let you have your time alone."

"Stay." She held on to his hand when he started to pull it away.

They sat engulfed in their own memories for a long time before she finally said, "What happened to your grandpa?"

"Heart attack. Doctor said he was gone instantly. Granny ran the ranch until this spring. Then she turned it over to us."

So much had happened between that last night out at Henry's barn and that moment and she wanted to know everything. "Do you ever wish for one more hour with him to ask him important questions?"

"Oh, Lila," Brody sighed. "Him and my dad both. Daddy died in a tractor accident. I couldn't talk fast enough if I had another hour with either of them, especially right now. After he was gone, I threw myself into the ranch work. That's all I know or ever wanted to do anyway. My folks and Granny both had huge places with plenty to do, so I never had to worry about a paycheck."

"Lived with your folks all this time until you moved over to Hope Springs?"

"I moved into the bunkhouse when Grandpa died.

When Jace graduated from college, he moved into it with me," he said.

"So Jace went and you didn't?"

"He's kind of felt guilty about that but Mama and I insisted. And he's really smart when it comes to agriculture business. What did you do after you graduated from college?"

"I took a job in Memphis for a couple of years, then moved over to Little Rock for a while and I've been in Panama City Beach since then."

The therapist told her that she moved so often because she was searching for happiness but until she found peace within herself, happiness would always be a step ahead of her.

Happy, Texas. Maybe she wasn't searching for the elusive euphoric happy but the place that was a tiny town in the panhandle of Texas.

"Come home with me," Brody finally said after several minutes of silence. "It's my night to read bedtime stories to the kids and I don't want to miss it. It's the second Father's Day without Adam and you of all people understand. But I don't want to leave you."

"Not tonight, Brody. You go on and read to those babies. They need you." She pushed away from him. "But for the record, I don't want you to leave either."

He kissed her on the forehead and straightened up. "Good night, Lila."

"Night, Brody," she said.

Was Kasey right? Could Lila really have both sides?

* * *

Brody sat in the middle of Rustin's bed with Silas in his lap, Emma hugged up to his left side and Rustin leaning over his shoulder as he read *Bedtime for Dogs*. There were lots of pictures and only a few words on each page but it still took almost half an hour to get through the book. Rustin and Emma had dozens of questions about each page and Silas wanted to point to the dog and jabber about it.

Finally, Kasey rescued him and put Silas into his crib, tucked Rustin in, and led Emma to her bedroom. While she got them settled, Brody went to the kitchen and popped the tops on two beers. He carried them to the living room and set Kasey's on the coffee table.

She plopped down on the other end of the sofa. "Thank you. I need this tonight. Father's Day is tough on me. Even worse than Christmas and his birthday." She took two long swallows before she set it aside. "I miss him so much, Brody."

"It doesn't get any easier, does it?" Losing Lila was one thing but she was still alive and able to come back. Kasey's loss was final, down to standing in front of a closed casket.

"Hasn't yet. After the initial shock wore off, I thought it would get better with the passing of time. It hasn't," she said. "Did you go see Grandpa and Daddy?"

"I did," he answered. "Lila was there at her father's grave. We talked."

It wasn't the first time that they'd held hands and talked for hours but in the past it had been either in the barn, under the willow tree, or in her bedroom. They'd talked about things that teenagers did in those days. Today had been different in so many ways and he'd used his words like Jace said. Not to banter or to tease, but emotionally.

"Argued or talked?" she asked.

"The latter. I can't imagine what you're going through but I know that I missed her horribly when she moved away. I'd finally given up on ever seeing her again when she came back to Happy."

"I knew that you had a crush on her, but I had no idea that you missed her like that," Kasey said. "Does she know?"

He shook his head. "There was chemistry between us back then that is still there but, Kasey—"

"When you get past everything that's keeping you two apart, there will be no more buts. However, you've got to work on all those things. Like talking to her. Like not keeping secrets from Mama. Like not caring what Mama or Granny thinks or anyone else for that matter. You have to let the past go and dwell on the future."

"That's a lot to do in one summer," he said.

"Yes, it is. We can't bring back the water that's already flowed under the bridge, can we? If we could, Adam would still be with me and I'd be in Lawton where folks treated me like I had a brain instead of looking down on me like I'm nothing but your kid sister," she sighed.

"You miss that life, don't you?" Brody asked.

"Yes, I do sometimes. I wasn't the odd Dawson kid with red hair who wasn't as pretty as all the Dawson girl cousins or even as her older brothers. I wasn't the only one who got married right out of high school. I was Kasey McKay who could organize a picnic or take care of the Fourth of July party at the recreation hall for the guys who stayed on base. And I was the woman in charge of ordering all the fireworks for the display," she said.

"And then Adam was gone and you had to move right back here," he said.

"Like Lila." She nodded. "Only she's come back where people remember her as that crazy kid who was always gettin' into trouble, not the teacher with a responsible job. Neither of us knows who we are anymore. Difference is that she gets to leave at the end of summer. I've got nowhere to go and three kids who are better off on this ranch than anywhere else. What can I do? Flip burgers or check out customers at a grocery store?"

Brody slid over next to her and put his arm around her. "Kasey Dawson McKay, this ranch is your army base. Without you, Jace and I would be lost. You're our rock. And as of right now, you can do whatever you want for a ranch picnic and fireworks display on the Fourth of July. Just don't leave us, darlin' sister. We'd be runnin' around like chickens with their heads cut off without you."

"I know you're just sayin' that to make me feel better, but thank you." Kasey smiled, her eyes watery.

"It's the truth. Cross my heart. When someone wanders onto the ranch and steals your heart, we'll have to hire five women to replace you," Brody said. "And I'm not whistlin' Dixie, sister."

"I don't reckon you've got a thing to worry about there. It'd take a big man to sweep me off my feet and he'd have to love my kids. Not many men are willing to take on a ready-made family."

"You never know," Brody said. "If I've learned anything, it's that life has a way of surprising you sometimes."

"Well, whatever comes our way—you, me, Lila—we'll figure it out as we go."

"Of course we will." He grinned. "Want to watch a movie? I'll even let you pick it out."

"And you won't bitch if it's a romance?"

"Not tonight," he answered.

He and Jace both had been protective of their little sister since the day their mama brought her home from the hospital. At three and five, they had no idea what to do with a girl baby but their mama said they had to watch out for her and they'd done their best. Now it was time for them to recognize that she wasn't a kid anymore.

"What if I'm not in the mood for something all sweet and sappy but I want some kickass stuff?" she asked.

"Then I might not snore."

"How about that old *Blue Collar Comedy Tour*? Would you snore through some redneck comedy?" she asked.

"Never. If you'll find it, I'll make some popcorn and pour us a couple of Cokes," he said.

"Laughter might help." She stood up and stretched, then opened the door to the place where the DVDs were stored.

"Hey, did you ever watch this *Lethal Weapon* movie? Granny must have left it behind. It's got Mel Gibson in it and he looks real young," Kasey yelled.

"Nope. Heard of it but never watched it. Want to trade redneck humor for kickass?"

"I think I do. If we don't like it, we can stop it and put in the other one."

Lethal Weapon.

That was Lila in a nutshell. She could destroy a man's heart or protect it, depending on how he treated her.

* * *

Lila padded barefoot from the bathroom to the living room of her apartment. Wearing boxer shorts and a tank top, she got comfortable on the sofa and towel dried her long hair and then tossed the wet towel on the coffee table. Duke and Cora took it as an offering and proceeded to use it to climb up on the table to play a game of king of the mountain, knocking each other off the table.

She got bored watching them and flipped through the old DVDs on the shelf below the television. Most of them needed to be tossed in the garbage but one with Mel Gibson and Danny Glover on the front caught her eye.

"*Lethal Weapon Four*. The last one." She put it into the player. "I remember this, Daddy. You and Mama sent me to bed early so you could watch it. I was in the sixth grade and I snuck out of my room and crawled on my hands and knees over to the cabinet. I peeked out around the side and saw some of it before Mama caught me and sent me back to my room."

The cats got tired of playing and flopped down on the edge of the towel they'd pulled from the table. She gathered both of them in her arms and laid them down beside her on the sofa. Her phone rang as the first scene of the movie started, so she hit pause. Duke grumbled in his sleep but he didn't wake when she reached across him for her purse on the end table.

"Hello, Mama," she said.

"Did you go to church tonight?"

"I sure did. Are you checkin' up on my soul?"

"Did you go to the cemetery?"

"Yes, ma'am. Daddy and I had a visit and then Brody Dawson showed up and we had a visit too," she said. "But I imagine that you already knew that and that's why you're calling, right? Who told on me?"

"It doesn't matter who. What matters is that you stay away from him. He's just flat out not the man for you," Daisy fussed. "You're lookin' at another heartbreak. You went inside a shell and didn't come out for years when we moved away all those years ago."

"I thought I kept my feelings hidden pretty good," she said.

"Honey, you don't hide things from a mama. When you have kids, you'll understand that," Daisy said.

"I can handle myself, Mama." She quickly changed the subject. "Guess what I'm fixin' to watch?"

"Depends on where you're going to watch it. Are we talkin' about Henry's old barn or television?"

Lila sighed. "*Lethal Weapon 4*. You remember when you caught me..."

Daisy giggled. "Yes, I do. That wasn't long before your dad died. It was the last movie that we watched together. I'm glad that you went to see him today."

"First Father's Day I've been able to do that since we moved away," Lila said seriously. "I know you miss him, Mama, because I do."

There was a long, pregnant silence and then Daisy said, "Well, I'd best let you get to watchin' the movie that you didn't get to watch almost twenty years ago."

"I wish you were here to watch it with me," Lila said softly.

"Me too, honey. And if that café doesn't sell by the middle of August, we'll watch it together before you go back to Florida. I've decided to move back to Texas if it doesn't have a buyer by the fifteenth of August."

"Seriously, Mama? You'd leave Aunt Tina and all those kids and grandkids?"

"It wouldn't be easy but I'm getting an antsy feelin' since you've been there. Kind of like something is calling me back to my roots."

"The café is going to sell. I just know it will. But I'll take this movie with me when I go and when you come down for Christmas, we'll watch it then, okay?" She would love having her mother right there with her that evening. December seemed so far away. By then nine months would have passed since spring break when she saw Daisy last. Then it had only been a short three-day visit and Daisy and Aunt Tina had worked every day except Sunday while she was there.

"It's a date," Daisy said. "Maybe I'll buy the first three next time I see them on sale and we'll have a marathon one day. Your dad would like that."

"Sounds good to me. Good night, Mama."

"'Night, kiddo."

Lila wasn't five minutes into the movie when she said, "Good grief! Mel's character is every bit as cocky as Brody Dawson used to be. Maybe those fifteen minutes I got of this movie is what made me like the bad boys."

Chapter Eleven

Brody hadn't planned to go with Kasey to Walmart but as she and the kids were leaving, Emma fell off the porch steps and scraped her knee. He couldn't stand to see her cry and the only thing that she said would make it better was if he'd go with them and if she could have a purple bandage on the tiny little cut.

When they all arrived at the store, Kasey situated Silas in the cart and then pointed to the side. "Emma, you hold on right here and don't let go."

Emma crossed her arms over her chest and sucked in a lungful of air. "I want to go see the toys."

"Me too," Rustin said.

"You want to see toys or go for ice cream? We can't do both," Kasey said.

"Ice cream," Rustin said quickly.

"Toys!" Emma pushed him and he fell on his fanny.

Like a feisty little rooster, he popped to his feet, hands

knotted into fists ready to fight until Brody got between them. "Okay, kids. No pushin'. No arguing. Give me half the list and I'll take Emma with me, Kasey."

Kasey divided the list and handed half to him. "After that, you don't deserve to get ice cream or go see the toys either."

"I want to go with Uncle Brody," Rustin declared.

Brody started to put Emma into her seat but she wiggled free of his arms and ran back to her mother.

"I'm not a baby. I'll go with Mama if I have to ride in the basket like Silas."

"Testy today, isn't she?" Brody said.

"Didn't get her nap and everything Rustin does aggravates her today. I remember when you and Jace did the same to me," Kasey said.

"Okay, big girl, you've made your decision. Even if your legs get tired, you don't get to ride in the cart," Brody told her. "But if I look around and you've disappeared, there will be no ice cream or toys and I won't read to you tonight."

"Granny Hope is reading to me tonight." Emma stuck her nose in the air.

"She won't either. Remember what I told you. You got to listen to your uncles and granny but…"

"Mama's word is the law," Emma sighed.

"That's right and both of you better behave." Kasey gave her the mama look. "Now I'm taking Silas to the grocery section."

"No, no, no!" Silas screamed. "Want Memma." He stretched out his hands and tears rolled down his cheeks.

"Take them both and go on. He'll settle down when they're out of sight," Kasey sighed. "It's been a day."

Brody nodded and walked in the other direction. With Rustin telling him all about what kind of ice cream he was going to order and Emma butting in every chance she got to talk about Lila and the ice cream party they'd had with her. Brody made his way to the area where the things on his list were located. He'd put two bottles of tear-free baby shampoo in the cart and was looking for a special kind of kid's toothpaste when someone tapped him on the shoulder.

"There is my friend!" Emma pointed toward the end of the aisle.

"Lila!" Rustin waved.

Brody wondered how in the world perfect little demons could trade their horns in for haloes in a split second. It was pure magic and he'd like nothing better than to put it into a bottle to give to Kasey for her birthday.

* * *

"Well, what a treat, gettin' to see my favorite kids tonight." Lila beamed.

She parked her cart beside Brody's and quickly hugged both of the children. "Hello, Brody. I saw Gracie and Paul back at the pharmacy. Guess everyone in Happy is out shopping tonight."

"Yep," Rustin said. "And then we're going for ice cream."

"And you're going with us," Emma declared.

"I'm afraid I've got to get back to my kittens. Duke and Cora will miss me if I stay too long."

"I could go home with you and read those kittens bedtime stories if you'd go with us," Brody said.

"Uncle Brody reads a real good story," Rustin piped up.

"And they have strawberry ice cream," Emma whispered.

"I guess I could but are you sure, Brody? I wouldn't want..."

Kasey parked her cart beside Brody's. "Hey, Lila, good to see you. I just bumped into Mama. If I'd known she was coming, I would have sent my list with her and saved a trip. You about ready, Brody?"

"Soon as we get the toothpaste." Rustin tossed two boxes into the cart. "That's it, Mama, and now can we go for ice cream? At McDonald's so we can play?"

"Lila is going with us," Emma said. "And I don't want McDonald's. I want the ice cream store and then we can go to the park."

"I should probably be getting home," Lila said. "Storm is brewing and dust is already flying out there."

"Nonsense," Kasey said. "Get the rest of your stuff gathered up and we'll wait until you get to the store before we order and then we'll go to the park for half an hour."

"The park sounds like so much fun. Can I push you on the swings, Emma?" Lila asked.

"Yes," Emma said with a tilt of her chin. "And then I'll push you."

"It's a deal." Lila smiled. "I'll get on with the rest of my shopping and meet y'all at—it is the ice cream place right beside the park, right?"

"That's the one," Brody said. "They make a mean banana split."

* * *

Lila remembered laundry soap and hairspray but forgot at least five items on her list, which meant she'd be making a trip to Tulia to one of the dollar stores later in the week.

Her brain ran in circles all the way to the small ice cream place. It was not a date. It was only ice cream with a family. If it was a real date, Valerie would have Brody committed and Hope would take the ranch away from him. She parked her truck and sat there for several minutes.

Through the window, she could see Kasey and the older two kids on one side of the booth. Silas was in a high chair at the end, leaving Brody alone across from his sister. That meant she'd be sitting with him but it was still not a date. Grown-ups sat beside each other at all kinds of events without it being anything that folks would gossip about.

Decision made, she hopped out of the truck, grabbed her purse, and slammed the door. The wind was blowing even more now, sending all kinds of dirt swirling through the air. She hurried into the store and was halfway to the booth when Brody stood up. His eyes lit up like they used to when she walked into Henry's old hay barn. He met her in the middle of the store and draped an arm around her shoulders. She wasn't a bit amazed when hot little shivers danced down her spine.

"Thank you for coming. The kids are being little devils today and Emma would have thrown another fit if you hadn't come, plus I wanted you here with me," he said.

"Then I'll do double duty?" She grinned.

"Triple. I've volunteered you to help carry the ice cream back to the booth as the lady gets it ready," he said as they walked past the booth. "I've got the list right here." He showed her a napkin with writing on it. "Kasey says if we'll order and then bring it to the booth, she'll corral the three monkeys."

"We ain't monkeys. We're childrens," Rustin declared loudly.

"I'll be a monkey if they eat ice cream," Emma said.

"They eat bananas, not ice cream, so you can't be a monkey," Rustin argued.

"Girl monkeys eat ice cream. Boys don't," Emma argued.

"Enough!" Kasey said in a tired mother's voice.

"Brody, this might not be such a good idea," Lila said on the way to the counter.

He laid a hand on the small of her back and escorted her across the floor. "What? Me ordering and you totin'? I trust you not to stumble over your feet and waste good ice cream."

"You know what I mean," she said, enjoying every delicious little shiver that his hand created.

He gave the girl behind the counter the order and then drew Lila even closer. "The end—except for your banana split, unless you want to share with me."

"Sharing is fine." She nodded.

Oh, Lord! What had she just agreed to? If anyone saw them eating from the same bowl... She took a deep breath and reminded herself that she was thirty years old and so was Brody.

"You tell her what toppings we want, then." His hand slipped around to rest on her waist.

She was amazed that she could utter a word with all the heat his hand created but she managed to rattle off strawberry, caramel, and chocolate.

When everyone had their order, Kasey put a bib on Silas and Lila slid into the booth with Brody right after her. Then Kasey sat beside him so that she could help all three kids: Silas at the end in a high chair and the other two across the table from them.

Brody was a big man and the booth wasn't one of those huge ones, so their sides were plastered tight together. It was a miracle that the heat between them didn't melt every bit of ice cream in the whole place.

Brody filled a spoon with ice cream and moved it toward Lila's mouth. She had no choice but to open wide. She'd barely gotten her mouth shut when Gracie and Paul McKay entered the store and headed straight toward them.

"Nana!" Emma squealed.

"Hey, kids." Gracie smiled. "Imagine finding all y'all at an ice cream store. I saw your van outside, Kasey. Can we steal the kids for a couple of hours? We'll have them home by bedtime. We'd take them to the park but the dust storm out there now is just the tip of the iceberg. There's a big one going to hit in about an hour. What we're seeing in the sky isn't clouds at all but dirt."

"That would be great. I can get some computer work done this evening without having to stop every five minutes." Kasey nodded. "Drag over a couple of chairs and join us."

Paul was already busy getting two from a nearby table and placing them on either side of Silas's high chair. "We had to run in to get prescriptions at the drugstore. I guess y'all heard about the new church pianist coming in. I'm glad to hear that we'll have another person who can play. That way if Gert needs to be gone, it won't be such a big deal."

"Just don't try to fix her up with me. I'm not interested." Brody grinned.

"She is not my friend," Emma said bluntly.

Rustin pushed her arm. "She can be my friend."

"Mama, he hit me," Emma tattled.

"Did not!"

"Did too."

"Whoa!" Brody said. "Let's eat our ice cream without fighting."

"Emma! You haven't even met her," Kasey scolded.

"She can't be my friend because Lila is." Emma glared at Rustin.

Paul chuckled. "So how'd you get tangled up with this bunch of renegades, Lila?"

"Met 'em in Walmart," she answered.

"Lila is my friend," Emma said seriously.

"And a mighty good one," Gracie told her. "How's your mama? Any way we could talk her into coming back to Happy and running the café rather than selling it?"

"She's been thinkin' about that." Lila wondered how quick it would be all over Happy that she was out with Brody. Maybe she'd better hightail it to Australia with him. Valerie Dawson was a pretty good shot with a rifle, the last she heard.

"Well, tell her to think real hard," Paul said.

Lila smiled and nodded. Daisy had grown pretty fond of the whole family out there, so it wouldn't be easy for her to move back to Texas.

After they'd eaten their ice cream, everyone drove away from the parking lot. Paul and Gracie had shifted Silas's car seat and Emma's and Rustin's boosters to the backseat of Gracie's van and waved as they headed out toward the park. Kasey had driven off in the van on her way back to the ranch. That left Lila and Brody standing beside her truck.

"I thought you drove the van for Kasey," she said.

"No, I like to bring my own vehicle in case I want to go home before they do."

"Thanks for invitin' me. I love bein' around the kids." The wind swept her hair across her face and blew dust into her eyes. "I'd forgotten about sandstorms in this part of the world. We'd better get on out of here before it gets really bad. Thanks again."

"Anytime." He pulled his hat down tighter, opened the door, and took a step closer, shielding her from the wind. "One more thing. Will you be my date for the Hope Springs Fourth of July ranch party?"

"I know I keep saying this but…"

He ran a finger down her cheek. "Yes, it's a good idea. We've got to get over this thing between us or embrace it and we can't do either by running from it. Can't rewrite history or do a thing about it. But it doesn't have to ruin the future."

She laid a palm on his cheek. "It's tough playing second fiddle to a woman who is going to play the church piano. Besides, what is your mama going to say about that?"

He grabbed her hand and kissed the palm. "Darlin', you will never be second fiddle to anyone and Jace can have Tara if he wants her. And I don't really care what Mama or Granny has to say. Just tell me that you'll go with me."

"Pretty good pickup line there and the kiss on the palm is a nice move. Yes, I will go with you and thank you for asking me. I'll wear my runnin' shoes so when your mama brings out her rifle, I'll at least have a fightin' chance," she laughed.

"I'll lock Mama's firearms in a safe place and pick you up at nine that morning. But we'll see each other before then." He brushed a soft kiss across her lips and disappeared around the back of her truck into a fog of sand blowing half of New Mexico into the Texas Panhandle. She started the truck and licked her lips. They tasted like a mixture of chocolate and sand. Not a bad combination; not bad at all.

The passenger door opened and Brody's big frame filled that side of the truck. Without a single word, he leaned over the console and wrapped his arms around her. Their lips met in a scorching hot kiss that made her knees weak. It was a good thing she was sitting and that her truck was not a stick shift because she couldn't have walked and she sure could not have held down the clutch. The weatherman on the radio said something about a fierce sandstorm and then Jennifer Nettles started singing "Unlove You."

He looked deeply into her eyes when the words said that it wouldn't work and would be nothing but hurt but that she couldn't unlove him.

"I can't unlove you either."

"Like it says, we have other lives," she whispered.

"We can change that," he said.

"What are we talking about here?" Lila asked.

Brody kissed her again. "One of those alternate endings to an old story." He got out of the truck and walked away, his head bent against the blowing dust.

Chapter Twelve

Before she pulled out of the parking lot, she found her Jennifer Nettles CD in the console and slipped it into the stereo and listened to that same song over and over all the way home. Lila could have written that song when she was sixteen, but that night every word became a part of her soul as she drove home with dirt swirling around her. She'd parked in the garage and hit the remote to close the door when she noticed a shadow in her side window.

Her door opened suddenly and with a flick of the wrist, Brody unfastened her seat belt. Then he scooped her into his arms like a bride and carried her toward the door into the apartment.

"You sure you want to carry me over the threshold, cowboy?" she whispered.

"Right now I'm not sure of anything except that I want to hold you in my arms and I want more than one kiss," he said.

She reached down and opened the door and his lips closed on hers.

"The same room as when we...," he whispered.

"Yes, the same," she said.

He carried her to the bedroom, shut the door with the heel of his boot, and sat down in an old rocking chair with her in his lap. Light from an almost full moon flowed through the window that he'd crawled in and out of dozens of times all those years ago.

"God, I missed you so much, I thought I'd die some nights." His voice was deeper than usual.

"But was it just rebellion because we weren't supposed to be together?" she asked softly.

Half of his face was in shadows, the other half lit by moonlight coming through the window. The story of their lives right there. One side lived in secret, the other in the light of day. One wild side, one responsible. Tonight she had a passionate desire to feed the hungry wild child.

She slowly ran her hands under his T-shirt. "How are you not married?"

He tugged her shirt out of her jeans and his calloused hands felt like fire on her skin. In a split second her bra was undone and he had free rein of her whole back. "How are you not married?"

"I almost was...once. You?"

"Never, not even almost." He nibbled on her earlobe. "But I want to hear about your near misses."

"Not now," she panted.

Effortlessly, he stood up with her in his arms and moved to the bed. "Is this the same..."

"Oh, yes, the same one where we both lost our virginity." She smiled.

He removed her shoes and socks, kissed her toes, one at a time. "I remember that night very well. You didn't cry."

"Why would I? It was wonderful."

Her jeans went next and then her shirt and underwear, all tossed on the floor. Her breath came in short spurts but she wanted him as naked as she was, so she pushed him backward on the bed.

"My turn." She sat on his knees with her back to him and removed one of his boots, tossed it across the room, and then tugged off his sock. He massaged her back the whole time.

Lord have mercy! He had learned some impressive moves since the last time they were together. She flipped around to undo his zipper and turned loose an erection that took her breath. Tugging his pants down to his ankles and then shoving them off the bed, she decided that a long, slow bout of foreplay was not going to happen. She crawled back up his long frame and held out her hands. He put his in them and she pulled him forward. Effortlessly, he went from lying down to sitting and removed his shirt. It was nothing but a blur as it joined the other clothing thrown haphazardly around the room.

"Dammit!" he swore under his breath.

"What?" she asked.

"I don't have a condom."

"No problem. I'm on the pill." She covered his mouth in a long, hard kiss that left her aching, just like words to the song in her head said. "I want you, Brody," she whispered.

He flipped her over on her back and her long legs

wrapped around his waist as he slipped inside her and they began to rock together. His mouth found hers and the last thing that crossed her mind was that she loved, loved tall men and then there was nothing but a scorching desire to put out the flames in her body…and only Brody Dawson had ever had the power to do that.

He took her right to the edge of release, then slowed down. She tightened her legs and he groaned. "Lila, I can't…," he said hoarsely.

"I know, me neither. One, two…"

"Three!" He managed a smile as they both hit the heights together. When he could breathe again, he rolled to one side, taking her with him and holding her tightly against his side.

"You remembered," she panted.

"So did you." He snuggled his face down into her hair. "One. Two. Three. We go together."

"Yes," she mumbled, and shut her eyes. She was back in Brody's arms, where she belonged. Past and future didn't matter—only the present.

* * *

Brody awoke to the sound of someone tiptoeing down the hallway. His first thought was that Jace had come in late, but then he realized that Lila's long leg was thrown over his. The footsteps stopped at her door and a female voice whispered softly, "Lila, darlin', are you awake?"

Every hair on his neck stood straight up. Even after more than a decade, he would recognize Daisy's voice. In a few seconds, she chuckled softly and then he heard the wheels of a suitcase cross the hall. The hinges on that door didn't squeak like Lila's did but there was no mistaking the latch when she closed it.

He rolled out of bed, landed on his hands and knees, and quickly found his clothing, jerking each item on when he located it. The door across the hall opened again and Daisy cussed when she stumbled over a kitten; then her tone changed and he could hear her high-pitched apology to the cat.

He unlocked the window and, holding his breath, slid it open enough to crawl out. God, he felt eighteen years old all over again.

The clock on the dash of his truck said it was five a.m. and the sun was barely peeking over the horizon. He broke every speeding record he'd ever set on the way to Hope Springs and had just sat down on the porch when Jace came out of the house.

"You're awake awfully early. Did you put a pot of coffee on?" Jace asked.

"Not yet. Had the dust storm stopped when you got home?" Brody answered.

"Only lasted about an hour, but that was enough. Kasey got home and then Paul and Gracie came in about ten minutes after her with the kids. They were going to keep them longer but Emma's bandage fell off and she wanted her mama. I got involved in a television movie and didn't go to bed until midnight," Jace answered.

"Reckon we ought to get back inside and get a pot of coffee going. Kasey is an old bear if it's not ready first thing when she gets to the kitchen." Brody stood up, stretched, and rolled his neck to get the kinks out.

Jace frowned. "You were wearing that shirt when you left last evening. Where did you spend the night?"

"A cowboy does not kiss and tell."

"You better not let Mama— Speak of the devil." Jace pointed to the truck coming down the lane.

"Let Mama what?" Brody groaned when he saw Valerie's bright red truck coming toward the house.

"Hey, I'm just sayin' and I don't have to spell it out for you. I can see the way you look at Lila but remember, she leaves at the end of summer. We ain't kids anymore and Mama has never liked her. Family gets complicated."

Brody waved when the truck came to a stop. "I wonder what she's doing here at dawn."

"Have no idea but Granny is in the passenger seat."

Brody quickly crossed the yard and opened the door for his grandmother. "Y'all are sure out early this mornin'."

"I left my cell phone in the kitchen. We're on our way to have breakfast at the café and then we're going to the cemetery to get the family graves in shape before it gets hot this mornin'," Hope said.

"Want me to run inside and find your phone? Why didn't you holler? I'd have brought it to you."

"Didn't know it was missin' until this mornin'. It's really your grandpa's phone. I had mine so I could make calls but I carry his around with me," Hope explained. "He had some pictures of the two of us together on it and sometimes..." Her voice cracked. "Yes, please go get it for me."

"Be right back," Brody said.

"Whoa! Before you leave, I heard that you had ice cream with Lila last night. What's goin' on?" Valerie asked.

"Sure was a demon dirt storm last night." He smiled.

"Don't change the subject. I want answers." Valerie crawled out of the vehicle and got right into his face.

"Answer is that I had ice cream with Lila and Kasey and the kids. Paul and Gracie were there too. I'm not sure what's going on but I've still got a lot of feelings for Lila and I intend to see where they go before she leaves at the end of the summer."

She looked like she could chew up railroad spikes and spit out staples right at him. "I won't have it, Brody."

"It's not your call, Mama. I've invited her to the Fourth of July festival."

Valerie inhaled deeply and let it out slowly. "I don't like it one bit."

"Well, I don't like it that you're being obstinate about something that's in the past," he shot back.

She crossed her arms over her chest just like Emma had done. Females! Didn't matter how old or young they were, they could be a handful.

"You're just like your daddy. He'd argue with a damn stop sign," Valerie said.

"Get back in the truck, Valerie," Hope yelled out the window. "He's not a little boy. He can make his own decisions and live with the consequences."

"Thank you, Granny. Sure you don't have time to come in for a cup?"

"No thanks. I've got my heart set on some of Molly's sausage biscuits this morning," Hope answered. "We'll visit later. And don't forget, the Dawson family reunion is this Saturday."

Brody shook his head. "No, ma'am. I'm lookin' forward to it. Jace and I will be over Thursday evening to help Jack get the barn ready. If y'all need anything between now and then, just yell. And I'm giving you a heads-up, Mama. I intend to ask Lila to be my date for that too."

"Well, crap!" Valerie got back into the vehicle.

Brody jogged to the house and brought out the phone, handed it to Hope, and took a step back. "See y'all later."

Valerie kept her eyes straight ahead and didn't even acknowledge him. Hope gave him a broad wink and a big smile.

"I love you, too, Mama!" Brody yelled as she drove away. Then he crossed the yard and flopped down on the porch beside his brother.

"You totally forgot that this was the week for the family reunion, right? Lila is messin' with your brain. I can't believe that you fought with Mama like that," Jace chuckled. "Jack called this mornin' to remind me about the reunion. Are you really going to ask Lila to be your date?"

"Jack is a good foreman. We'd have never made it without him when Daddy died," Brody said. "And, yes, I'm going to ask Lila."

* * *

Lila reached out to wrap her arms around Brody but all she got was an armful of pillow and covers. Her eyes popped open wide and her heart fell to her knees. Same ole, same ole! A booty call and then gone when she awoke. What ever made her think he would change? In the past, it had been necessary. If her mother had caught them sleeping together, her hot temper would have burned down the café. But now they were adults and her mother was in Pennsylvania for God's sake.

Her alarm sounded and she hit the button to turn it off and crawled out of bed. More than a little angry, she headed toward the bathroom, took a quick shower, and then with only a towel around her body, she padded back to her room. Her phone pinged when she was tugging on a pair of jeans, but she ignored it. If it was Brody, she wasn't ready to talk to him. When she was fully dressed and had her long black hair pulled into a ponytail, it pinged again.

Sure enough, there were six messages from Brody. The first one said: *Call me.*

The last one said: *We have to talk. I can explain.*

"There is no explainin'," Lila muttered on the way to the café kitchen. Duke and Cora were sleeping together on the sofa, but she didn't take time to stop and pet them.

She pasted a smile on her face even if she didn't have one in her heart. "Good mornin', Molly!"

"I'm not Molly but good mornin' to you." Her mother pulled a pan of biscuits from the oven, set them on the cabinet, and then opened her arms. "Surprise!"

"Wow." Lila's heart skipped a beat and then raced. Sweet Jesus! Was that what Brody wanted to explain? She walked into her mother's arms and hugged her tightly. "When did you get here and where's Molly?"

"Five minutes until we open the doors and there's already trucks out there in the parking lot, so you get the short version. I wanted to see you, so Molly and I hatched a plan. I'd get into the airport at the same time she did and she'd loan me her vehicle for a week. She's going to Florida for a test to see if she likes it there. I came here for the same reason. We meet again next Monday evening at the airport."

Lila was speechless but finally found enough voice to at least ask, "And what time did you get here?"

"About five this morning. I knocked on your bedroom door but you didn't wake up. Thought I heard you as I headed toward the kitchen to get things going, but it must've been those two kittens runnin' around. Cute little fluff balls, by the way." Daisy stepped away from Lila and stirred a pot full of sausage gravy.

Lila's phone vibrated in her hip pocket. She pulled it out to see another text from Brody: *Have you gone to the kitchen yet?*

Her thumbs moved like lightning: *Yes. No explaining necessary.*

His came back: *Thanks. Call you later.*

She headed toward the dining room to turn on the lights, adjust the thermostat, and open the door for business. *How did you get this number?*

Lights on and she was flipping the sign around when she got the next one: *Stole it after you went to sleep.*

She sent a smiley face and tucked the phone back into her pocket.

The first two people to enter the café were Valerie Dawson and her mother, Hope. Lila hoped neither of them heard her quick intake of air and that they didn't know where Brody had spent last night.

"Good mornin', Lila. We're here for the pancake special that Molly makes on Tuesday mornin's," Hope said.

"What gets you ladies out this early?" she asked as she came to their table with two steaming mugs of coffee.

"We're makin' sure the Dawson graves are cleaned up. The family likes to go to the cemetery while they're here for the reunion." Valerie's tone had a definite chill to it.

"Hey, I saw a black cat out there in the cemetery. Y'all ever seen it?" she asked.

"That would be Chester O'Riley's old cat. He lives in the house right beside the graveyard," Hope said. "I heard that you got a couple of kittens out at Henry's old barn."

Lila nodded. "Cora and Duke. One is black and the other is white. Cute little things."

"Speakin' of Henry's barn, did you or Daisy ever hear anything about where he went when he left Happy?" Hope asked.

It seemed strange that Hope was eager to engage her in conversation when Valerie's whole body language said that she'd rather be talking to the devil than to Lila.

"Mama told me about him leaving town but it went in one ear and out the other. I hadn't thought of him until I came back this summer," Lila said.

"To answer your question, we have no idea where he went or why." Daisy pushed through the swinging doors that separated the kitchen and dining room. "How are y'all doin' this mornin'?"

"Daisy Jo." Valerie shot icy looks toward Daisy.

"Valerie." Daisy nodded. "I haven't been called that since I left Texas."

"Well, you'll always be Daisy Jo to us. That's what your mama called you," Hope said. "I came for pancakes and crispy bacon and a side order of biscuits and gravy. And what are you doing in town? Coming back for good?"

"I don't know yet. Molly is decidin' if she really wants to leave. I'm decidin' if I want to return. It's a test. What do you want, Valerie?"

"For Molly to stay and you to go," Valerie said without a hint of a smile.

"Well, some things never change, but I was talkin' about food," Daisy said.

"I'll have the big country breakfast with three eggs," Valerie answered.

Daisy propped her hands on the table and leaned in until her nose was only inches from Valerie's. "Just for your information, I'm not in the market for a husband, a significant other, a boyfriend, or even someone to date, so if you're seeing someone, he is totally safe."

"That is enough," Hope said. "Good God, y'all are both well past fifty years old and you're actin' like a couple of teenagers. Get over it, Valerie! And, Daisy Jo, you stop bein' bitchy."

"Mama!" Valerie gasped.

"Hope!" Daisy's voice went high and squeaky.

"We'll have those orders right out." Lila looped her arm in Daisy's and led her to the kitchen. "What just happened?"

"She accused me of trying to seduce Mitch Dawson in high school and she's never gotten over it and neither have I."

Lila bit back a giggle. "So that's why she didn't want me and Brody to date. Because you were still mad at his dad."

"Maybe." Daisy poured pancake batter on the grill. "But I didn't want you dating Brody either. I'd rather see you in a convent as married to a Dawson."

"Why?" Lila asked.

"They all think they are only a notch below God and the angels and you'd spend your whole life tryin' to be what they want you to be rather than who you are. We've got a whole week to have this conversation. Take this to them and if Valerie asks, I did not poison her eggs but I might next time."

"Well, you sure flunked this test with flying colors." Lila smiled.

"Or I passed it. I'm not moving back here and it didn't take a week to make me figure it out," Daisy said.

"I'm surprised that you stayed as long as you did with the kind of anger you two have," Lila said.

Daisy shook a spoon at her. "Don't get me started."

"Yes, ma'am." Lila picked up the orders and got the heck out of the kitchen.

Chapter Thirteen

Someday when Lila had daughters, she might understand her mother but that Wednesday evening, she was glad to see Daisy drive off to church and leave her alone. Working with Daisy was a whole different thing than vacationing with her a couple of times a year. Or maybe it was simply that when they were both back in Happy that Daisy reverted to the mother of a teenager rather than treating Lila like she was a grown woman.

"Which is understandable," Lila told Duke and Cora that evening. "This wild streak inside me is hard to keep reined in when I'm here, so I'm not surprised that she thinks she can run my life like she used to."

Cora bit Duke's ear, so he latched on to her tail and the fight was on. Black and white fur all mixed together made Lila laugh but she needed to get outside to clear her head.

A few minutes later she was headed out toward the canyon with intentions of riding through it without getting sidetracked. But when she reached the lane back onto Henry's old place, she slowed down and turned into it. She told herself it was because she wanted to see that big white mama cat, but the voice in her head said that she was lying.

That same niggling voice said that she shouldn't go into the barn when she saw Brody's truck parked in the shadows of a big oak tree, but she didn't listen that time either. She parked beside the barn doors and hung her helmet on the handlebars.

The white cat came out immediately when Lila sat down on a bale of hay and she stroked its pretty fur from head to the tip of its tail. "So are we here alone? Did someone leave that truck and go off with a friend? Too bad you can't talk."

"I'd trade places with that critter." Brody's voice came down from the loft.

"I saw your truck. How long have you been here?"

"I decided to swing by after replacing fence posts all day. Join me."

Without hesitation, she left the cat and started up the ladder toward his voice. He reached down to help her from the top rung into the loft and sent a shot of pure unadulterated fire through her body. She noticed the quilt spread out over the loose hay in the corner.

"I wasn't expectin' anyone, but I have to admit I was hopin' you might feel the vibes of me wanting you to come out here tonight." He kept her hand in his and led her to the quilt. "Sit with me."

She let him pull her down onto the quilt and a soft breeze fluttered her ponytail. She'd been in this same spot more than one time.

"Remember all the times when we used to spend time here?" he asked.

"Oh, yeah," she whispered. "How many other women have been here with you on this same quilt since I left?"

His free hand covered his heart. "I'm hurt that you'd even think I'd let another woman look at our quilt."

She giggled. "This isn't really that same old quilt that you kept in your truck, is it?"

"It really is the same one—our quilt." He nodded. "And, honey, no other woman has even laid eyes on it. This is my secret place where I come when I'm lonely and want to think."

She'd never thought so much about what Brody went through when she left. She'd always figured that he'd gotten over her within a week and moved on to someone else. "What do you think about?"

"Everything," he said. "Important decisions have been made sittin' right here but mostly I think about you, Lila."

"What are you battling with tonight?" she asked.

"It's not the breath you take but the moments that take your breath away," he said. "I've been thinking about that phrase all day. And I realized that just about every breathtaking memory in my life involves you."

She turned toward him and let her soul sink into those blue eyes. His dark lashes fluttered and then rested on high cheekbones. And then his lips found hers in a long, passionate kiss that raised the heat at least ten degrees. His tongue touched her lower lip and she opened her mouth to allow him entrance. That kiss led to more, each one getting hotter than the last.

Just when she was ready to start unsnapping his shirt,

his phone rang loudly, breaking the mood. He ignored the first five rings. Then within a second, it started again.

"Dammit!" he said as he fished it out of his shirt pocket. "This had better be good, Jace."

He listened for a minute and then hung up. "Our prize bull and two heifers are out on the road. I have to go help get them corralled. Will you wait here for me?"

"I could go help," she said.

He hesitated half a second as if he was weighing the idea and then he nodded. "I'd like that but only if you'll come back here with me when we get done."

She planted a kiss on his cheek. "Want to take the cycle?"

"It would scare them half to death. Jace is bringing the old farm truck. They know that sound. We just need to get them roped and tied to the back. I'm sorry we got interrupted."

She patted him on the knee. "Ranchin' is a twenty-four-hour job, Brody. I understand that. Let's go get the cattle off the road."

He held her hand and she kept pace with his long legs as they left the barn. The moonlight silhouetted an old bull and two cows grazing on the grass beside the road. That old adage about the grass always being greener on the other side of the fence flashed through Lila's mind.

"Hey, Lila." Jace grinned.

"Jace." She nodded.

One of the heifers suddenly raised her head and bawled, then trotted off toward town. The other one headed in the other direction. The bull sauntered to the back of the truck as if he understood exactly what he was supposed to do. Jace quickly wrapped a rope around his neck and tied him to the truck.

"I'll turn around the one going toward town," Lila said over her shoulder as she jogged in that direction.

"I'll keep the one headed in the right direction toward the ranch," Brody yelled.

Lila managed to get ahead of the cow and take a stance right in the middle of the road. The heifer lowered her head, eyed Lila, and started to charge but Lila waved both arms and yelled. The cow stopped in her tracks and simply turned around and began to run back the other way with Lila right behind her.

She caught up with Brody near the lane going back to the ranch and found that the problem with the fence was right beside the cattle guard. "It's a wonder only two got out. I see a dozen or more," she said breathlessly.

"Hey." Jace's voice carried through the darkness. "I came back for the truck. I got Sundance in the corral. I can get this fence fixed in no time."

"I'll stay and help," Brody said quickly.

Jace bumped shoulders with him. "I've got this. You want to use the truck to take Lila back to wherever y'all were?"

Lila could see that Brody was battling with the decision—stay and help where he was needed or go with her. "I can walk back to the barn and get my cycle. I know the way."

Brody reached over and took her hand in his. "Thanks, Jace. I'll be home in a little while."

"See you at breakfast. First one to the kitchen gets the coffee going." Jace waved him away.

"Well, that was fun," Lila said. "But honestly, Brody, I can go back alone or else stay and help y'all fix the fence."

"Jace has got it and I want to spend time with you," he said.

"But it's not easy for you to let him, is it? Tough cowboy that you are, you think you've got to take charge of everything," she said.

Brody gently squeezed her hand. "You know me too well."

"Right back atcha, cowboy," she said.

The sky was filled with twinkling stars surrounding a moon with darkness on one side and light on the other. Lila felt as if that was her life that evening. Light flowing around her in the present and darkness where the future was concerned. Maybe, she thought, she should concentrate on the present and not worry about what the future holds.

"You're awfully quiet," Brody said when they turned to go down the lane leading back to the old barn.

"Just enjoying the moment," she said softly.

He stopped, dropped her hand, and tucked his knuckles under her chin. She tiptoed to meet him part of the way when he bent to kiss her. Like always, her knees went weak, her palms resting on his chest became clammy, and her pulse raced.

"I'm enjoying the moment too," he said when the kiss ended. "Would you go to the Dawson family reunion at my folks' ranch with me on Saturday?"

She cocked her head to one side. Had she heard him right?

"Brody, going to the Hope Springs thing for Independence Day is one thing. Everyone in the whole county is invited to that. The Dawson family reunion is personal."

Valerie might really get out the gun if she showed up with Brody, but then if they were going to test the waters of the future, they'd both better stop thinking about her or Hope or even Daisy.

"I'll introduce you to my whole family." He squeezed her hand.

"Are you sure about this?" Lord have mercy! The Dawson family reunion with Valerie and Hope both there—Lila might as well sign her own death warrant and pick out her burial clothes.

"Never more sure about anything in my life, Lila. Please," Brody whispered.

A star shot across what was left of the moon, leaving a trail of brilliance in its wake. Was that her sign? She and Brody had hoped to see a falling star many times when they were teenagers and God saw fit to throw one through the sky that night. It had to be an omen.

"Okay." She nodded.

"Thank you." He leaned over and brushed a soft kiss across her cheek. "I'll knock on your door at six-thirty."

"If you change your mind—" she said.

"I won't." That time he stopped the words with a steamy string of hot kisses.

When she finally drew away, she said, "I would have floated all the way to the clouds if you had invited me to your family reunion when we were in high school."

* * *

"I'm not that kid anymore," Brody said as he took her hand in his again and began to walk the rest of the way to the barn. "I want to go forward, not backward."

"Sounds good to me." She stopped at the bike. "I should be going."

"Come inside for just a little while with me." His heart was about to float right out of his chest and he couldn't bear to let her leave—just another hour, maybe two so that he could hold on to the feeling.

She looped her arm in his and he led the way back inside the barn, and let her go ahead of him on the ladder. When they were in the loft, he pulled her down to rest in his arms as he stretched out on the quilt.

"I was a fool," he said. "You know what they say about not missing the water until the well runs dry."

"What happened after the well went dry?" she asked.

"I tried to get you out of my mind with hard work. So what kind of girl were you after you left?"

"I turned into a quiet nerd in college."

"That's hard to imagine," he chuckled.

"Mama said that no one knew I was Lila Harris, that crazy kid from Happy, Texas, who caused all kinds of trouble. She said I could be anyone I wanted to be, so I became the quiet Dee Harris and molded myself to fit into the character that she was," she said. "I made excellent grades, graduated with honors, and had my pick of teaching jobs."

"And the Harley?" he asked.

"I didn't get it until last year. Every so often that Lila girl would surface and want to go on a ride with her daddy down through the canyon. I bought it so that she'd be quiet and leave Dee alone."

"I can't imagine anyone ever keepin' Lila quiet and I sure don't see you as Dee."

Lila nodded. "Brody, in six weeks, I'm going back to Florida. I don't know if I'll stay there for another year or move to another state, but wherever I am, it'll most likely be far away from this part of the world. Are you sure you want to start something with no future?"

"So you like teaching better than runnin' a café?"

She rolled over and propped up like him, her face just inches from his. "What do you think?"

"There's schools all around us," he said. "Lila, I can't imagine why you'd want to hide yourself in another person. You're beautiful, witty, fun, and we were just kids who did crazy things. We never hurt anyone with our shenanigans."

"And Lila was also the poor girl who lived in the back of her mother's café that no one asked to proms or family reunions or even to a rodeo."

"I'm sorry," he said. "Brody was a fool who didn't listen to his heart but he won't make the same mistake twice. Let's give it the six weeks and see where it goes. What have we got to lose other than time? And when summer is done..."

"We can wave good-bye without tears this time," she said.

If he had a lucky bone left in him, maybe there would be no good-byes. "What are you thinkin' right now?"

"Something that your smart little sister said," she answered.

"And that would be?"

"That we might be able to have both the inner child and the responsible adult if we want," she said.

"So maybe you could be responsible for everyone else and be my wild child?" Her lips called to him. His body ached for her. But that night shouldn't be about sex. He needed to show her that he was willing to court her properly, and that was more than sneaking into and out of her bedroom for a fast roll in the hay.

She flipped over on her back. "This business of being both is confusing. What if I forget who I am at your family reunion?"

He traced the outline of her lips with his forefinger. "Might liven things up."

"You sure?" Her mouth tingled from his touch.

"You're so beautiful," he whispered as he leaned down and kissed her softly.

She wiggled around until her head rested on his chest. "You know what I missed most when we left?"

"Me?"

"Well, there was that, but I missed the smell of hay and hot summer nights."

"I missed you, Lila. Everything about you. Your wet hair hanging down your naked back when we went skinny-dippin'. Your wit and the way you never let me get away with anything," he said. "I missed holding you and not just for the sex. I flat out craved even half an hour with you nearly every evening. No matter how much I tried to lose myself in work, it never eased the pain."

"I think you were the reason I invented Dee Harris. If I changed it all, the heartache of leaving Happy and you wouldn't kill me. If I was someone else, a studious girl with no background or memories, I had no reason to hurt." She yawned.

Lying there with her in his arms and not saying anything else should have been awkward, but all the words in the dictionary were useless. Nothing could begin to describe the peace in his heart and soul. He pulled her closer to his side, not caring that the night was hot or that the only thing they were doing was enjoying being close.

She mumbled something and then her body went limp when she fell asleep.

He smoothed her hair, drew her closer to his side, and closed his eyes, hoping that she believed in second chances.

* * *

Lila awoke with a start. She squirmed out of Brody's arms and sat up, wrapping her arms around her knees.

"Good mornin'," Brody yawned. "Did you sleep well in this five-star hotel?"

"Yes, I did. What time is it?"

Thank God it was still dark. Hopefully, still early enough that her mother was still at the church affair or else she'd gone to one of her friends' houses to catch up on the gossip.

"Still night," he said.

"I've got to get home. Mama is drivin' me crazy with advice already. If she thinks I've been with you, she'll never shut up."

"You should ask me for a date," he said.

"What?"

"I asked you to my family events. I'll make my mother face the fact that there is an us—as in Lila and Brody. Maybe you should do the same with yours," he said.

"Good advice. Would you go with me to church on Sunday night? I will come and get you at six-thirty and we'll be there by the time it starts," she said.

"Wow!" He grinned. "That's a pretty big step, going to church. I mean the family reunion is one thing, but a public thing like sitting together in church? You expectin' to share a hymn book too?"

"I don't share a songbook on a first date. I save that for the third date and only then if I really like the guy," she teased.

"Well, then, I suppose I'm free on Sunday night but only if I can take you and Daisy to Tulia for ice cream afterward."

"Why go all that way? We'll just open the café and invite Mama to join us," she said.

"Long as I get to pay for it so it's my treat, that's fine." He draped an arm around her shoulders.

"Then it's a date. I'll tell Mama when I get home," she said. "And when are you telling Valerie to expect me for the family reunion?"

"I already told her I was invitin' you," he drawled.

"Are you kiddin' me?" she gasped.

"Nope. Told her that I'd invited you to the Fourth of July picnic and that I was asking you to be my date for the reunion."

"And?"

"She didn't like it but that's her problem. Mine was convincing you to go with me." He pulled her tighter into his embrace and kissed her on the tip of her nose.

"I really do have to go, Brody." She rolled to her feet and started for the ladder but stopped after a couple of feet. "Want me to help pick the hay off that quilt?"

"No, it's so dry, it'll shake right off. Give me a minute and I'll walk you out to your bike. I still have trouble believing that you ride that thing."

She shimmied down the ladder and waited at the bottom for him. In the darkness she had to use her imagination to really see the way he filled out those snug jeans. Could she really say good-bye to him at the end of the summer with no tears?

He tossed the quilt into the bed of the truck on the way to her bike and took her hand in his. Would even the simplest touch of those big, rough hands ever stop sending delicious hot little shivers through her heart?

She threw a leg over the seat of her bike and settled onto it, but he didn't let go of her hand. He leaned in and captured her mouth in a scorching kiss that made her weak in the knees. She pulled her hand from his and wrapped both her arms around his neck and opened her mouth slightly to allow his tongue entrance. He made such sweet love to her mouth that she wanted to take him back to the hayloft or better yet to the bed of his truck since it was closer.

Then he took a step back. "Text me when you get home."

She nodded as she settled her helmet onto her head. "Betcha I beat you."

"I'm right next door." He grinned.

"I've givin' you a fightin' chance against my Harley."

He took off toward the truck and she left a dust storm for him to follow. When she reached the end of the lane, she leaned into the curve and gave the cycle more gas when she straightened up. Glad that there were no cops out at that time of night, she didn't even look at the speedometer. She braked at the café parking lot, slinging gravel against the old building in a spray.

"So much for sneakin' into the apartment," she giggled as she grabbed her phone and hurriedly sent a text: *I beat you.*

One came back immediately: *Only by a few seconds.*

Her thumbs typed: *You owe me something wonderful.*

She put the phone back in her pocket, removed her helmet, opened the garage door, and pushed the bike inside. Her phone pinged and she grabbed it to read: *Name the time, the place, and the poison and I'll pay up.*

She eased the back door open and took off her boots. She made it to the living room to find her mother standing in the middle of the floor with her hands on her hips.

"God I hate that bike. I bet you were down in that damned canyon, weren't you? Actually, I don't want to know. You're home and safe and I'm going to bed. Kids!"

"Good night, Mama."

"I'm glad I made the decision not to come back here. I'd die of a heart attack in a week worryin' about you. If I'm eighteen hundred miles away, I won't know what you're doing," Daisy fussed. "At least if you were riding too fast in that canyon, you weren't with Brody Dawson."

"See you bright and early, Mama."

"I don't know which is worse. The bike or Brody." Daisy got in the last word as she slammed her bedroom door.

Chapter Fourteen

Lila tied on an apron and tucked an order pad into the pocket before she flipped on the lights and unlocked the doors to the café that Thursday morning. No one was in the parking lot yet so she went back to the kitchen, stuffed a biscuit with crispy bacon, and ate it as she watched Daisy crack eggs into a bowl.

Lila took a deep breath and faced her mother. "I'm going to the Dawson family reunion on Saturday night with Brody," she said.

"Well, that ought to go over like a cockroach in the punch bowl at a church social," she said. "It might be the smartest thing for you."

"Really?" Lila had expected a hundred reasons why she shouldn't go and lots of talk all day about the issue.

"Sure," Daisy said. "It will show you that those people ain't never going to accept you. You'll always be my daughter and Valerie would rather have Lucifer's sister for a daughter-in-law than my kid. Go on and be miserable."

"And you won't say 'I told you so' one time, right?" Lila finished the biscuit and made another one.

"Oh no. I'm going to say that at least fifty times on Sunday. You never would listen when it came to Brody Dawson," Daisy said.

The bell above the door dinged and Lila laid her biscuit to the side. "Well, just be careful you don't say it in front of Brody. I asked him to go to church with me on Sunday and we—as in me and you and him—are coming back here for ice cream afterward."

"Are you nuts?" Daisy whispered.

"Not according to my therapist!"

Lila made her way through the swinging doors into the dining room. "Good mornin', Paul and Gracie. How y'all doin' today?"

"Coffee for us both and the breakfast special," Gracie said. "We're on the way to Amarillo to get some things for Hope and Valerie for the Dawson family reunion and thought we'd splurge and have breakfast out this mornin'."

Lila pinned the order on the merry-go-round in the window and poured two mugs of coffee. "Sugar or cream?"

"No, just black," Gracie said. "We started helping with the reunion when Adam got in the family. Since our family is down to just the two of us, we like having the Dawsons take us in."

"That's sweet of them," Lila said, glad that several more folks were arriving so she'd have an excuse to walk away.

"Order up," Daisy yelled.

From then until after the noon rush, there was someone in the café all the time and Daisy was kept busy. But at two o'clock things slowed down enough that Daisy brought two burger baskets to the front. She pointed at the drink machine and then at the food.

"You know what I drink," she told Lila.

"Sweet tea for both of us." Lila nodded. "No lettuce and extra pickles, please?"

"I raised you, kiddo," Daisy told her. "I know how you eat your burgers."

Lila carried the tea to the booth and sat down across from her mother. Each of them stretched forth their long legs and propped their feet on the other side and sighed at the same time.

"Been a morning." Daisy dipped a French fry in a small container of ketchup.

"Felt more like a weekend than a Thursday." Lila poured ketchup over her fries.

Lila had just bitten off a bite of burger when the bell above the door rang. She looked around to see Brody swagger into the café. Looking like he'd spent the whole morning in the hay fields or maybe building fences, his white T-shirt was smudged with dirt and his hair wet with sweat. His forehead had a definite line between dusty and clean where his hat had been all morning.

She didn't realize she was mentally stripping him out of his clothes until Daisy kicked her under the table. Shifting her gaze from him to her mother, she tucked her chin and shot a mean look across the table.

"Something wrong, Lila?" Brody headed around the counter to the drink machine.

"Not a thing." She smiled. "What can I get you?"

"Y'all keep your seats. I'm just here for a glass of ice tea and I can get it myself," he said.

"Kasey don't make tea at the ranch?" Daisy asked.

"Yep, but I had to come into town to get a load of feed and I'm thirsty," Brody answered. He poured a tall glass from the drink fountain and carried it to the booth where he slid right in beside Lila.

"How you been Miz Daisy?" he asked.

"Busy," Daisy answered tersely.

Under the booth, his hand rested on Lila's knee. She took a big gulp of iced tea but it did nothing to cool her off.

He squeezed gently. "Lila tells me that you'll be here until Monday. You need a ride to the airport?"

"I've got Molly's car. I'll drive myself and she'll be here in time to cook breakfast on Tuesday," she said.

"She hates Florida and can't wait to get home to Texas. Crazy thing is that Georgia doesn't like it so much either and she might be coming back to Happy also. They might buy the café after all."

"Why does Molly hate Florida?" Lila asked.

"Too much sand. Molly says it's in everything from her hair to the corners of her suitcase. It's like it follows her." Daisy almost smiled.

"Well, would you look at that? I wonder what Clancy is doing in Happy, Texas." Daisy beamed.

Lila whipped around so fast to look out the window that it made her light-headed. She dropped the French fry in her hand and gasped at the sight of her ex-boyfriend walking toward the cafè. "Mama?"

"Hey." Daisy shrugged. "We still talk occasionally."

"Why?" Lila glared at her mother.

"Should I leave?" Brody asked.

She grabbed his free hand and held it on top of the table. "No, stay."

It was Daisy's turn to glare and if looks could kill, Brody would be nothing but a bag of thirsty bones on the floor right then. The bell rang and Clancy entered the café, glanced around, and smiled when Daisy waved him over to the booth.

"Well, hello, Clancy. Can I get you something?" Daisy pulled a chair out for him.

"Got a drink back down the road," he said. "I'm good. Keep your seat, Daisy. Hello, Lila."

"Clancy, meet Brody Dawson." Lila made introductions. "Brody, this is Clancy. He and I are colleagues at the school where I work in Florida."

Brody slid out of the booth and extended a hand. "Pleased to meet you, Clancy. I take it that you're friends with these folks or is it family?"

"More than friends, right, Dee?" He shook with Brody and then sat down. Wearing perfectly creased dress slacks, a pale blue shirt open at the collar, and loafers, he looked exactly like he did every day at school. Not a blond hair was out of place and his cute little mustache was trimmed.

Brody's phone pinged and he checked the message. "That's Jace. The kids we've hired to help us this summer are down to the last fence post, so I'd better get back to the ranch with what I've got loaded on the truck. See you Saturday, Lila." He stood up. "Nice to meet you, Clancy."

"Lookin' forward to it," Lila answered. "Call me later?"

"Of course." Brody dropped a kiss on her forehead and started toward the door.

"So what are you doing in Texas?" Lila asked, but her eyes stayed on Brody as he crossed the floor.

"I came to see you, Dee. Why would he call you Lila?" Clancy asked.

Brody stopped at the fountain and filled a takeout cup with ice and tea. He took his time, throwing a wink over his shoulder toward Lila before he finally laid a five-dollar bill on the counter. He waved at the door and she couldn't keep her eyes or mind off him as he made his way across the parking lot.

"I asked you a question," Clancy said brusquely.

"Because that's what I'm known as in this town. Why would you drive fifteen hundred miles to Texas to see me? If you're going to fire me, you could do that by phone," Lila said.

Clancy chuckled. "Darlin' Dee, I'm not going to fire you. I can't wait for the end of summer when you come on home where you belong."

"Does Belinda know you're here?"

"Blunt." Clancy's grin got bigger. "Like always. Texas didn't change that a bit, did it, Daisy?"

"When she crosses the border into Texas, it gets worse," Daisy said. "I've got to get back to the kitchen. You two have things to discuss. And, Lila, we'll talk later."

"Oh, yes, we will," Lila said, and then turned her attention to Clancy. "What's going on? Did my mother call you?"

For some insane reason, an old song by Vince Gill played through her head—"Which Bridge to Cross (Which Bridge to Burn)." She thought she'd burned the bridge between her and Clancy when they'd broken up last year. If she hadn't at that time, she sure enough had the torch in her hand now and he'd better run because she was about to set fire to the damn thing.

"No, actually I called her last week and she said she was coming to Texas for a week. Then we talked on Monday. I got a flight from Pensacola to Amarillo today just to see you. I've only got about an hour before I have to head back to the airport, but what I wanted to say needed to be said face-to-face," he said seriously.

"I'm listening." She imagined skipping across the bridge like a little girl and pouring gasoline from a red can as she went from one end to the other.

"I missed you." He scooted closer and ran a hand down her arm. It did nothing but irritate her.

"What about Belinda?" Sorry sucker was two-timing his girlfriend of four months. He deserved to get a little gasoline on his expensive shoes, so in the video playing in her mind, she doused them down good.

"Things are going well. We like the same things, love the same old movies, the same books, and we have so much in common. We're both coaches at the school, so we understand what the job means," he said. "But there's this thing between me and you that I need to resolve before I take it to the next step."

"Which is?" Mentally, she flicked a candle lighter and a flame shot out from the end.

"Which is asking her to marry me. Are you listening to a word I'm saying?" He squeezed her arm too tightly.

"Congratulations. I'm happy for both of you." She jerked her arm free and scooted over to the other side of the booth.

"Is that Brody cowboy the reason you called it quits with me?" Clancy raised an eyebrow.

"Could be." She'd seen that look on his face before when he didn't get his way.

He combed back his hair with his fingertips and not a single strand fell over his forehead like Brody's did when he did the same thing. "I really love you, Dee."

"Then why are you marrying Belinda?"

"I won't if you'll give me another chance. We had something good and I can't get you out of my mind and heart. It's not easy for me to sit here and say this when I saw the way you looked at that dirty cowboy," Clancy answered.

"You shouldn't have come to Texas," Lila said.

"Is there hope for us after school starts? If you get that rancher out of your sights, you might see things different. A marriage shouldn't be based on a high school whim," Clancy said.

"There is no hope for you and me," she said.

Flaunting the fact that he had money enough to fly to Texas and back in one day did not impress her one bit.

"Then I wish you the best and I'll go now."

"Thank you and give my best to Belinda," she said.

"A good-bye kiss? It might change your mind." He stood and pushed the chair back in place.

She shook her head. "Not a good idea."

Propping his hands on the booth, he leaned close to her and whispered, "We could have had something really good."

That was as far from the truth as black was from white. What they would have had would have been far from good and would have probably ended in divorce.

"I want something that will take my breath away and if I can't have that, I'll do without," she said.

In an instant, his hands left the table and he was plastered next to her in the booth, her face cupped in his hands and his tongue halfway down her throat. She pushed him away so hard that he slid off the end of the booth and sprawled out on the floor.

"You just made the biggest mistake of your life." Clancy's voice went cold as ice as he got to his feet.

"Or I just made the smartest decision of my whole life. I can't believe that you came all the way to Texas to try to get back together with me when you're living with Belinda." She wiped the feel of his lips away from hers. "She deserves better."

"I care too much about you to see you throw away your life on a worthless, dirty farmer," Clancy said. "You know I could give you a good life, if you would just get over this silly teenage infatuation."

In her vision of the bridge, she wrung every last drop of gasoline from the can and poured it out.

"You sound more like a parent than a boyfriend and that's a little creepy." The imaginary torch she'd held in her hands hit the bridge, sending it into a blaze. "I've got to get back to work. Have a nice flight home."

She made her way out of the booth, sidestepped around him, and headed toward the kitchen. The decision to not go back to Florida for the new teaching year was made in that instant. She would reopen her employment files at the college and teach in central Pennsylvania, as badly as she hated the winters there, before she taught with Clancy as her principal for another year.

"Then this is good-bye?" he asked on his way across the floor.

"Exactly." *Run, Clancy, run. The fire is on the way.*

"Just remember I tried, Daisy," he called out as he slammed the door.

Lila pushed through the swinging doors to the kitchen and popped her hands on her hips. "What were you thinkin'?"

"Keepin' you from a life of misery," Daisy shot back. "What did you tell Clancy? He loves you and he'd do right by you."

"Oh, like he's doing right by his current girlfriend?" Lila said through gritted teeth. "I can't imagine how she'd feel if she knew he was only going to propose to her if I wouldn't take him back."

Daisy's brows drew down into a solid line. "He said that?"

Her mama just got a glimpse into the real world. Not every man out there was like Billy Harris who adored his family and who let them be a part of the decisions.

"Pretty much. You talk about Brody's family feeling like they are above me socially, well Clancy is a thousand times worse." Lila propped a hip on a bar stool. "What'd he tell you?"

"That you had commitment issues, whatever that means. You kids talk a different language than we did at your age," she sighed.

"He's right," Lila said. "I do have trouble giving my heart to someone."

Daisy searched in her purse for her phone. "I'm going to call him and give him a piece of my mind. I'm so sorry that I even talked to him."

Lila took the purse from her hands. "Remember what you've always told me?"

"About what?" Daisy's dark brows drew into a tight line.

"Anyone who stirs in a shit pile..." Lila got tickled.

Daisy finished the old saying. "Has to lick the spoon."

Arms around each other's shoulders, they laughed so hard that tears ran down their cheeks. Finally, Lila wiped her mother's face and then her own with a bar rag.

"Everything works out as it should, Mama. Ignoring him is the best thing we can do. This helped me decide that I'm definitely not going back to Florida, though. I'll take a job wherever I can find it next year," Lila said. "I can't work with him after this."

"Come to central Pennsylvania. I promise I'll...," Daisy started.

Lila crossed the room in a couple of long strides. "You're the mother. If you didn't meddle and worry, I'd call the undertaker."

Daisy wrapped Lila in her arms. "Thanks for not being mad at me. Now get on back out there. I hear truck tires on the gravel."

"And if it's Brody?"

"I don't want to see Clancy again but..."

Lila handed Daisy the towel. "When you were my age, you had a ten-year-old daughter. And your mother didn't run your life."

"She tried," Daisy said, "but I was every bit as stubborn as you. She didn't want me to buy this café or put an apartment behind it."

Lila waved over her shoulder and she went back out to the dining room. "Well, hello, Brody Dawson. Haven't seen you in days."

She could almost hear Daisy's sighs.

"We good?" he asked.

"We are very good." Two bridges had been burned but she was very interested in rebuilding one of them.

Brody had come back to check on her. That meant more than a Sunday date, the Dawson reunion, or the Fourth of July party. Not caring that Paul and Fred were on their way into the café, she walked right up to him and wrapped her arms around him.

"Want to talk about anything?" He drew her close.

"Not a thing. I just want you to hold me for a minute so that I know you're really here," she said.

"I'm here for you always, Lila," he whispered. "As long as you need."

The door opened again and two of Daisy's old friends, Laura and Teresa, rushed inside from the blistering heat with Fred and Paul right behind them.

"Well, hello, Brody," Laura said.

Lila stepped back away from him. "Hello. What can I get y'all?"

"Ladies." Brody nodded toward them and turned back toward Lila. "I'll see you Saturday night, right?"

"I'll be ready." Lila beamed. "Don't work too hard."

He rounded the end of the counter and kissed her on the cheek.

"Does Valerie know about this?" Laura raised a dark brown eyebrow that matched her hair—all but that inch of gray roots shining at the part, anyway.

"Lord, she's going to have a hissy," Teresa whispered. Laura's opposite, she was tall and thin with dyed red hair cropped at chin length and a face so full of wrinkles that it looked like a road map of Dallas.

Drying her hands on her apron, Daisy pushed back the swinging doors and motioned them back into the kitchen.

"Good enough for her, the way she's acted toward me and Lila. Not that I'm for my girl going out with Brody but Valerie don't get to call the shots. Y'all come on in here and we'll make us a batch of sweet potato fries to nibble on while we have a visit."

Lila carried two glasses of sweet tea to Fred and Paul's booth. "A big order of fries?"

"Sounds good, sweetheart," Fred said. "It's my turn to buy, so make the ticket out to me. He's wishy-washy like an old woman. Changes his mind all the time."

"And you're one of them DOC people," Paul shot back at him.

"OCD, obsessive-compulsive disorder. Get it right, old man," Fred said.

"Only someone who had it would know how to spell it," Paul joked. "And does Valerie and Hope know that you and Brody are makin' out in public?"

"Why would you ask that?" Lila asked.

"Because we need to know whether we should warn the volunteer fire department," Fred teased. "Those two women are going to burst into flames when they hear what we just now saw."

Paul lowered his voice and his eyes shifted around the café. "I heard that you might be going to the Dawson family reunion. That true?"

"Might be." Lila patted him on the shoulder.

Lila listened to their banter and yelled the order through the window rather than pinning it up. She'd barely gotten that done when her phone rang. Seeing Brody's picture put a smile on her face.

"Hello," she said.

"Just thought I'd let you know that I did tell my family

that you're my date for the family reunion and for the Fourth of July picnic at Hope Springs. There's no surprises," he said.

"Tell that to Laura and Teresa. I'm not sure they believe their eyes," she laughed. "What do I hear in the background?"

"George Strait and I are enjoying the morning now that Conrad has driven out of Happy," he answered.

"Clancy, not Conrad," she said. "But that doesn't matter. He's gone. And I think that is 'Check Yes or No' playing. Am I right?"

"If I gave you a note with the words 'will you be my girlfriend' and there were two boxes at the bottom with yes by one and no by the other, which would you check?" he asked.

"Well, I checked no when Clancy handed me the note today. I haven't gotten one from you yet, so I don't know. Maybe you'll have to write the note and see which box I check," she answered. "Order is up. Got to go."

"Maybe I will write that note," he said.

* * *

Brody let out a whoosh of air that he didn't even know he was holding until he put the phone back in his pocket. It rang immediately and he jerked it out, hoping that he'd hear her say that she'd check yes on that childish note.

"Hey," he said.

"Come on to the springs. Sundance is belly deep in the water and refuses to get out," Jace said.

Brody parked the truck and one of the high school boys he'd hired for the summer came running over.

"Glad to see you with the wire. We strung the last of what we had."

"Got to go get that pesky bull out of Hope Springs. Wouldn't happen to have a rope, would you?"

"Sure thing, Mr. Dawson." He removed his keys and tossed them at Brody. "Take my truck. Rope is behind the seat. The clutch is a little tight so you got to stomp it real good. We'll get this unloaded and keep on workin'."

"Mr. Dawson. If that don't make me feel old," Brody complained as he started the ten-year-old vehicle, jammed it into gear, and took off across the bumpy pasture toward the springs.

Jace was sitting at the edge of the water when he parked the truck. Boots were set off to one side and his jeans were soaked all the way to the waist. "There ain't no coaxin' or cussin' him out of there."

Brody grabbed the rope and headed that way. "How'd he get out of the corral?"

"I have no idea but I'm ready to put him in a steel pen with no gate," Jace groaned. "I might as well go on out there and rope him since I'm already wet."

Brody handed him one end of the rope and kicked off his boots. "I'll go this time. It's so damned hot that I'll enjoy the cold water."

"Kasey called. Who was the citified feller who came to see Lila?" Jace wrapped the rope around his broad palm twice.

"Don't know much other than she put him packin'." Brody waded out into the water and sucked air when the bull kicked backward and drenched him from the neck down. "You sorry sucker. You want to act like a rodeo bull, then I'll ride you out of this water."

Sundance shook his head and bawled.

"Feelin' feisty, are you," Jace laughed.

"Yes, I am." Brody slipped the rope around the bull's neck.

"Hey, I was talkin' to Sundance, not you. He's already mad. Just push and let me get him tied to the truck and he'll come out of there."

"I'm going to teach him a lesson." Brody mounted his back, holding on to the rope with one hand.

Sundance went completely wild. His back feet shot toward the sky and his nose went straight down into the water. He snorted, slung water and bull snot everywhere as his hind legs hit the water with a splash. Twisting his head toward his tail one way and then reversing the process, he tried to shake Brody off.

"Hey, we could use him for rodeo stock," Jace hollered as he removed his phone from his shirt pocket and started recording.

Brody hung on, getting angrier by the minute as he watched Jace film him rather than checking the time to see if he'd managed eight seconds. Then suddenly, the bull's back legs reached for the sun and his head went into the water again. His hide and Brody's jeans were sopping wet, so there was no way Brody could hang on another minute. He slipped into the cold water and his straw hat floated down the stream.

"Guess your family jewels is a bit cold now too," Jace laughed.

"Delete that video," Brody panted.

"Okay," Jace said, and hit a few keys. "Deleted."

"Thank you."

"But I did send it to Lila before I deleted it."

"You..." Brody shook his fist at Jace and ran toward his brother.

Sundance, now rid of the burden on his back, walked out of the water, his head held high as he strutted off toward the pickup truck and stopped at the rear.

Brody had Jace in a headlock when he realized that Sundance was staring at them. "Would you look at that crazy fool? He's waiting for us to tie him to the back of the truck and lead him back to the corral."

Jace wiggled free and plopped down on the grassy bank. "Why shouldn't I send that to Lila?"

"You didn't see that guy, Jace. He was everything that she probably needs in her life. All spruced up." Brody fell down beside him, flopping onto his back. "She deserves better than a crazy old rancher who gets mad and rides a bull out of icy-cold water."

"Maybe so, but she put him goin', didn't she?" Jace lay back beside his brother. "If that bull moves an inch, I swear this is when he goes to the market to be made into bologna."

"That don't mean she can't reconsider. He looked at her like she was... Well, he looked at her like I feel when she's in my sight. Like there's no one else."

"She loved you first and you know what they say about first loves. Let's get this old cuss back to the corral." Jace stood up and offered a hand to his brother.

"Thanks, brother."

"Just helpin' my elders," Jace teased.

"Hey, I'm not old yet." Brody slid into the truck seat.

"You'll always be older than me," Jace said as he headed toward the back of the truck.

Brody grabbed his phone from where he'd tossed it

onto the passenger seat and found a message from Lila: *Call me.*

She answered on the first ring. "What was that all about? I was afraid you'd drowned when you went into the water like that. I swear it was worse than the fear in my heart when you rode at the bull riding and fell off."

"You care!" he chuckled.

"I don't want you dead. And I bet you and that bull both will have to warm up for a long time before..." She paused for a breath.

"Before what?" he asked.

"Call me later when your HDTs are thawed."

"HDTs?" he asked.

"Hangin' down things," she said as she hung up.

The screen went dark and he roared with laughter.

"What's so funny?" Jace asked.

"Nothing." Brody had no intention of sharing the moment. "You going to drive or ride on the tailgate and keep him moving?"

"I'll tailgate and then we're going to the house to get cleaned up. Mama says we're supposed to be over at her place at six to start helping get things ready for the reunion. I'm steering clear of her. She'll be fuming or trying to lay a guilt trip on you. I don't want to hear either one," Jace said. "And for a man who's about to get strung up by his mama, you sure got a happy expression on your face."

"I'm doin' now what I should've done in high school. I just hope it's not too late." Brody got inside the truck and started driving slowly back to the barn.

Chapter Fifteen

The pile of clothing grew on Lila's bed as she tried on outfit after outfit. Who would have thought that she'd have so much trouble picking out an outfit for a family reunion? Jeans and a shirt should do fine but thinking about a first official date with Brody had her insides twisted into a knot. She was checking her reflection in the mirror when Daisy pushed her way into the room. She handed a cup of chamomile tea to Lila and then sat down in the rocking chair.

"Thought that might calm your nerves," Daisy said. "This is not a date with the governor. It's just Brody Dawson."

Lila set the cup on the dresser. "Thanks, Mama, but I'd be less nervous if it was the governor. Does this look all right? Is it too short?"

The bright red sundress left her shoulders bare. The waist fit snug and the skirt lay in gentle folds, stopping at the top of her knees. She'd shaved her legs, put a few curls in her long, black hair, and applied a minimum of makeup.

She was every bit as nervous as she had been when she dressed for her first date with Brody twelve years ago. Her mother had brought her a cup of tea that night, too, and then held her while she wept when he didn't show up. She glared at the tea, refusing to take a sip for fear it would jinx the whole night.

"You look beautiful. But, honey, I'm sure the almighty Dawsons wouldn't take too well to you comin' to their affair in your bare feet, so you better find a pair of shoes to match that dress. Or, you could just blow this silly notion off and go to dinner with Laura, Teresa, and me," Daisy said.

Lila slipped her feet into a pair of leather sandals and groaned. "Molly was right—I really should have gotten my hair trimmed and my nails done. My toes look horrible and I don't even have time to do them myself now."

"Wear cowboy boots. Those fancy ones I bought you for Christmas a couple of years ago. They've got that red inlay in the front," Daisy suggested.

"Oooh, good idea." Lila pulled the boots from the closet and shoved her feet down in them.

"Now that completes the outfit," Daisy said. "Wipe off that light colored lipstick and put on clear red. It's on my dresser."

Lila checked the mirror. Daisy was right. The outfit called for red lipstick.

"I hate to see your heart broken again, but I guess you've always had to learn your lessons the hard way," Daisy said. "It's tough on a mama to see her kid hurting."

"Sometimes the only way to get past the pain is to wade through it to the other side." Lila raised her voice as she crossed the hall. "Right now I'm standing right in the middle of the river, not knowing what to do. Behind me is the past. Ahead is the future and the water is rising."

"That sounds like something your father would have said," Daisy said. "Now you're ready. I hear his truck driving up. I'm going to play the mama card even if you aren't a teenager. You will not go rushing out there to meet him and if he honks rather than coming to the door like a real date should, then I'm going to shoot the tires out of his truck."

"That's a step up." Lila extended a hand and pulled her mother to her feet. "You would have shot him, not the tires, when I was younger."

Daisy led the way down the hall to the living room. "The mama of a grown daughter can only do so much."

The phone rang at the same time that Brody knocked on the door. "You answer that and I'll get the door," Daisy ordered.

Lila grabbed the phone and said, "Happy Café. Lila speaking." Lila held up a finger to give her a moment. "Yes, ma'am, we are interested in selling the café. You heard right and I'll be glad to see you tomorrow morning at ten-thirty. Bye now."

She turned to find Brody standing in the middle of the floor. He held a bouquet of wildflowers tied with a bright red ribbon in one hand and a black cowboy hat in the other. The top button of his blue and white plaid shirt was left undone, showing a tuft of dark hair. Her eyes had trouble moving away from the belt buckle engraved with a bull rider.

"You look amazing." He stuck the flowers out toward her. "I picked these for you."

"Did I hear that you were meeting someone about the café?" Daisy asked.

"Yes. They're coming tomorrow morning." Lila smiled. "Thank you so much for these, Brody. Give me a minute to put them in some water."

"I'll do it for you and they'll be on the dresser in your room when you get home this evening. I'll shut the door to keep the cats out." Daisy took them from him.

"Thank you, Mama," Lila said, but her eyes didn't leave Brody's. "They are beautiful."

"Not as beautiful as you are. Does she have a curfew, Miz Daisy?" Brody asked.

"Only if I do," Daisy said.

Lila hugged Daisy and whispered, "Wish me luck."

"Never, not with that guy," Daisy told her.

"Ready?" Brody asked.

"As I'll ever be. Excited but nervous."

He settled his hat on his head and held the door open for her. "You have a good time, Miz Daisy."

"I'm sure I will," she said.

When they were near the truck, he put both hands on her shoulders and turned her around. His gaze started at her toes and traveled slowly to her hair and then back to settle on her lips. "You take my breath away, Lila. You're stunning."

"You clean up pretty good, cowboy, but I got to admit, I kind of like a little dirt on your shirt."

His lips landed on hers for a brief, sweet kiss as he helped her into the truck. "I like you in your tight jeans and tops, too, but, darlin', you look like something out of a movie in that outfit."

She flipped the visor mirror down and checked her lipstick as he rounded the hood of the truck and took his place behind the wheel.

"Brody, I'm really stressed about this." She put the mirror back up and fastened her seat belt.

He drove to the highway and turned right. "Would you have been if we were still in high school and I'd asked you to our reunion?"

"Of course, but I bluffed my way through things better in those days," she answered.

"I've got a confession. I felt like a kid tonight when I knocked on your door. My hands were sweaty and I almost threw the flowers behind the garage. I should have thought to go to Amarillo and get you roses. You deserve something more than wildflowers picked from our back pasture." He parked the car at the end of a long row of other vehicles in the pasture beside the ranch's sale barn. "Ready?"

She shook her head.

"Hey, any woman who would be willin' to climb on a bull that refuses to get out of Hope Springs and ride the critter with me isn't afraid of anything." He grinned.

She hit the button to undo the seat belt and threw open the door.

"Whoa, darlin'," he said. "You see all those cowboys around the barn door? They need to see me bein' a gentleman or I'll have to beat them off with a stick all evening."

She sat still until he made it around the truck and held out his hand. Putting hers into his turned the whole world around. The jitters in her stomach settled. Her heart stopped racing.

"Is that your cousin Toby with Jace?" she asked.

"It sure is, but he's married now so I don't have to worry about him." With an arm slung around her shoulders, Brody led her toward the barn.

She tried to take it all in with a glance but it was impossible. A group of cowboys had gathered around Toby and Jace, and they were all staring at her. Kids were running around everywhere, but she didn't see Emma or Rustin. Country music was playing. The aroma of smoked brisket filled the air.

"A band?" she asked.

"Just a local group. It's not Blake Shelton," Brody said. "But I'm askin' right now for every dance."

"Yes," she said without hesitation.

"Lila Harris?" Toby smiled. "Is that you?"

Toby was a Dawson—tall, sexy, great angles to his face and gorgeous eyes. But in Lila's eyes, he fell far short of Brody when it came to looks and charm.

"It is really me," she said. "You haven't changed a bit, Toby Dawson. And I hear that you're married."

"I am," he said. "You'll have to meet my Lizzy. We're expecting our first baby in a few months."

"Congratulations! And Blake?"

"He and Allie are here somewhere. They have a little girl already." Toby nudged Brody on the shoulder. "You'd best keep her close, Brody. We still got lots of cousins who'd just love to steal this one from you."

"Don't I know it!" Brody nodded. "We'll see y'all later, I'm sure."

"Lila?" Hope was suddenly right there in front of them when they walked inside the barn. Her eyes started at Lila's red lipstick, then traveled to her boots and back up again.

"Doesn't she look beautiful tonight?" Brody flashed a smile.

"She's always been a pretty girl. I do like those boots and I'm a sucker for red lipstick," Hope said. "Girls today ain't got a bit of style with all them browns and pinks on their lips."

"Thank you." Lila nodded.

"You should wear more red." Hope looped her arm through Lila's. "Brody, you go on and visit with your cousins a little bit before Jace says grace and we're turned loose on the food. I'm going to take Lila around and show her everything."

Rustin appeared out of nowhere and tugged at Hope's hand. "Granny, I'm hungry. When are we going to eat?" Then his eyes grew big and he yelled, "Emma, Lila is here!"

Emma squealed and she ran across the barn toward them.

Lila dropped down to a squat and hugged both kids at the same time. "This looks like a great party. What's your favorite thing on the food table?"

"The baked beans," Emma said.

"Chocolate pie but you got to eat everything on your plate before you get any," Rustin said seriously.

"You're not my boss, Rustin, but you can dance with me." Emma pulled him out to the dance floor.

Hope wrapped her hand around Lila's upper arm. "They're cute kids. We'd like to have a dozen more on Hope Springs."

Lila was stunned speechless. Hope might be telling her that she wanted her to produce twelve little Dawson kids or else she was being nice to lure her to her death in a dark corner of the barn. Lila wasn't ready for either one of those options right then.

"Hey, Valerie, look who I found," Hope called out to her daughter, who was in the midst of several women.

Valerie's quick glance said that she'd rather be home with a migraine than attending a reunion with Lila.

"We'll be around to introduce you later." Hope waved as she kept walking toward the stairs leading to the buyer's balcony. "Now it's your turn to hold my arm. My knees ain't what they used to be."

Lila took the steps slowly and waited for Hope to get a firm stand on every one before she moved on. Was the old gal going to push her over the top railing to her death or did she have a gun hiding between the bleacher seats?

"I used to sneak up here with my boyfriend," Hope said when they reached the top. Three layers of wooden benches ran the length of the balcony. During the fall livestock sale, the buyers could have a bird's-eye view of the cattle being offered.

Without thinking, Lila glanced to the top bench on the far end—the one where she and Brody always had a making-out sesssion.

Hope giggled. "That was our favorite spot, too, but we'll sit right here on the bottom seat because my legs need to rest."

Lila waited for Hope to get comfortable before she removed her hand from her arm. Then she sat down beside her and looked down at a barn full of people. There was Valerie still visiting with a group of women that Lila didn't know.

From the way Kasey was motioning with her hands, she was giving the caterers their last orders before they took all the lids off the food dishes. Kids were running every which way and the band was playing one country music song after another.

Then she spotted Brody talking to Jace and Toby. He kept scanning the barn and finally as if a sixth sense got a hold on him, he looked up. She waved and he grinned—she had no doubt that they were sharing the same memory. Her cheeks filled with high color but she couldn't take her eyes off him.

"Looking down from here puts a new perspective on things. Getting away from the forest so you can see the trees. Henry was my neighbor, you know. We grew up right across a barbed-wire fence from each other. Even graduated from high school together."

Lila shook her head. "I guess I did know that but it never dawned on me that y'all were the same age."

Hope sighed and blinked a few times. "We were very different."

Lila sucked in a lungful of air when she realized why Hope was talking and why they were sitting in the balcony. Henry Thomas had been her boyfriend at one time. Holy crap!

"Do you love my grandson, or are you going to break his heart to pay him back for the way he treated you?" Hope changed the subject so abruptly that her question shocked Lila.

"I'm not that kind of person."

"Okay, then do you love him?"

"I've been terrified of you in the past, Miz Hope. I respect you in the present but that is something I'm not going to discuss with you. It's between me and Brody," Lila answered.

Hope giggled. "Yep, I knew I was right. You've grown into a responsible woman who would do good on Hope Springs. Now if you can stand up to Valerie like that, you'll be fine."

"Yes, ma'am." Lila let the air out of her lungs slowly.

"Hey, what're y'all doin'?" Brody asked as he cleared the top step.

"We're visitin' away from all that gawd-awful noise. That stuff ain't country music. Why don't they play some Hank Williams or some Ray Price," Hope fussed. "You can help me get back down the stairs. I bet it's time for Jace to say the blessin' on the food, ain't it?"

"Kasey says in fifteen minutes. I've got time for one dance with Lila before then," he answered, and raised an eyebrow at Lila.

She hoped that her smile told him that everything was all right.

Hope headed off in Valerie's direction when they reached the bottom of the steps and Brody pulled Lila onto the wooden dance floor. He twirled her around a couple of times, then brought her back to his chest. He sang along with the band when the lyrics talked about them getting a little wild on Saturday night and then she went to church on Sunday in ribbons and pearls.

"Ain't this the truth?" he said.

"I don't own any pearls and never did wear ribbons in my hair but we did get a little wild on Saturday nights," she answered breathlessly. The whole world had always disappeared when she danced with Brody, whether it was at the Silver Spur to a live band or in an old hay barn to the music of a truck radio turned up as loud as it would go.

Barely taking a breath, the singer went right into Sammy Kershaw's "Don't Go Near the Water." Lila swished her red skirt a few times and then Brody grabbed her hand.

She caught Valerie glaring from the sidelines but she didn't care. She wasn't going to take Brody to the springs after dark for a night of hot, passionate sex under the willow trees and then a time of skinny-dipping to cool off, so the woman could back off.

Jace hopped up on the bandstand and rang a cow bell to get everyone's attention. When the noise settled, he picked up the microphone. "Welcome to the Dawson family reunion. Looks like we all took that verse in the Good Book about going forth and multiplyin' very literally."

Laughter rang out and he gave it time to settle down before he went on. "Rustin, that would be Kasey's son, has been tellin' me for nearly an hour that he's starving and his sister, Emma, says that she is hungry to death. So without any more comments, I'm going to say grace and y'all can hit the food tables. As usual, Prairie Rose is catering the meat and the drinks but we thank all the rest of you for bringing a covered dish to go with it. Now if you'll bow your heads."

Brody whipped off his cowboy hat with all the other men in the barn and laid it over his heart but he kept Lila's hand in his left one. Jace said a brief prayer and then folks began to form a line in front of the tables.

"If I remember right, you eat when you're stressed. Hungry?" He kissed Lila on the forehead.

"Starving," she answered.

"Then we'll eat and then I want my older aunts who

aren't from Happy to see that I am with you. Maybe they'll stop trying to fix me up with every woman in their church or at their school or— You understand."

"Oh, yeah, I do," she said. "You brought me here so all your relatives would stop trying to get you married off?"

"I brought you to the reunion because I want to spend the evening with the most beautiful woman in Texas. The other is a little bonus," he said. "What did Granny want to talk to you about or is that confidential?"

"Did you know that she and Henry Thomas dated?"

He looked as stunned as if she'd hit him between the eyes with a shovel. "Did she say that?"

"Not in so many words but I figured it out."

"We had a conversation a few days ago and that does make sense. But Henry?" He frowned.

"About as likely a match as Brody and Lila, right?" she asked.

"Oh, honey, we make a beautiful match." He grinned.

"Brody!" Hope waved from a table where she'd claimed a seat. "You kids bring your plates and sit here beside me."

Brody nodded. "The queen bee has summoned us. You don't mind, do you? We can go skinny dippin' afterwards."

"In your dreams, cowboy," she said. "This is a real date. We will stay in plain sight all evening and you will take me home and come straight back here."

"Then they'll all think you're respectable, right?" he asked.

"What do *you* think? You're really the only one that matters to me."

"I feel like my world has stopped spinning and it's

tilted right on its axis again. I like you the way you are and anyone who doesn't can go to hell." He handed her a plate. "I told you everything would be okay."

"I'll be respectable but I insist on a good night kiss." She grinned. "I've waited too many years for this date to be left at the door with no kiss."

"Yes, ma'am. Eat hearty so you'll have the energy to dance all evening. I've waited too long for this night to waste a single minute of it. And before you say a word, yes, it's my fault that it didn't happen sooner."

She loaded her plate and waited at the end of the table for Brody and they crossed the barn together. Forget about hiding in the shadows. Everyone in the whole place could see her. She felt like turning around and running when Hope motioned to the chair right beside her. Brody set his plate down and pulled out a chair for her before he took his place on her right.

"Where is your mama this evening? You should have brought her with you," Hope asked.

"She's out with Laura and Teresa."

"Just between me and you"—Hope leaned over and whispered—"I'd rather be with them. This is too many people for me at one time. I can BS my way through it for Valerie's sake but I like smaller groups."

"A little BS and a lot of 'ain't that nice' gets us through," Lila said.

Hope laughed loudly, drawing a lot of attention to the table, and then she leaned around Lila to speak to Brody. "Darlin', would you go get me a couple of hot rolls? I forgot to put any on my plate and Gracie makes the best yeast bread in the state."

"Sure thing, Granny. You need anything, Lila?"

"Maybe another glass of tea," she answered.

When he was halfway across the barn, Hope leaned over to whisper softly, "And now everyone in the place knows that we're talkin' and playin' nice. But, sweetheart, know this, if you hurt my grandson or break his heart, you'll answer to me, and that's not BS. You treat him right and you've got a friend in me for life, but if you don't, well, I can be a real bitch."

"Tell him the same thing and you won't have a thing to worry about," Lila said.

Hope patted her on the shoulder. "Glad we had this talk and the one in the balcony. You've got brass as well as class."

Brody returned and took his seat; then he leaned over and whispered, "What was she sayin' when I left? Your face went all serious and I was afraid you were going to leave."

"Just girl talk," Lila said. "This is excellent potato salad, Miz Hope. Which one of the relatives made it?"

"I did," Hope said. "Brody loves bacon, so I fry a couple of pounds good and crispy to add to the mixture."

"I'd love to have the recipe," Lila said.

"I'll write it off and send it with Brody tomorrow night when y'all have your second date," Hope said.

"You think we're going to have a second date?"

"You've invited him to church tomorrow and that's a date in my books. Brody, did you hear that Henry's sister isn't going to renew Paul's lease this fall? She says that she's got other plans for the ranch. Wonder if Henry might be ready to come back home?"

"First I've heard of it," Brody said.

"If she's interested in selling that ranch, we'll sure

make her a good offer. It would be a nice addition to Hope Springs. I'll call her in the next week or so," Hope said.

Jace sat down on the other side of Hope and soon they were deep in a discussion about the possibility of buying the Texas Star.

Brody draped an arm across the back of Lila's chair and asked, "You remember the night before the fall sale when we snuck away and went to the buyer's balcony?"

"That was the closest we got to gettin' caught. I thought for sure your dad would…"

"I never got dressed so fast in my life except the other night when your mama snuck in the apartment. If she'd opened that bedroom door..."

Kasey startled both of them when she leaned down between them and whispered, "Granny is being really nice tonight. What did you put in her tea, Brody?"

Both of his hands shot up defensively. "I'm innocent. I didn't spike her tea. How you doin', sis?"

"This is my first family reunion without Adam. It's kind of strange. We used to sneak off to the buyer's loft and make out." Her smile didn't erase the pain in her eyes. "Even after we were married and had kids."

"I wonder how many kids we'd disturb if we flipped on the lights in the balcony," Brody said.

"Don't do it. Let them have the thrill that we had," Kasey said. "It's good to see you, Lila."

"Hey." Jace touched Lila on the arm. "I wanted to come on over and ask you to save me a dance later this evening."

"Her dances are taken," Brody said quickly.

"Hey, now!" Lila spoke up. "I've got an extra one right now if you want to dance, Jace."

He held out a hand. "Yes, ma'am."

The band was playing the very song that had been playing in her mind when Clancy was in the café—"Which Bridge to Cross (Which Bridge to Burn)."

"Sounds like maybe this is special for you tonight," Jace said as he drew her close for a two-step. "Brody was worried."

"Truth is I burned the bridge between me and Brody years ago. The one I burned with Clancy is still smoldering but it's gone. I don't care about that one but I wouldn't mind rebuilding the one with Brody," she said.

"I've got nails if y'all run out and if there's anything I can do to help, you just call me. I like seein' him as happy as he is right now," Jace said.

"Thank you. Reckon you've got any pull with your mama?"

"Now that's something you and Brody got to do on your own. She's my mama and I love her but she can be a handful. Granny used to be even worse but she is mellowing since she retired," Jace chuckled.

* * *

Brody leaned forward and put his hands on the table so he could watch them. Not because he was afraid his brother would try to steal his woman, but Brody enjoyed just seeing Lila move around the floor. The song was so appropriate for the night. He didn't have a single bridge to burn. But Lila had two before her and it scared the hell out of him when he thought of her going back to Florida and being around Clancy.

He had eyes for only her, moving so gracefully. Jace

said something and her body language said that she was very serious when she answered him. Then she smiled and nodded when he made another comment. Brody wanted to cut in and ask her what they were talking about, but he just watched from a distance. The next one and all those after belonged to him.

The song ended and Jace brought her back to the table. "I told her to make sure that you need to resole your boots when tonight is over since you're being selfish. She dances like a dream. No wonder you always kept her to yourself in high school."

Lila patted him on the shoulder. "Thank you, Jace."

"You're very welcome," he said. "Hey, you ever think about all those crazy things we did when we were kids?"

"Happy memories." She smiled.

"Yep, they are. Can I get y'all a beer?"

"Love one," Lila said.

"Just leave them right here on the table," Brody said. "We're about to hit the dance floor if this gorgeous woman will let me step on her toes again."

"Will do." Jace disappeared toward the bar.

Brody led her out to the middle of the floor. "We'll dance a couple of times and then go back to the table and drink those beers while they're still cold. And then I'm going to kiss you."

"Oh, so you've got the whole evening planned, do you? Are you trying to prove that you're brave enough to bring the wild girl to a family reunion in spite of what everyone might think?"

"Nope. I'm trying to prove to you that I mean business this time and I don't care what anyone or anything thinks of our relationship," he said.

"So this is a relationship?" she asked.

She'd expected the clouds to part the day that Brody said something like that. But not even the crowd on the dance floor parted. The only way that anyone would even know what he'd said would be by the way her heart had tossed in an extra few beats. And no one could even see that happening.

He sank his face into her hair. "It's whatever you want it to be. I'll take what I can get."

She looped her arms around his neck and his slid down to her lower back when the singer started Tracy Byrd's song "Holdin' Heaven."

"It's the truth. I really am holdin' heaven in my arms."

"You know why, don't you?" She looked into his eyes.

"Because you're in my arms?"

"No, sir, if you're holding heaven in your arms, then I'm an angel, and honey, I traded my halo and wings for horns back when we had sex the first time," she laughed.

"Then I should have a set of long horns right along with you," he laughed.

He didn't wait until they were at the bar to kiss her. His dark lashes closed slowly and then his lips were on hers in a kiss so hot that it would have melted the devil's pitchfork. She leaned into it, not caring if she was at his family reunion and everyone was watching them. This night had been a long time coming and she deserved her Cinderella evening.

* * *

They were the only ones on the dance floor when the band closed out the evening at eleven-thirty with a request from Brody. "Bless the Broken Road," by Rascal Flatts, a slow country waltz, brought Brody and Lila together in the middle of the floor.

"This was playing that year when you left," he whispered. "But it didn't have the meaning that it does today."

"Do you think that God did bless the road that led me back home to Happy?"

"I do," he said.

She laid her head on his chest and listened to the steady beat of his heart.

Home.

She'd called Happy home.

Her pretty red dress didn't turn into rags at the stroke of midnight. His truck didn't instantly become a pumpkin. But when he kissed her at the door, she felt as if she had truly had her Cinderella night.

"Good night, Lila," he whispered hoarsely, desire in his voice.

"Good night, Brody." Her whole body wanted more.

"I really don't want to let you go," he said.

She leaned into his arms, her face resting on his chest. She could have stood there until dawn simply enjoying that steady heartbeat. "We both know this night has to end at the door. But there's always tomorrow."

He brought her palms to his lips and kissed each one. The warmth of his breath, the feel of his lips on the tender part of her skin, and the slight scruff on his face against her fingertips made her wish that all time would freeze—that they could stay right there in that scene forever.

"Until tomorrow." He dropped her hands and walked to his truck.

She watched until even the sound of the vehicle had

faded, leaving nothing behind but a lonesome old owl and a coyote vying for attention off in the distance. She opened the door and made it to the living room before she melted into a chair and kicked off her boots.

"Only a few minutes late," Daisy said from the sofa where Duke and Cora both rested in her lap. "Lipstick is gone and you've got a faraway look in your eyes. Valerie must have been at least halfway decent."

"It was magic, Mama, and I held my own with Valerie Dawson."

"Good for you!" Daisy pumped a fist in the air.

Lila could hardly believe that her mother had made that gesture.

"Don't look so surprised. Tina has grandkids and that's what my favorite one of the bunch does when things are good," she said.

"You want grandkids?" Lila asked.

"When you're ready but I'd really like for their name to be something other than Dawson," Daisy said. "But if it happens to be, then by golly, I'll be the favorite because Valerie won't have anything to do with them. That's the only good thing about it, though."

Lila's phone pinged in her purse and she took it out to find a message: *H.O.L.Y.*

"And that would be?" Daisy asked.

"A text from Brody."

"More magic?"

"Just the title of a song."

"I worry about you," Daisy said. "Even if it was magic, I still worry that you're trying to re-create the fun times of when you were a kid. Now you're grown, Lila. It's time to say good-bye to the past."

"Tonight I did just that, Mama. I don't want to go back but I do want to enjoy the present and look forward to the future. I don't give a damn if Valerie Dawson hates me or if Hope threatens me," Lila said.

"What did Hope say?" Daisy's eyes flashed anger.

"Just that I'd better not break Brody's heart."

"What about all the times he broke yours? Where was she with all her threats back then? Did she tell him to ask you to the prom or not to stand you up that last night?"

Lila kicked off her boots. "Tonight was wonderful. I want to think about that."

"So what does that text mean?" Daisy asked.

"Did you stop listening to country music when you moved away from Happy?" Lila asked.

"You know I've always loved jazz. Etta James and Sam Cooke. I can handle those beer drinkin' songs but they aren't my favorite."

Lila found the song on her phone, turned the volume as high as it would go, and set it on the coffee table. She leaned back in the chair and watched her mother's face as she listened to lyrics that said he was high on loving her.

"That's pretty damned romantic," Daisy said.

"It is, isn't it?" Lila said. "I'm going to get a shower and go to bed. Folks will be flocking in here tomorrow morning lookin' for gossip about the family reunion."

"On a church mornin'?" Daisy frowned.

"Oh, yeah, and then there will be even more at noon, so I hope you fixed lots of chicken and dressin' today." She stooped to get her boots and stopped long enough to pet her kittens on the way down the short hallway to the bathroom.

"So"—Lila turned around—"did you have a good time this evening?"

"Always enjoy spending time with old friends, but I'm gettin' too old for this late night crap. I'd rather spend the evening watchin' an old movie with a shot of whiskey in my hand," Daisy said. "I'll see you in the morning and, honey, I figured that we'd be swamped tomorrow so I did fix plenty."

"Love you." Lila yawned.

"Right back atcha, kiddo. Always have and always will," Daisy said.

* * *

The church was packed that morning with every pew full but Brody would have gladly let Lila sit in his lap if she could have left the café. He didn't even have to close his eyes to visualize her in that cute little dress that she'd worn the night before.

"Good mornin' and thank you to the Dawson family for draggin' all their relatives to church this mornin'," the preacher said.

A few giggles erupted and then there was silence.

"I'd like to talk to y'all about family this mornin'," the preacher said, and read a few verses from the Bible in front of him on the oak pulpit.

Brody could agree that family was a good thing but that morning he couldn't get his mind off Lila and the way she'd fit into his arms the evening before, the way she'd leaned into the good night kiss, the way she'd drank a beer with him at the bar without even glancing at all his single Dawson cousins. And especially the fact that she'd shaken her head when more than one of those cousins asked her to dance.

He folded his arms over his chest and attempted to listen to the thirty-minute sermon that lasted every bit of six hours. He nodded off twice and Hope had to poke him to wake him. Finally, the preacher asked Jace to deliver the benediction.

Jace kept it short and when he finished, the whole congregation said a hearty "Amen."

"What is wrong with you?" Hope frowned as they stood to their feet with the rest of the crowd. "You didn't hear a word the preacher said."

"I was daydreaming about Lila," he answered honestly.

"Dammit!" Valerie whispered under her breath.

"In church, Mama?" Brody scolded.

"Don't take that tone with me and believe me when I say I'm not ready to fold yet." Valerie shook her finger at him. "I haven't changed my mind about that woman. She's going to leave at the end of summer and you'll be left with a broken heart. There are other women around here who are a lot more suitable for you and for Hope Springs."

Brody slung an arm around his mother's shoulders. "Mama, I love you, but I'm going to keep seeing Lila, so get used to it. I'm going to the café for dinner today."

* * *

The truck felt like an oven when he settled into his seat. Only a little more than twelve hours ago, Lila had been sitting there in the passenger seat. And then there was that kiss—that wonderful, amazing good night kiss. He started the engine, switched on the A/C and drove straight to the café.

His step was lighter than it had been in a long time when he pushed the door open into the café. Every seat was full and every booth crowded, so he stood in the doorway for several minutes trying to decide whether to stay or go on home.

"Hey," Lila said as she passed by him. "You stayin' or goin'?"

"Jace is holding down the ranch for me so I'm stayin'," he answered.

"If you'll man the drink machine until this rush is over, we'll have dinner together in the kitchen, my treat. Mama made chicken and dressin'," she said.

He unbuttoned the cuffs of his shirtsleeves and rolled them up. "You got a deal."

She kissed him on the cheek. "You're a lifesaver."

A low buzz of whispers started with Valerie's and Hope's names floating around as folks hurriedly got out their phones to call and text the newest gossip.

Chapter Sixteen

It was hard for Lila to believe that she'd been back in Happy less than four weeks that Sunday evening as she flipped through hangers in her closet. The calendar said that it was June 25, which meant she should give notice in Florida and get her résumés in soon for other jobs. The best ones had probably already been taken.

She finally chose a cute little sleeveless dress with twenty-seven buttons up the front and since it had red trim, she decided to wear her boots again. They'd brought her good luck the night before and on a whim, she applied her mother's red lipstick. She really intended to drive her truck out to Hope Springs to get Brody for their church date but the Lila who'd kissed him in front of a packed café took one look at her Harley and changed her mind.

She got her dad's beat-up old helmet from behind the seat in her truck and tucked it into a saddlebag. "I hope you don't mind, Daddy. I don't do this lightly and no one else has ever gotten to wear this but...well, I think you'd understand."

Not a cloud floated in the summer sky that evening. The sun was sinking toward the tops of the trees, putting a glare in her rearview mirror. She had second thoughts about her decision to ride the bike as she turned into the lane for Hope Springs and rode across the cattle guard, but it was too late to turn around.

Brody was sitting on the porch with Kasey and Jace when she parked outside the yard fence. He stood to his feet and shook the legs of his jeans down over his boot tops, settled his hat on his head, and crossed the yard.

"You goin' to let me drive that thing?" he asked.

She removed her helmet and shook out her hair. "If you leave your hat at home and wear a helmet."

He slung his cowboy hat toward the porch. Jace caught it like a Frisbee and laid it on the top step.

"You kids don't stay out too late now," he teased.

Emma ran to the fence and crawled up on the bottom rail. "Lila! Can I go with you?"

"You have to wear boots and a helmet. Mine are too big for you but when you get big enough, you can ride with me," Lila said.

"Rustin, did you hear that? I'm goin' to ride bulls and get me a motorcycle like Lila has when I get big."

"Helmet is in the saddlebag," Lila said.

Brody pulled it out and cocked his head to one side. "Is this what I think it is? Does this big B in the lightning streaks stand for Billy?"

"It does," she said with a serious nod and moved back so that he could straddle the cycle.

"I'll wear it with pride." He jerked it down over his head and they exchanged a meaningful look. "It's been a few years since I've been on one of these things," he said.

"Gas is a little sensitive." She flipped her hair up under the helmet as she settled it on her head.

He turned it around, revved it a couple of times, then popped the clutch and the front wheels shot off the ground several inches. She wrapped her arms around his waist. She doubted that riding a bull behind him would be any more exhilarating than a bike ride with him.

Her skirt whipped around her thighs as he opened it up on the straight stretch of highway from the ranch to town. When he parked it at the church and removed the helmet, his eyes were twinkling. Nothing could ever take away their need for adventure but could a relationship survive two people like Lila and Brody? Or would it burn itself out, leaving nothing behind but a pile of ashes and two broken hearts?

"That was amazing. Now I can see why you were so mad when your mama sold your dad's cycle and didn't give it to you." He put the helmet back in the saddlebag.

"She was a smart woman. We'd have gotten into all kinds of trouble if we'd had a motorcycle. We probably wouldn't be alive today, as crazy as we were then. I'm just glad that she let me keep his helmet."

He popped down the kickstand and dismounted. "Ain't that the truth? Shall we go inside and get saved and sanctified?"

"You're expectin' a lot out of one single preachin'." She took off the helmet and fluffed out her hair with her fingers.

"Do you know how sexy you are when you do that?"

"Really?" She tilted her head to one side.

"Oh, honey!" He groaned. "Let's skip church and take this bike out to the barn or better yet to the springs," he said.

"Can't. Mama is saving us a place," she said.

He slipped his hands around her waist and swept her off the cycle as if she were one of those tiny women who weighed only slightly more than a feather pillow. When he set her on the ground, he cupped her chin in his hand. The soft, sweet kiss left her wanting more and seriously considering his offer.

"Didn't you hear me? I said we are sitting with Mama," she said breathlessly when he clasped her hand in his and started toward the church.

"You think I'm not tough enough to sit on the same pew with your mother?" He opened the door for her and stood to the side but he didn't let go of her hand.

"She's pretty mean."

"Since you held your own last night with my mama, I'll do my best not to crawl under the pew and cower in fear," he teased.

Several heads turned when they went inside the church but after the news of a kiss that morning right out in public, holding hands didn't seem like such a big deal. Daisy was sitting near the middle on a pew all by herself. She nodded at them when Brody stood to one side to let Lila enter ahead of him before he took the spot at the end.

"You aren't late," Daisy whispered.

"Neither are you," Lila said.

"Please tell me I did not hear a motorcycle out there in the parking lot."

Lila shook her head. "Can't tell lies in church, Mama."

"And you wore a dress. The whole town probably knows what color your underpants are," Daisy fussed.

"White. Bikini with lace around the top. Since it was Sunday I left the red thongs in the drawer," she said.

"Great God!" Daisy gasped.

"Yes, ma'am, he is." Lila smiled.

"It's Happy, Texas. I swear to Jesus, it makes people crazy."

Lila nudged her. "There's a song that says that you're always seventeen in your hometown."

"Well, whoever sings it is a genius," Daisy whispered.

Lila sang with the congregation and made an effort to focus on the preacher's Sunday night sermon about how everyone should be thinking of how fast time flies. He snapped his fingers and said that it wouldn't be long before it was time for each and every one of them to leave this earthly world.

"Ever had sex on a Harley?" Brody whispered.

His breath sent shivers down her backbone. "No, but I'll give it a try if you're willing."

"Oh, yeah!"

Daisy elbowed her on the upper arm and she straightened up. She wasn't the only one who was the same in her hometown. So was her mother.

As soon as church services were over, Lila leaned over and said, "Mama, it's only two hours until you have to leave. Let's sneak out the side door. We'll meet you at the café."

"Let me tell Laura good-bye and I'll be right behind you," she said.

* * *

Brody parked the cycle in the garage and got off, and they both removed their helmets at the same time. Lila hung them on the handlebars and moistened her lips with the tip of her tongue. His mouth closed over hers and the only thing that mattered was that he was with her right then at that moment. He was a big, tough cowboy but in the hot garage, his heart and soul melted.

If he could live right there for the rest of his life, he would have been a happy cowboy. Just let him have Lila to come home to every evening after a long day of ranching or even fighting with Sunday and the world would be all right.

The kiss ended and he held her close to his chest for another moment. "It's been an amazing weekend. I've loved every minute of it. I can't even begin to think of you leaving at the end of summer."

"I agree," she said, and took a step back when the sounds of a car engine approached. "That would be Mama turning into the parking lot."

"I think your mama might know that we have already kissed each other more than once," he said.

"Surely not," she teased as she crossed the garage floor and unlocked the door. "Well, look who's here to meet us. Here, you can hold Cora. She's a sweetheart." She picked up both kittens and handed him the white one.

"Hey, I figured y'all would already have the ice cream ready for sundaes." Daisy followed them into the apartment, and crossed the living area and into the café kitchen. "I'm having a triple dip and then I'll sleep all the way to the Harrisburg airport."

"You going to work tomorrow or are you going to rest a day or two?" Lila asked as she hugged Duke to her chest.

"Put those cats back out in the apartment. If we got a surprise inspection and they found cat hair in this place, we'd get a citation and we ain't never had one," Daisy said.

"I'll take them back." Brody picked up Cora by the scruff of her neck and carried both of them across the utility room.

"So," he said when he returned. "Are you ready to go back to Pennsylvania?"

"I'm ready to be back in my routine even if I'm not ready to tell Lila good-bye. I hate that part even worse than she does," Daisy answered. "I'm not on the schedule until eleven for the noon rush, so I'll sneak in a few more hours of rest before I have to go in."

"Did you get back with that lady who called to reschedule?" Lila asked.

Daisy nodded. "I did but Molly asked me to wait a week before I make arrangements for you to talk to her. She and Georgia are thinkin' about buyin' me out. I hope they do."

Lila put her kitten on the sofa and led the way into the café. "I can't imagine why they wouldn't like Florida. It's a perfect retirement place."

"It's not Happy," Brody said. "They were born here and they know everyone in the place. The café has been the hub of all the gossip and news since you first put it in, Daisy, and they miss their place in the fun."

"You're probably right." Lila got out the ice cream.

Daisy split three bananas and laid them in the fancy

glass boats. "I was born here and was in the middle of that hub for years and I still miss it. Someday, maybe when I retire, I'll come back home. But that's a long way off and who knows what'll happen between now and then. Well, that's everything except the cherries for the top," Daisy said. "We might as well make this a classic banana split to celebrate, right?"

"Yes, ma'am." Lila bent to get the jar of maraschino cherries from the bottom rack in the refrigerator. The tail of her dress slid above her knees, showing a lot of those sexy legs. Brody got a visual of them wrapped around him and the pressure started to build behind his zipper. He quickly turned around and made himself think about ice cream.

"Crazy, ain't it? If Molly and Georgia decide to buy the place, they'll be coming home from pretty close to the same place in Florida that you'll be returning to," Daisy said.

Lila set the cherries on the table. "I'm not going back. If Clancy won't let me out of the contract, I'll take a year's sabbatical. Maybe I'll work on my master's degree."

"Oh?" Brody's heart threw in an extra beat.

"If he lets me out of the contract, I might try Montana or Wyoming next, or maybe I'll go back to Conway. I kind of liked it over there." She scooped out a perfect round of ice cream.

"Why Wyoming?" Daisy asked. "I'd think you'd get tired of taking those tests every time you move."

An empty feeling, as if someone had ripped his soul out and threw it in the trash, hit Brody in the chest. He'd been living in the present, but soon he and Lila would have to face the next step. And he'd have to figure out how to live without the hope of seeing her every day.

"Why don't you teach around here? You haven't tried Texas yet." He took the scoop from her. "Here, let me do that."

"Seventeen," Daisy said.

"What's that mean?" Brody deftly put three mounds of ice cream on each banana.

"The song," Lila answered.

"You mean that one by Cross Canadian Ragweed?" Brody asked.

"That's it," Lila said. "It says that you'll always be seventeen when you go home again."

"I'm not," Brody said.

Daisy topped off her banana split with a layer of whipped cream and then carefully carried it out to the dining room. "No, but Happy has seen you mature from a reckless teenager to a responsible adult. Folks saw her leave and then when she comes back, she is that same girl because there was nothing in between."

He handed Lila the chocolate syrup. "How's that a reason not to teach in Texas?"

"Not all of Texas, just Happy. No one will look at her like a responsible adult. They'll whisper behind her back and remember the stupid things that she did."

She passed the chocolate back to him and finished her toppings. "Mama's right, you know."

His phone rang. "Excuse me, this is Jace. I have to take it."

He stepped away from the table but locked gazes with Lila while he talked. "You can take care of that, Jace. I'll be home after a while."

When he slipped the phone back into his shirt pocket, she raised an eyebrow. "If you're needed at the ranch..."

"We've got a cow that's calving out of season. Jace knows how to pull a calf and Granny is there to help if he needs it. Let's go join Daisy." He smiled.

"So if they let you out of the contract, you'll move again? Want me to take a long weekend and fly down to help?" Daisy asked when they'd sat down across the table from her.

"I'd love it," Lila answered. "I'll let you know tomorrow or the next day. I'm going to call Clancy. I don't think he'll have a problem with it after his visit here."

"I'll be glad to take a few days off and help you," Brody said quickly. She might have put Clancy going but the man could swoop in with a lot of promises and smooth talk and convince her to stay in Florida. Then he'd have a whole year to win her back. As badly as Brody hated to be away from her, anywhere was better than Florida.

"I'll take all the help I can get but first I have to find another job." Lila ran a hand from his knee to his thigh under the table.

He shoveled ice cream in his mouth to cool him down and to keep from moaning. He'd miss her touch, the way her hair smelled and everything about her when she was gone. Skype was a good thing but it would never take the place of having her right there beside him sending desire through his body with nothing but her touch on his leg.

Chapter Seventeen

A flash of lightning shot out of the dark clouds as Brody drove the motorcycle out of town that Sunday evening after their ice cream date. To the north, Lila could see stars and a sliver of a moon. But to the southwest where the storms usually originated, the sky was black with only an occasional burst of light. She counted when the next streak zigzagged as if trying to reach for the treetops. Ten seconds. That meant the storm was ten miles out. Depending on whether it was traveling slowly or with the speed of a bullet, it could hit in a few minutes or take half an hour.

The first drops of cold rain hit when they were halfway between the café and the ranch. Then the hail started pinging off her helmet and stinging her back when it hit with the force of the high wind pushing it. Brody turned into Henry's old ranch and drove straight to the barn.

She hopped off the back of the bike as soon as he stopped and slung the barn door open wide enough that he could drive inside. By the time he'd parked, she had her helmet off and was wringing water from her dress tail.

"That's some cold rain and biting hail." She shivered.

He quickly hung his helmet on the handlebars and gathered her into his arms. "I know where we can wait out the storm."

"Tack room?" she said.

"Oh, yeah."

With his arm still around her, he headed that way. Not watching where she was going, she stumbled over the white mama cat and had to do some fancy footwork to keep from falling and pulling Brody down with her.

"Poor old thing must crave company," Lila said. "You should take her home with you. Kasey's kids would love her and she wouldn't be lonely."

"Why don't you take her home? She could snuggle up next to you at night and keep you warm," he said.

"That's your job." Lila groped around for the string that would turn on the light. Finally her fingers found the same old wooden thread spool at the end of a length of jute twine and she gave it a tug. "Well, would you look at this," she said.

There was a small electric heater in the corner, a tiny air conditioner in the window, and a futon on one wall with a quilt tossed over the back.

"Paul turned it into a poker place a few years ago. Said he needed a room for the boys on the nights when the girls gather at his house for those church meetings every month," Brody said.

"I don't remember anything in here but lots of musty old saddles and a couple of horse blankets." She wrapped her arms around herself trying to get warm.

He hugged her close to his own chilly, wet body. "Hail produced a cold rain. You're shiverin', Lila. Let's get you out of those wet clothes."

Brody slowly removed her dress and draped it on the back of a chair. His warm hands on her chilled skin as he unfastened her bra and removed it made her shiver even worse but it had nothing to do with the weather. He gently hooked a thumb under the edge of the elastic on her bikini underwear and strung warm kisses from her belly button to her toes as he pulled them down to her ankles.

Then he stood up, grabbed a quilt, and whipped it around her body. "As warm as it is in here, your things will be dry by the time the storm passes."

She adjusted the quilt like a sari and undid the snaps on his shirt one at a time as she started undressing him. Running her fingers through the soft black hair on his chest, she tiptoed and kissed him on the chin. Then she quickly undid his belt buckle and pulled his jeans off, admiring all the hard muscles from his broad shoulders down his ripped abdomen and the V that led down below his flat belly. Then she took his hand and led him to the futon. In a blur the quilt left her body and she sat down, pulling him down with her. She moved into his lap and covered them both.

His fingertips grazed her jawline, tilting her chin for the perfect angle so that his mouth could cover hers, and she leaned into the kiss. The tip of his tongue touched her lower lip, asking permission. She opened slightly and he eased inside as the hail and rain made beautiful music on the barn's old tin roof.

His work-roughened hands lightly skimmed from her shoulders, ever so slowly down her bare arms. When they reached her fingers, he made slow circles on the tender part of her palms as he deepened the kiss. Her body on fire, she pressed closer to him, her breasts against his chest.

Then his hands were on her back, massaging and working kinks out from her shoulders all the way to her butt and then down the backs of her legs. The kisses got hotter and hotter until she couldn't bear it anymore. She wiggled a few times and guided him into her but he controlled the movement with a long, slow gliding motion.

"My God, Brody," she panted.

"Good?" he asked as he maneuvered her onto her back and laced his fingers in hers, holding her hands above her head. "There is no one else on the earth right now but me and you."

"*Good* isn't even close," she said.

Talking stopped and they moved together until she was frantic with need. He slowed down and let her cool down just enough to catch her breath, then started building the speed again until she squealed his name and dug her fingernails into his back.

The heat as she tumbled into steaming hot desire into complete and utter satisfaction was more than she'd ever experienced, even with Brody. He rolled to one side but the futon was so narrow that they were still plastered together. She kicked the quilt off to one side and slung a leg over his body to keep him from falling off on the rough wooden floor.

"That was amazing," he whispered.

"I know." She stifled a yawn. "Don't you love the sound of rain on a tin roof?"

"Mmmm," he said as his blue eyes fluttered shut.

* * *

Brody awoke to her soft breathing. The rain had stopped and he could see stars shining in the window above the air conditioner. As hot as it was and as much as he would have loved to have had cool air, he didn't want to wake Lila. That would mean they'd have to go home and he didn't want to ever let go of her.

"Hey." She opened her eyes slowly. "What time is it?"

"Have no idea. Phones are on the table over there," he said. "Let's lock the door and live here forever."

She snuggled down deeper into his arms. "Sounds like a plan to me, but I bet Molly would send out the National Guard if I wasn't in the kitchen by opening time. It'll be strange not havin' Mama there."

"So that means our date is over?" Brody asked. "I think it better be. I'll get dressed and walk home. You can take the bike." He sat up and rolled the kinks out of his neck. "I love sleeping with you. I love the way you fit in my arms."

"Me too." She left the futon and went straight for her clothing.

"Seems a shame to cover something that beautiful." He grinned.

"Right back at you," she told him. "I'll take you home, Brody. You don't have to walk." She checked the time on her phone and gasped. "Holy smoke! It's four o'clock."

"Be best if that loud bike don't go roarin' down the lane at this time of morning, don't you think," he said.

* * *

She made it home by four-thirty and went straight to the shower. When she came out with a towel around her head and one around her body, two kittens were sitting on the floor staring at her.

Duke meowed.

Cora laid back her ears.

"Young lady, you don't get to give me those kind of looks either," Lila said. "It was worth losing a little sleep over. Besides I liked sleeping with him. Not as much as I like the sex but having someone to snuggle with is nice."

Duke meowed again.

"See, there, Duke agrees with me. He likes having you to sleep with." She bent forward and dried her hair.

At five o'clock she heard pots and pans rattling in the kitchen. She dried her hair and dressed in jeans and a T-shirt, laced her shoes, and fed the kittens. Duke put his paw on Cora's head and tried to push her back but she wasn't having any part of that.

Lila left them tumbling around on the floor and went straight to the kitchen where she wrapped Molly in a fierce hug. "I'm so glad to see you."

Molly stepped back and narrowed her eyes. "I leave and everything goes down the toilet."

"Mama left this place clean as a pin. What's your problem?"

"Nothing to do with my kitchen. I told you to stay away from Brody Dawson."

"Ah." Lila grinned. "I missed you, too, Molly."

"Who said I missed you or anything about this place. I just hated the sand more than I do..." She fussed. "I'm lyin'. I didn't like the sand or the beach or anything about that place and I found out real quick that I love Happy, Texas, and do not want to leave it. And Georgia agrees with me."

"So where are you going when you go on another vacation?" Lila opened a drawer and took out a clean apron.

"Maybe to the mountains or maybe I've been broke from suckin' eggs and I'll stay where I'm happy from now on and that's right here where I know everyone and they all like my cookin'," she said. "I hear that Hope is coming around to being civil to you but that Valerie isn't. That right?"

Lila tied an apron around her waist and tucked an order pad into her pocket. "That's about it."

"Valerie means well. I can remember when Hope was a lot like her. She sure didn't like Mitch Dawson there at first and Mitch's mama wasn't very happy with the marriage either. It's the way of mothers—always interfering, but they do it out of love." Molly flopped a bowl full of biscuit dough on the counter and started rolling it out.

Lila laughed. "How do you know all that when you've only been home a few hours?"

"I keep my ears open. Speakin' of that, I heard your motorcycle comin' past my place about the time I was havin' my first cup of coffee and gettin' ready for work this mornin'. I expect you were out at Hope Springs all night," Molly said. "He's goin' to break your heart, girl. You know the old sayin' that goes 'Fool me once, shame on you. Fool me twice, it's my own blamed fault'?"

Lila glanced at the clock. "Time to open the doors and I don't think that's the way that sayin' goes."

"Close enough," Molly said. "It's goin' to be your own fault."

"Note taken," Lila said.

"Smarty pants," Molly huffed. "Turn on the lights and let's get this week started."

"So is Georgia comin' home too?" Lila poured herself a cup of coffee and carried it with her.

"Soon as she can get here. She had all her belongin's moved down there. Thank goodness her house hasn't sold and she hadn't signed on the dotted line to buy one down there. Do you know what it costs to buy a place in that state?"

"Not much more than here unless you want beachfront," Lila said.

"Do you own a house?" Molly asked.

She'd thought about buying a little cottage on the beach and had decided she might give it more serious thought if she stuck around for five years.

"Oh, no, I rent a garage apartment and it's furnished. I could put all my belongings in the back of my truck. I can't afford the taxes on a place in that area—not on a teacher's salary."

"Well, thank God for that. When are you comin' home to Happy, then?" Molly asked. "If me and Georgia buy this café, we'll hire you as a waitress. You probably make as much in tips as you do teachin' and Lord knows, you don't have nearly the hassle. Teachin' a teenager anything is like nailin' Jell-O to the smokehouse door."

"You got that right, Molly, but what on earth gave you the impression I would ever come back here permanently?"

Molly grinned and pointed. "That right there."

Lila whipped around to see the first customer of the day getting out of his truck in the parking lot. In the dim morning light he was nothing but a silhouette settling an old Stetson on his head but that swagger left no doubt that it was Brody, and the feeling deep inside Lila left no doubt that Molly was right.

Chapter Eighteen

Good mornin'!" Lila said cheerfully when Paul and Fred entered the café that Tuesday morning. "Y'all boys ready for a cup of coffee?"

"Oh, yeah, and we'll have two of Molly's big country breakfasts with all the trimmin's," Paul said. "I'm buyin' this world traveler breakfast this mornin'. Our wives are at the church with the Ladies' Circle so there ain't no food at home."

Fred chuckled. "It's an excuse for Mary Belle to tell them all about the cruise and I'm glad I ain't there."

Lila filled two mugs with coffee and took it to the guys. "So two big breakfasts? Anything else?"

"That should do it," Fred said. "I got tired of all that fancy food on the ship after the first week. It was pretty good there at first but all them choices kind of bewildered me. I'm ready for some of Molly's cookin'. You ever been on a cruise, Lila?"

She shook her head. "Not yet but it's on my bucket list."

"It's all right. Mary Belle liked it better than I did and she'd go again. I told her if we made it to our seventy-fifth I'd consider another one but only if it lasted one week and not two," Fred said.

"You and Brody could go on one," Paul whispered. "All cooped up like that would tell you if you were really meant for each other."

The blush was instant with two red spots filling her cheeks and burning like wildfire. "I'd better get that order in. Holler if you need any more coffee before it gets ready."

"What's happened since I've been gone?" Fred asked. "Brody and Lila? Really?"

"Hey, I can hear you," Lila said.

Paul, with his salt-and-pepper hair, leaned forward until he was practically touching Fred's snowy white mop and lowered his voice. Lila couldn't hear a word they said but whoever made the comment about old women being the biggest gossips in the world was dead wrong. Old guys could outdo them any day of the week.

Her phone rang and she pulled it out of her hip pocket. "Hello, Mama. Breakfast rush over?"

"Just about but there's still a few stragglers. I tried to call last night but it went to voice mail. Georgia is coming in early and I told her she could use the apartment. Got a problem with that?" Daisy asked.

"They're buyin' the place, so I guess I shouldn't have," Lila answered.

"That's not what I asked."

"No, Mama, not a problem at all," Lila said.

"What's wrong with you this morning? I hear something in your voice."

"Nothing—just dreading the move and hoping that the school board in Conway, Arkansas, offers me a contract. They gave me every hope but things could go wrong."

Hope—the word brought visions of Hope Springs and Brody to her mind. She dreaded telling him good-bye, even if it wasn't final. Just thinking about it brought tears to her eyes.

"And if they do, it's not too late to go somewhere else. I heard on the radio yesterday that Oklahoma, Kansas, and Texas still have jobs open everywhere. There was a number to call but I didn't write it down," Daisy told her. "I'd just as soon you lived far away from Happy so this thing you and Brody have started again would die in its sleep, but I'm glad you aren't going back to Florida this fall. That Clancy sure snowed me."

"So you think we couldn't survive a long-distance relationship?" Lila asked.

"Most people can't. I've got customers. Talk to you later. Hug my grandkittens for me."

She was gone before Lila could say another word.

"Order up!" Molly called out as she slid two platters of food onto the serving window ledge.

"I didn't even put the order on the roller," Lila said.

"I heard them," Molly said. "And they've gone to talkin' about that cruise and cows now. Talk of you and Brody didn't last long."

"You've got ears like a bat," Lila laughed.

Molly shook a wooden spoon toward her. "And Georgia's are even better, so you'll have to be even more careful when she gets home. You might need to meet Brody out at his bunkhouse."

"Molly!" Lila blushed.

"Just callin' it like I see it." She shrugged.

When things had quieted down in the café, Lila poured herself another cup of coffee and took it to the back booth. She sat down on one side and stretched out her long legs to prop her feet on the other side. Her phone had pinged half a dozen times that morning but there was no way she could check messages in their busy hours.

The first one was from Brody and put a brand-new blush on her face. The second one was from Clancy saying that he would be glad to let her out of her contract. Third, fourth, and fifth were from Brody asking her to call him as soon as possible.

She hit the speed dial for Brody and he answered on the first ring. "Hello, gorgeous. I sure hated to leave before daylight. I wanted to watch you wake up."

"Me too. What are you doing right now?" she asked.

"Jace and I are finishing a corral for this pesky bull and tryin' to get a fence built that he can't get through and then we've got cows to tag and two pastures that need to be plowed. Ranch work is like wipin' your butt on a wagon wheel—there's no end to it. At least that's what Grandpa always used to say. But if I get done by dark, would you like to ride down to Tulia for an ice cream? I could be there at nine."

"I'll be ready."

*　*　*

Brody whistled all the way from Hope Springs to the café that evening. He knocked on the back door and she opened it immediately. One step and she was in his arms, his lips were on hers, and their hearts were both racing. Then she stooped to pet the cats that were right at her feet.

"Are you okay, Lila? Is something wrong?"

"Georgia is stayin' in the apartment until her stuff arrives on Monday. I hope she likes cats."

"If she don't, they can stay in the bunkhouse until you get ready to go to Florida," he said. "And, darlin', you look beautiful tonight in that red dress."

"Thank you," she said.

"Don't worry, darlin'. We can spend time away from here when Georgia moves in." He kissed her pretty red lips again and they left the apartment together.

He opened the passenger door on his truck for her. "I reckon I should've brought along my pistol to keep some handsome cowboy from stealin' you away from me."

"Then I should have brought my pepper spray to keep the women from trying to take you away from me. Reckon we should call in our pizza so we don't have to fight off the crowd?" she teased.

He started the engine and backed the truck out enough to turn around and start south to Tulia. "I know I've said it before but I'm really going to miss you when you have to leave. I can't imagine how Kasey gets through the days, knowing that she'll never see Adam again."

"Think she'll ever get a second chance at love?" Lila asked.

"I hope so but it'll have to be a really special man. It'll have to be something like what we have got."

"What we have is special, but is there going to be an

us after I'm gone? Do you really want a long-distance relationship?" Lila asked.

He laid a hand on her shoulder. "More than anything in this world."

"But is it an us like we were in high school or is it something more? Have we simply gone back to wild sex and the way we were or is this something lasting and real?"

"What do you want it to be?" he asked.

"I'm askin' you." She turned so that her eyes met his.

Men, especially Dawsons, didn't normally do all that analyzing their feelings crap. They took things as they were and moved accordingly.

"I've loved every minute of this summer with you, Lila, and it's not like we are still in high school. Admit it. We've been to church together, to my family reunion, and out on dates. That much has changed but..."

"There it is," she said.

"What?" he asked.

"In a real relationship there are no buts," she told him softly, and looked away. "Let's not ruin the evening with an argument. I'm lookin' forward to an evening with you, one that doesn't have a single *but* in it."

What's wrong with you? the voice in his head screamed loudly. *She's an amazing woman and you're in love with her, so why don't you man up and tell her so.*

Because I want it to be more than words. I want it to come from so deep in my heart that she doesn't doubt it for a minute because I never want to hurt her again like I did last time. I love her too much for that.

"It's not so far from here to Conway. We can do weekend trips a couple of times a month," she said.

"And you'll have two weeks at Christmas and spring break." What he wanted to say was that he wasn't sure he could live without her for two weeks at a time. And the way Clancy looked down on Lila, like he was the king and she was one of his servants, aggravated the hell out of him.

"Do you want a big wedding if you get married?" he asked, and then wondered if he'd said the words out loud and where they'd come from.

Her head snapped around and her brown eyes were huge. "Where did that come from?"

He grinned. "A picture of you in a big white dress flashed through my mind."

"All those times you could have—and probably should have—proposed and you choose now? Why?" she asked.

"Who says I proposed? And when should I have asked you to marry me?" he asked.

"Well, there was the time when we lost our virginity."

"We were both too damn young to think about marriage," he said.

"Yes, but you should have at least told me that we were headed that way in the future."

"You didn't propose to me, either," he said. "What about all the other times?"

She laid a hand on his thigh. "The morning Mama and I left."

"We still weren't even old enough to get married without parental consent. Can you imagine your mama and mine signing those papers? Besides, you wouldn't roll down the window. And…"

She held up a finger to hush him up. "But you should have offered."

* * *

He wrapped his hand around her fingers and kissed them, the heat from his lips warming her from the depths of her heart. He kept her hand in his, holding it on the console separating them. “And if I had proposed tonight?”

“I would say no.” Lila hoped that she would be able to tell him no. Her mind knew that they needed more time—her body, not so much.

“Why?” His voice came out in a raspy whisper that made her wonder if he might be testing the waters instead of teasing.

“Because you’d only be sayin’ it to keep me from leavin’ and because if you were askin’ for all the right reasons, I still would not. We need to see if we can survive a long-distance relationship before we talk about a commitment like that. So let’s have a good time while we can.”

“Lila, are we okay?”

“I think so,” she said.

“Think or know?” He kissed the tip of her nose first and then moved on down to her lips. There was no thinking or knowing when his lips were on hers. If he’d have proposed even in a teasing manner right then, she would have said yes and followed him to the courthouse as soon as it opened the next morning.

“The jury is still out,” she panted when the kiss ended and grabbed for the door handle.

Chapter Nineteen

Lila awoke on Wednesday morning to find Duke and Cora sharing the same pillow with her. Duke's little paws rested in her hair on the left side while Cora purred into her ear on the right side. She carefully moved them over to the other side of the bed and headed for the bathroom for a morning shower.

The cats were sitting side by side when she started across the living room floor. She'd only been in Happy for a month. How could so much have happened? When she first arrived, all she could think about was selling the café and getting out of the town. Now she dreaded telling Molly, Fred and Paul, Kasey and her kids—but most of all Brody—good-bye. Knowing that Georgia was coming home and she really wasn't needed at the café was like a big awkward elephant sitting on her chest. Her heart hurt and she had trouble breathing.

"I've been lookin' at this all wrong," she said out loud.

All she had to do was load her cats, pack her clothes, and get in the truck and drive away. That way she didn't really have to tell anyone good-bye. Maybe that's why she moved so often.

She was struggling with the idea of simply going after work one evening when she opened the door into the café kitchen.

"Well, good mornin'. What's the matter with you? You look like you're about to cry." Molly narrowed her eyes at her.

"Nothing's wrong," Lila answered.

"Don't give me that crap. You look like you lost your best friend. Did you and Brody have a fight?"

Lila put on a clean apron and shook her head. "No, ma'am. Things are good between us."

"Is it because Georgia is coming home? I told you that we really want you to stay on here. You can choose your hours and live in the apartment, free of charge as long as you like."

Lila layered a sausage patty, a slice of cheese, and a scoop of scrambled eggs inside a biscuit. "I appreciate that. I've got to take a few days after July Fourth and get moved out of my apartment in Florida. I've got an interview in Conway, Arkansas."

"That's good, isn't it? Closer to here if you and Brody do stay together."

"I'm not sure what's a good thing right now. My world is kind of crazy."

Molly shook a knife at her. "I told you that gettin' mixed up with Brody was not a good thing."

Was that knife an omen? Should she simply leave? It wouldn't be like the last time because she and Brody had the foundation of a relationship. There would be phone calls, texts, and Skype. But there wouldn't be those painful last-minute tears. Plus, if she got back to Florida and cleared out her apartment by the first of July, she wouldn't have to pay another month's rent.

She'd weighed the pros and cons until closing time at the café and decided that leaving that night made sense. She wanted to hug Molly and tell her that she wouldn't be there the next morning but she couldn't make herself do it. She did take time to write her a note before she packed everything into the truck and got the cats into the old wooden crate.

"We'll stop at the first store we come to and I'll get you a proper carrier and a new toy to keep you entertained on the ride. If you don't whine, I'll even buy you some cat treats." Talking out loud helped take the sting out of driving away from the café.

She couldn't leave town without talking to her father first. Stopping at the cemetery, she got out of the truck and sat down in front of his tombstone. "I never did tell you good-bye. Not even at your funeral and I can't do it tonight. Remember when you would leave and I'd beg you not to go away? We'd touch each other on the forehead and we'd say 'see ya later.'" She traced his name with her forefinger. "I love that cowboy so much. Am I doing the right thing, Daddy?"

No answers came floating down from the big white puffy clouds above her. The sun didn't stand still in the sky. Her phone pinged a couple of times but she ignored it.

"Evidently you're tellin' me to figure this one out on my own, aren't you?" she finally said as she rose to her feet. "See ya later, Daddy. I promise I won't wait twelve years to come back this time."

The kittens had decided to claw at the crate and whine about being cooped up. "Y'all might as well settle down. We'll be driving most of the night and I expect you to stay awake and talk me out of making a U-turn anywhere between here and the Louisiana border. I didn't bring you to listen to you fuss at me the whole way."

Duke meowed pitifully.

Cora glared at her.

She stopped at the edge of town and pulled off to the side of the road. In five minutes she could be back at the apartment. Tears rolled down her cheeks. If leaving without even saying the words out loud created this kind of pain, she didn't want to even think about seeing Brody waving in her rearview mirror like she remembered from the last time she left Happy.

She pulled back out onto the highway and flipped on the radio. Every single song had a message to her heart but she kept going until she got through Tulia. Then she saw the flares and hit her brakes hard. She counted four cars ahead of her truck but the traffic was lining up behind her pretty fast. A semi blocked both lanes of traffic but it didn't obliterate the flashing lights of half a dozen police cars, along with a couple of ambulances not far ahead of the traffic jam.

"Okay, guys, is this an omen? And if it is, what's it tellin' me? To turn around and go back to Happy or is it telling me that there will be obstacles in the way of this long-distance relationship?"

Not a single meow came from the backseat.

"Some help you are," she fussed.

It took thirty-two minutes to get the semi pulled out of the way and the ambulances going back south with their sirens blaring. For the next half hour the traffic was horrible and it was nearly midnight when she stopped to buy the things she'd promised the cats, along with a bag of chocolate donuts, a couple of apples, and two bottles of cold Dr Pepper. That much caffeine and sugar should keep her awake for several more hours.

She set the new carrier with a fluffy throw in the bottom, along with a little bowl of treats and a new toy on the passenger seat. She managed to get a kitten in each hand and relocate them. They nosed around, ate a few of the little treats, sniffed the toy, and went back to sleep.

She smiled for the first time since they'd left Happy. She'd bought some ribbon and a leash so they could get out and run around later but right then she needed to get more miles in before she stopped for a rest. She turned on her phone before she started the engine. Six messages and four missed calls from Brody. One call from Molly and two from her mother.

She hit the button to call her mother first.

"Where are you?" Daisy answered. "Molly went back to the café to get some sugar and found the note you left. What were you thinkin'?"

"I'm on my way home. I'll stop in Shreveport or sooner if my eyes get heavy. What was I thinkin'? That I couldn't bear another good-bye," Lila answered.

"What about Brody? Did you kiss him good-bye?"

"No." Her voice cracked.

"That's good enough for him."

"Why would you say that? He came back that morning we left to apologize but I didn't want to hear it," she said.

"You're taking up for the man who broke your heart?"

"I guess I am, Mama."

"You love that cowboy, don't you?" Daisy sighed.

"Always have. Probably always will. Can we talk about this later when just the sound of his name won't make me tear up?" She wiped away a fresh batch of tears.

"Turn around and go back, Lila."

Had she heard Daisy right? Surely she wasn't throwing in the towel and admitting defeat where Brody Dawson was concerned.

"I can't. Something in my gut says that we need this time apart to see what happens and where this is going. If it is meant to be, I'll know it. If not, I'll survive on the memories," she said.

"I know this is hard for you and hearing the pain in your voice is making me cry with you," Daisy said. "I wish I'd stayed in Texas all those years ago. I may have ruined your life."

"You did the best you could with what you had to work with that day, so don't have any regrets. You were only thinkin' of me when you left, not yourself. I'll text after a while. Bye now. I'm going to get back on the road. I'll text you when I check into a hotel. I love you, Mama."

"Call Molly. She's worried sick that she offended you," Daisy said.

"I will. I promise." She hit the END button before Daisy could say anything else.

Molly answered on the first ring. "I'm sorry for whatever I did."

"It wasn't anything you said or did. You've been great, Molly, and I've loved working with you but I couldn't endure a bunch of tears and good-byes."

"When are you comin' back?"

"Don't know that I am," Lila said.

"Oh, yes, you are. It's just a matter of time," Molly said.

"We'll see. Thanks for everything. I need to get back on the road."

"Don't drive when you get sleepy. Get a hotel room."

"I promise I'll be careful," Lila said. "Tell Georgia hello for me."

"Hmmmph," Molly snorted. "You can tell her yourself when you come home."

She waited another hour to send a text to Brody: *Too late to call. We'll talk tomorrow morning.*

Seconds later the phone rang.

"I thought we were good." His voice sounded raspy.

"We were. We are. But you said it when you told me you were lost and your heart hurt when I left the first time. Imagine how hard it would be to go through that again."

"I am going through it again," he said.

"So am I but I have to get moved out of my apartment and we need some time apart."

"How long is some time?"

"I don't know. I just couldn't say good-bye, Brody."

There was a long silence before he said, "I understand. Does that mean you're coming home to Happy for the rest of the summer after you get this job in Arkansas?"

"It means I'm leaving Florida. I'm not sure where I'm going. I'm at a rest stop right now and I need to get back on the road."

"Be careful, darlin', and call me every couple of hours so I know you're okay," he said.

"I'm a big girl, Brody. I've been traveling alone for years. I'll text you when I get to a stopping point. If you're awake, you can call me."

"Lila, I don't like this."

"Neither do I, Brody."

She hit the outskirts of Shreveport at four in the morning. She'd thought she'd feel a tremendous sense of relief when she crossed the line from Texas into Louisiana. The inner wild child would disappear and she'd be another person.

It didn't happen.

Her eyes felt like they'd been worked over with eighty-grit sandpaper but she couldn't rationalize paying out money at that time of night for a hotel. Checkout in most of them was noon and only a few would let her take the cats in without a hefty deposit. Three or four hours' sleep, maybe just until the sun rose, would get her on into Panama City Beach by bedtime.

She saw a sign for a roadside rest at the next exit. She whipped over into the right lane and slowed down. The place was empty except for a van with a family who looked as if they'd been traveling longer than she had. A little red-haired girl must've slept through the night because she was running circles around a picnic table where her daddy slept on top of it.

The child reminded Lila of Emma but her mama wasn't a thing like Kasey. The dark-haired lady was sitting on a quilt next to the picnic bench with a second little girl in her lap. The lady watched the little girl run off energy and smiled as Lila passed by them on her way to the ladies' room.

Someday Lila would have a family like that. It

wouldn't matter if she and her husband were too strapped for money or time to get a hotel room on their travels. The important thing would be if they had each other. The family had left when she went back outside.

The kittens were quiet, so she rolled down the windows a few inches, threw the seat back as far as it would go, and shut her eyes. She wiggled around until she was semicomfortable, tucked her hands under her cheek, and was sound asleep in seconds. The sun pouring in the window and Duke howling awoke her four hours later.

"Okay, guys, let's try out this new thing." She put collars on each of them and tied a ribbon to each before she took them outside and tied the other end to the leg of the picnic bench. She expected both of them to fight against the collars but they were too fascinated with the grass, a butterfly, and the new things to fuss. Duke was the first one to scratch out a hole in the loose dirt under the bench; then Cora followed his lead.

"Good kitty cats," Lila praised them.

She kept them in sight and went back to the truck to get the new water dish and food bowl. When they'd finished eating and romping, she took them back to their carrier and removed the collars and ribbon leashes. They were not happy but they didn't have a choice. It was still a long way to Florida and she didn't want them getting lost amongst the luggage.

She rolled the kinks from her neck and fastened her seat belt. The second Dr Pepper she'd bought was warm but it washed down half a dozen donuts. She wouldn't need food again until noon. She was on the road again, trying to put the disappointment she'd heard in Brody's voice out of her mind without much luck. By supper time she'd be back in her apartment but right then she wished she was helping with the breakfast rush at the Happy Café.

I miss you, Brody. It's only been a few hours but I miss you so much. Why does love have to be so hard?

Chapter Twenty

On Thursday morning, Brody awoke to the same empty feeling he'd taken to bed with him on Wednesday night. There had been hurt the first time Lila left Happy, but this time it went beyond simple pain and he had no idea how to make it go away. He put a pot of coffee on, made a peanut butter and jelly sandwich, and carried it with him to the corral where Sundance was penned up.

He sat down on the other side of the fence and ate two bites of the sandwich before he tossed it to the side for the ants or the squirrels. Whichever got there first was welcome to it.

"I'm back, old friend," he told the bull.

Sundance made his way over to the fence and tried to poke his head through the railings.

"Grass ain't a bit greener on this side," Brody said. "She's gone and I don't know what to do or say to make her come home for good. I feel like half my heart is gone.

Hell no! That's not right. She took the whole thing with her when she left. I hate good-byes, too, but if she'd have talked to me, we might have avoided ever havin' another one. Movers could have taken care of her stuff and she had a job at the café."

The big Angus bull hung his head over the top rail.

"Nothing we can do now. I sent a text an hour ago and she hasn't responded yet. What if she doesn't? What if she gets down there and Clancy convinces her to stay? I don't know why I'm talkin' to you. You don't have any answers and every time you get a chance, you break out of the corral and get into trouble."

Brody chuckled. "I guess that's why—we're a lot alike. We don't like being penned up and we know what we like. Well, thanks for the visit. I don't know what I'm going to do, but I'm not going to figure it out here."

He started back to the house and checked his phone but there were no messages or missed calls. He didn't want to talk to Jace or Kasey, so he detoured and walked over to Henry's old barn. He heard Blake Shelton's voice singing from his first album before he even peeked inside the door to see Paul loading feed.

"Hey." Paul waved and reached inside the truck to turn down the music.

"I like it loud but Gracie won't let me play it like that when she's in the truck." He grinned. "I heard Lila left last night without tellin' nobody, not even you. Thought maybe Henry might reappear."

"Why would you think that?" Brody asked.

"Just a feelin' I had. I know that they left and then he disappeared but since it all happened in a few weeks, I've wondered if they were connected in some way. Guess I was wrong. There ain't no one at the house. I go through and check it every month or so just to be sure there ain't been no vandalism."

Brody grabbed a pair of gloves from a hook beside the door and hoisted a bag of feed onto his shoulders. "I'll help you get this unloaded since I'm here."

"How're you takin' it?" Paul asked. "Looked like y'all was gettin' pretty serious."

"I wish she would've stayed."

"Maybe the stars wasn't lined up right," Paul said.

They finished loading the feed and Paul removed a glove and stuck out his hand. "Thanks for the help and remember that old thing they say about lettin' something you love go."

"If it comes back, then it's real. If it don't, it wasn't?" Brody asked.

"Something like that. I remember once when Kasey and Adam were havin' a big fight. Can't remember what it was about but Gracie told him to love her enough that she'd come back. What'd y'all fight about?"

"We didn't. She hates good-byes," Brody said.

"I can sure relate to that. Telling Adam good-bye every time he left made me come out here to this barn and cry like a baby. Mamas are pretty smart when it comes to things like this. Speaking of, you talked to yours?"

Brody shook his head slowly. "Oh, no!"

"You might be surprised how smart she is about these things, son. Thanks again for the help. There's that white cat again. I sure wish someone would take her home with them. She's a sweet-natured old gal but Gracie ain't one much for cats. You think about talkin' to Valerie or Hope." Paul got into the vehicle and drove away.

Brody worked his phone from his hip pocket and had his finger ready to call his mother but he couldn't. He jogged back to the ranch, got into his truck and drove over to her place. He knocked on the back door and then pushed on inside.

Valerie was braising a roast and scarcely even glanced his way. "Good mornin', son. Coffee is in the pot. What brings you out this early?"

"Lila's gone."

"I heard." Valerie finished the job and slid the roast into the oven. "The only thing that surprises me is that you're here talking to me about it."

He removed the phone from his pocket and found the song that had come to his mind when Paul made that comment about mamas. "I want you to listen to this and then we'll talk." He laid it on the countertop and turned up the volume.

"So Much Like My Dad" started playing and tears ran down his unshaven cheeks. George Strait sang the words better than he could express them. His mother had always said that he was just like Mitch Dawson. By the time the song was nearing the finish, Valerie was wiping both her tears and Brody's away with a dish towel.

"Like it says, if I'm like Dad, then there must've been times when you wanted to get in the car and leave this place too. So please, Mama, she's gone and I need to know what it was that Dad said to make you stay, because I don't think I can live without her," Brody said.

Valerie poured two cups of coffee and set them on the table. "It's normal for people in a relationship to have arguments and times of doubt, son, but I don't know that I can help you."

Brody had a hard time swallowing all his tough pride around the lump in his throat. "How did he do it, Mama? I know it's personal, but I need to know if I'm so much like him."

Valerie motioned for him to sit down at the table. "He said the three magic words. *I love you.* That's what always made me stay with him. Have you told her that?"

"Not seriously," he said.

"As much as I've fought you being with her, I'm going to give you a piece of advice. You're both adults and if you love her, then go to Florida and tell her so. Not here in Happy where you're both still battling against being those two kids that you used to be, but in a different place where you're adults. Jace and Kasey can hold down the ranch for a few days."

He shook his head. "I can't go anywhere right now. The middle of summer is our busiest time for repairing fences, plowing and planting for winter pasture, and... well, you know, Mama. You've been runnin' this ranch for years, so I don't have to tell you how hard it would be to leave for several days right now."

"Do you love her or the ranch more? Or is this a pride thing?"

"Granny Hope expects me to be responsible when it comes to the ranch." He raked his fingers through his hair.

"You didn't answer me," Valerie said.

"I love her more than anything, but it might be a pride thing," he admitted.

"Pride is a dangerous thing, son," Valerie told him. "It can ruin a relationship."

"Will she be welcomed into the family?" Brody asked.

"If she loves you as much as you do her. God, Brody,

I can't stand to see you like this. I had no idea that you loved her this deeply," Valerie answered.

"Thank you, Mama." Brody hugged his mother.

The answer was simple. He just had to get to her to deliver it.

* * *

Soft, drizzling rain had darkened the Florida skies when Lila pulled into her parking space in front of her apartment. She was close enough to the beach that she could hear the faint sounds of the waves as they splashed against the shore. Leaning on the truck's back fender, she inhaled the salty air and felt the warm rain on her face. She'd miss evenings like this, but it was time to move on.

With a sigh, she opened the passenger door and removed the cat carrier. "Welcome to your two-day home," she said. "It's not as big as the Happy apartment, but it's a heck of a lot more room than you had in the truck. Give me time to get your litter pan out and I'll open the chute."

The word *chute* reminded her of Brody and the way that her heart stopped when he was thrown off that bull. Her mind circled around from that night to when they'd skinny-dipped in the cold water and how he'd looked wearing nothing but a smile in the moonlight. She sighed as she went back to the truck and unloaded kitten supplies. Then she carried them to the kitchen and showed them their food. Neither of them showed as much interest in that as much as snooping around in the new surroundings.

"Make yourselves at home." She yawned.

She sat down on the sofa and called Brody before she passed out from exhaustion.

"I've been waiting all day to hear your voice. Texts just aren't the same," he said.

"Me too. I'm already homesick," she admitted.

"You said home," he whispered.

"Happy has always been the home base, Brody. That doesn't mean..." She yawned again.

"I think it does, Lila, but I'm not going to argue. You sound tired, darlin'. Are you in your apartment?"

"Yes, I am. The cats are set free and happy and I'm going to take a shower and sleep a little bit before I start packing," she said.

"And tomorrow?"

"I got a call from the school in Conway. I've got an interview, so I'll head in that direction. I'm exhausted. I wish you were here."

"So do I, darlin'. You go on and get some rest," he said.

"I miss you so much."

"Me too, Lila."

She took time to send her mother and Molly a text and then she turned off her phone and fell on the bed without even taking off her clothes. She was asleep when her head hit the pillow and it was full dark that evening when she awoke. A black ball of fur rested in the crook of her neck and a white one was sitting beside her shoulder, staring at her.

"I'm awake and I still miss him so much that my heart hurts," she whispered.

Cora meowed loudly, waking Duke, who instantly started to purr. Her stomach growled, reminding her that it had been hours since she'd eaten anything but junk food. She was so hungry, she could almost taste the fish from Margaritaville. She hopped out of bed and headed straight for the bathroom.

Letting the warm water beat down on her back and shoulders for several minutes, she didn't fight the memories of the past month but let them play through her mind on a continuous loop several times before she got out of the shower and wrapped a towel around her body. She dried her hair and dressed in a sundress, applied a little makeup, and kissed both cats on the heads before she left.

With her motorcycle still strapped down on the back of her truck, she drove to one of her favorite places for good local fish. As usual, Margaritaville was noisy and pretty well packed when she arrived. But luck was with her because they had a table in the back corner. A young couple with glimmering gold wedding bands sat to her left. They could have been Brody and Lila in another lifetime. The waiter seated a small couple with a toddler in a high chair not far away. Then an old couple, gray haired and still holding hands as he helped her down the three or four steps into the dining room, was seated at a table for two right ahead of her.

Happy-ever-after was lived out in stages right before her eyes. She wanted that shiny gold wedding ring. She wanted that little blue-eyed daughter in a high chair. And she wanted Brody to hold her hand to steady her as she walked down the steps into a restaurant when they were old and gray.

She studied the menu so that the three couples wouldn't catch her staring at them. A motion in her peripheral vision caught her attention and before she could escape, she saw Belinda drag Clancy by the hand over to her table.

"Clancy told me you're leaving us. I was hoping to see you before you checked out at the school." Belinda stooped to hug her.

The last thing Lila wanted was to share her table but Belinda hesitated so long that it became awkward. "This is a table for four. Y'all can join me if you want."

"That would be wonderful," Belinda said. "So I hear you might be going to Little Rock."

"Conway, actually. It's about an hour from Little Rock. We'll see if they like me and if I like them."

Belinda sat down, crossed one long leg over the other, and then tucked her chin-length red hair behind her ears. "I can't imagine living anywhere but right here. And they have tornadoes in Arkansas."

"Florida has hurricanes," Lila said.

She should have at least a little streak of jealousy, right? But it wasn't there—not even a smidgen. If anything, she felt sorry for Belinda for getting tangled up with a narcissistic, egotistical fool like Clancy.

"But"—Belinda smiled—"they don't have a Margaritaville."

"A sacrifice I'll have to make for their fine Southern cookin' restaurants," Lila said.

"What can I get you?" the waiter appeared at her elbow.

"I'm having whatever the fish of the day is and a bottle of Jäger," she said.

"I want a bowl of gumbo and a glass of white wine," Belinda said.

"And I'll have the eight-ounce sirloin, baked potato,

and salad with house dressing and bring a bottle of red to the table," Clancy said.

"One ticket or separate?"

"Separate," Lila said quickly.

"Separate for all of us," Belinda said.

Lila was suddenly intrigued.

"Okay, then, I'll have that right out," the waiter said.

"I'll have to eat and run," Lila said. "I've got packing to do tonight if I'm going to get my room cleaned out and keys turned in tomorrow."

"We'll miss you," Belinda said.

"We can keep in touch," Lila said. "So how did the summer job go at the T-shirt shack?"

"Great. If I could make a living working there, I'd stop teaching in a minute." She and Clancy exchanged a look and then she sighed. "But minimum wage doesn't pay the bills and..." She let the sentence drop.

"And she's too smart to live that kind of lifestyle," Clancy finished for her. The tilt of his chin said that he was talking to Lila as much or more than Belinda.

"So you think that only stupid people can be sales clerks or waitresses," Lila pushed the issue. "You wouldn't want to introduce Belinda as, 'Please meet my girlfriend who works at the T-shirt shop on the strip,' would you?"

"No, I wouldn't or take home a waitress to introduce to my parents either," he said curtly.

Belinda turned to face Clancy. "That's crazy. It's all good work whether it's teaching kids or making the tourists happy."

"Society makes the rules. I just do my best to live by them." He laid a hand across the back of her chair.

"Oh, well, it's not important," Belinda said. "We are who we are and I'm a teacher. Now, Lila, tell me how did the waitress business in Texas work out?"

The waiter brought a glass of white wine, a beer, and an empty glass with a full bottle of red and set it on the table. He poured the wine and said, "Food should be ready in only a few minutes."

"Thank you," Clancy said. "Now, you were going to tell us about the waitress work, Lila? Still chasing after that redneck cowboy? You're so unsuited to a man like that."

She took a sip of the beer and turned to Belinda. "Being a waitress was amazing. I made a little more than my usual teacher paycheck, actually. And of course, we get all the good town gossip." Her smile faded as she addressed Clancy. "And the cowboy isn't a bit of your business."

Belinda sipped her wine. "Oh, really!"

"Had some good tippers and then some who only came in for a glass of sweet tea but I loved visiting with all of them," Lila said.

Belinda giggled. "I really will miss you. Anytime you want to come back to Florida you can stay with me."

"Thank you." Lila was glad that she'd gotten cornered by Belinda. In Florida she wasn't the wild child; she was a full-fledged bona fide grown-up. Neither of her personalities liked Clancy and that was a good thing to have settled. It wasn't just because she was living a different life in Texas that he'd gotten on her last nerve. He could do it in any state and with either of her twin personalities.

In Happy, she could be that wild child with Brody and still hang on to the grown-up woman. Like Kasey had said that day in the café, she could have both. But the only place she really wanted both was in the panhandle of Texas—that's where both pieces of her heart fit together.

She ate faster than usual and was able to pay her bill and get out of the restaurant in thirty-six minutes. Belinda expressed regret that neither she nor Clancy would be at the school the next day when she checked out but they had plans to visit her parents in Pensacola. Lila faked disappointment and smiled all the way to her truck.

"Here kitty, kitty," she called out at the door of her apartment. Duke and Cora came running from the bathroom and stopped at her feet as if asking if she'd remembered to bring them something.

"I didn't forget. I've got two pretty nice-sized bites of good grilled fish."

Duke growled and slapped a paw down on his bite, practically inhaled it, and then headed across the kitchen floor to help Cora with hers. She sniffed it daintily, walked around it, slapped it a couple of times to see if it would wiggle, and then pranced off, tail held high. Duke grabbed it in his teeth and tossed it into the air like a dead mouse, caught it on the fly, and ate it quickly.

Lila plopped down on the sofa and picked up a notepad from beside the house phone. Call the cable company, the phone company, and the Internet service provider first thing the next morning. Call the Sugar Sands and make a reservation for the next night because her lease actually ran out at midnight on June 30. Her cell phone rang and, hoping it was Brody, she quickly fished it out of her purse and answered without checking the ID.

"I'm awake and ready to talk," she said.

"This is Valerie Dawson and I'm ready to talk too."

The phone fell from Lila's hand and she had to scramble to grab it before it hit the ground. "Is Brody all right?" she whispered.

"Fine when I talked to him earlier today," Valerie said. "I'm butting in where I probably shouldn't but he's my son. You'll understand someday when you have kids."

Lila gulped a couple of times. "Okay, then what do you want to talk about?"

"I'm not sure where to begin or even what to say. I got the number from Kasey and...," she stammered.

Lila was sure that she was about to hear that she should stay out of Happy, leave Brody alone, he would get over his pain, yada, yada, yada. Lila shut her eyes and got ready for the tirade.

"I've judged you and that was wrong," Valerie said.

Lila's eyes snapped open. She was awake and this was not a dream. "Why are you telling me this?"

"My mother-in-law never did think I was good enough for Mitch. Right until her dying day, she awoke every morning and hoped he would divorce me."

Lila chuckled. "Surely not."

"Oh, yeah, she did," Valerie laughed with her. "I swore I'd never make my sons choose between his family and the woman they loved, but I did...and I apologize."

Lila's eyes shot toward the window. It didn't look like the end of the world but surely the apocalypse was on the way if she'd heard Valerie right. "Apology accepted. Why are you telling me this now?"

"Before, you two were so different and so young. Now I see things differently." There was a long whoosh of air on the other end as Valerie sighed. "I want to tell you that I won't be my mother-in-law. I don't know you very well but I'd like to remedy that if you'll come back to Happy for the rest of the summer. I won't stand in the way of whatever relationship you and Brody decide to have."

"Thank you," Lila said. "But I've got an interview in Conway, Arkansas, in a couple of days for a teaching job there. I'll have to find an apartment and get moved in before I can make a trip back to Happy."

"Could we talk again sometime?" Valerie asked.

"Yes, ma'am, that would be great," Lila said, still wondering if she'd awake tomorrow and figure out that this had been some kind of wild dream.

"Okay, then, good night. And before I hang up, Kasey said that she'd love to hear from you, so when you have time would you please give her a call?"

"I sure will," Lila said. "Good night to you too."

She hit the END button, tossed the phone on the pillow beside her, and rolled her eyes toward the ceiling.

Cora climbed the arm of the sofa like it was a tree and perched there. Lila stroked her pretty white fur and said, "Well, now, that should do it for this day. I've dealt with Clancy and Valerie in the same evening. Don't you think that should get me a gold crown even if it's only a plastic one?"

Cora purred an answer and the phone rang a second time. Lila checked it that time.

"Hello, Brody," she said.

"Hi, darlin'," he drawled.

His deep voice sent sweet shivers down her back.

"Gettin' packed and ready to roll out of Florida?"

"Slept all day and am just now getting started, but I

made a list. I'm going to turn in my key tomorrow by quittin' time at the complex office and check into a little place called the Sugar Sands on the beach for one night, then head out on Saturday morning."

"Sounds like you got things under control, then," he said. "I thought after twenty-four hours that the missin' you might get better. It hasn't but at least this time I can call and hear your voice."

"I'm not so sure anything is under control. But I do have a couple of stories to tell you." She went on to tell him about seeing Clancy and knowing that she'd made the right decision six months ago to break it off with him and then about the phone call with his mother.

"Nanny didn't like Mama. We all knew it and it made for tense times when we all went over to their house. I'm glad that Mama is coming around," he said. "I was just listening to Vince Gill sing 'Never Knew Lonely' over and over again. I can so relate to the words of the chorus that say that lonely can tear you in two. I feel like half of me is missing," he said.

"Me too." The lyrics of the song, especially that part about not being able to make up for the times when she was gone, played through her head.

He cleared his throat and she swallowed hard. "I'll try to get things taken care of in Arkansas if I get the job and come back to Happy in a couple of weeks."

"I'm not sure I can survive for two whole weeks," he whispered.

"Well, then, I guess maybe you'll just have to fly into Little Rock if you get to feelin' weak." She fought back new tears. Lord, she hadn't cried so often in more than a decade. "I'll gladly drive to the airport and get you."

"Don't invite me if you don't mean it," he said.

"You're welcome anytime," she said. "How about next weekend?"

"How about this one?"

"Don't tease me, Brody," she laughed.

Chapter Twenty-One

Lila had started out the month of June in Happy, Texas. That Saturday morning, the first day of July, she was sitting on a beach far away from Texas and the only place she wanted to be was at home in Happy.

She let a hand full of warm sand sift through her fingers. The waves were calm that morning, lapping up on the shore peacefully. Seagulls flew around overhead, their beady little eyes looking for food. Sandpipers darted in and out of the edge of the water, leaving their footprints in the sand.

She got one of those antsy feelings that said someone was close by. Glancing to the right, she caught a glimpse of the motel cat, belly to the ground as it stalked a bird. To the left, a seagull was picking at the sand. Then the black and white cat took off for the sea oats and weeds and the gull flapped its wings and joined its flock high in the air.

She looked over her shoulder and blinked several

times. That cowboy silhouetted on the deck looked so much like Brody in the early morning light that it was uncanny. His broad chest and that snowy white T-shirt—it made her ache for Brody. He left the deck and in a few long strides, he covered the distance and sat down beside her. She moved one of her bare feet over to touch his ankle.

He was a real person, not an illusion.

"When you said anytime, I hope you meant it."

"But I'm leaving in a few minutes," she whispered, still unsure if she was imagining things.

"Thought I'd hitch a ride and spend time with you, then fly home from Little Rock to Amarillo."

He was honest to God real, and he was right there beside her. In one fluid motion, she pushed him back and wiggled her way on top of him and then her lips were on his. His arms drew her so close that a grain of sand couldn't have found its way between them. Everything in her world was suddenly all right. Brody was there. He had come to Florida to spend time with her.

"I can't believe you're here." She ran her fingertips over his face and covered his eyelids with butterfly kisses.

"The welcome was a little delayed but..." He pulled her mouth back to his and rolled to one side for a better angle.

"Get a room," a voice above them said.

Lila glanced away from Brody into an old guy's grinning face. "We've got a room, thank you very much."

"Then use it." He moved on down the beach at the slowest jog she'd ever seen.

With a giggle she sat up and grabbed Brody's hand,

afraid that if she wasn't touching him he would disappear. "When did you get here? Where did you stay? Do you have a car? Did you really fly?"

He brought her hand to his lips and answered each question as he kissed her knuckles. "I got here about midnight, then took a car service to the hotel behind us. I stayed in room 101. Since it was a one-way ticket, I'm flying on a prayer that you wouldn't send me packing."

"Mama warned me about picking up strange men." She grinned.

"Well, then." He rubbed his chin. "Would you let just any old cowboy drive your truck?"

"No, I would not," she answered.

"If you let me drive, that would mean I'm not a stranger, right?"

"Seems that way." She smiled. "I could hire you to drive for me and maybe Mama wouldn't get upset."

He gazed out into the water. "I'll take that job. What's the pay?"

"I'm down on my luck, so maybe you'd do it for free meals and a ride to the airport when we get to Conway?"

He pulled his hand free and stuck it out. "Shake on it and it's a deal."

Without hesitation, she took his hand. "We are burning daylight, so we'd best herd the cats into their carrier, check out of this place, and get on the road toward Monroe, Louisiana."

"Is that our first stop?" he asked without letting go of her hand.

She nodded. "It is and then tomorrow morning we'll

go to Conway, get there early, take a look around, and check into a hotel. I have my interview on Monday morning at nine sharp."

"Plans are set in stone, then." He stood to his feet and brought her with him. "So we'd better go chase down Duke and Crazy Cora. Which one of those places are they in?"

"Room 102, right next to where you were last night," she said.

He took the first step across the beach toward the motel. "Only a wall separating us."

"Story of our lives." She stopped at the faucet to wash the sand from her feet.

"Maybe it's time to tear the wall down." He brushed the sand from his jeans and waited his turn.

"That'd be quite a task. You packed and ready?"

"I stay ready." He wiggled his eyebrows.

"I can't argue with that," she laughed. "I'll get the cats in the carrier and meet you at the truck after I check out. And, Brody, this is beyond amazing."

"Yes, it is." He nodded.

* * *

The truck bed was loaded with plastic bins in case it rained, and her motorcycle right in the middle of all of it. The backseat held a carrier with two squalling kittens, suitcases, and cardboard boxes. Brody's duffel bag sat on top of it all and he'd never been happier than that morning as he headed west with Lila sitting beside him.

He wanted to say those three words that his mother

said kept her from leaving his dad when things got rough but he wanted it to be a special time. Lila deserved the whole package—flowers, candlelight, and romance—when he finally said that he loved her. She shouldn't have to hear him say it over the top of whining kittens and the sound of traffic all around them.

"Does your mama know about this?" Lila asked after they were on the highway.

"She's the one who told me it's what I should do. She don't like to see her baby boy hurtin'."

"The big tough cowboy will always be her baby, won't he?"

"I hope so. When you have a son, will he always be yours?" Brody made a right-hand turn to head north.

She turned around and stared out the side window for a long time before she answered. "Do you want children, Brody?"

"A dozen wouldn't be too many for me," he said. "You?"

"More than one. I hated being an only child. I envied anyone who had siblings—still do." It was evident by the serious expression on her face that she struggled with the next words. "Do you really think we can make this long-distance thing work?"

"If we keep the lines of communication open, we can make anything work," he answered. "You can come to Happy once a month for a weekend or longer over holidays. I'll fly to Arkansas a weekend out of each month and we can talk every night. Easy has never been our portion, has it?"

She laid a hand on his thigh. "What about the ranch? Can you leave it for two or three days at a time?"

"You're more important to me than Hope Springs, and I can turn some responsibility over to Jace."

She nodded. "I'll have a week at Thanksgiving, two weeks at Christmas."

"We've got an extra bedroom at Hope Springs."

"You mean I don't get to sleep in your room?"

He brought her hand to his lips and kissed the palm. "That's your decision. My door will always be open."

She turned on the radio and leaned her head back on the seat with her eyes shut. "Let's not go to Arkansas or Texas. Let's spend the rest of our lives in this truck, traveling from one place to the other. I can waitress and you can make a few dollars working on a ranch. Maybe we'll get one of those tiny little silver trailers to hitch to the truck and live in it."

"What about all those kids?" he asked.

"When the first one is school age, we'll settle down. I know it's crazy and that it's my wild child talking but let's pretend just for this day that we never have to say good-bye again. Not even for two weeks or a month," she said.

"Sounds good to me. I hate being away from you, especially after this past month. Hey, there's a town not far ahead. Maybe they'll have a trailer for sale."

She straightened up so quick that she grabbed her head. "Wow! That gave me a head rush."

"What? The trailer or making it rock? We should look for one of those signs that says, 'If this trailer is rockin', don't come knockin',' shouldn't we?"

Lila put a finger on her lips and then on his cheek. "Definitely. Or maybe a bumper sticker. We could steal a 'do not disturb' sign from a hotel to hang on the door."

"We do need that trailer for sure. I don't think there's room for us to cuddle together in this truck. If we find one sittin' on the side of the road, then it's a sign that we need to turn this from pretend into real."

Brody allowed himself to indulge in the fantasy for a moment. After his long day being a ranch hand, Lila would come home at night and he'd rub the soreness from her feet. They'd shower together in the warm rain and laugh every time they'd bump into each other in the tiny space.

* * *

Lila's imagination went to the only travel trailer she'd ever been inside. The bed took up most of the area on one end and the other was nothing more than a tiny kitchen with a booth for a table. She shut her eyes and visualized Brody's long leg thrown over her in the hot nights of summer. In the bitter cold winter, they'd pile on more covers and make wild, passionate love to keep warm. He'd come home from a day of ranch work and she'd massage the knots from his shoulders.

"What were you thinkin' about?" she asked.

"That travel trailer. Everything you say and do makes me want you," he answered. "You ready for a stop? We just passed a sign that said there's a rest stop at the next exit."

"I'm good, but the kitties might need a bit of dirt to dig in," she said.

He slowed down and parked on the edge of the lot and she bailed out of the truck. She took the carrier with the cats inside to the pet area. She tied the bright red ribbons around each of the cat's collars before she wrapped the other end around the leg of a picnic bench.

Brody headed toward the building and came back with his arms loaded with vending machine snacks. "I'll watch the children while you stretch your legs and go to the ladies' room. I brought breakfast."

She jogged to the bathroom, where she looked at the reflection in the mirror the whole time she washed her hands. There was Dee, the schoolteacher with black hair and brown eyes, staring back at her. But in those same eyes, she could see Lila, who only came out to play when Brody Dawson was around.

"I don't want to be away from him," she whispered. "But there's nothing for me but him in Happy, so what do I do? I have to work and make a living. I really would be willing to throw everything to the wind and go with him if we found a trailer for sale. But he has a ranch to manage and lives depend on him."

She dried her hands and stopped at the vending machine for more junk food and two bottles of cold soda pop to keep them going until lunch.

"Hey, I told you that I bought breakfast," he said.

"We have to keep up our strength."

"And why would we need to do that?"

When he smiled like that, her heart kicked in an extra beat and her pulse raced. "Because you have to drive all the way to Monroe and I get real bitchy when I'm hungry. I don't want you to throw me out on the side of the road. And I promised you food for payment if you would drive."

He corralled the kittens back into the cage and shut the door, picked it up, and headed toward the truck.

"Gettin' to spend time with you is double payment, darlin'. But I am glad you remembered to get us something to drink."

"I saw a sign back there that says there's a truck stop ahead about five miles. We should fill the gas tank there," she said. "And who knows, we might even find a silver trailer for sale."

He resituated the carrier in the backseat. "Remember when we used to sneak away from everyone else and take my old beat-up truck down through the canyon?"

She crawled into the passenger seat and tossed her stash on the console. "And we'd stop at one of those lanes back to a ranch, eat corn chips, drink root beers if we couldn't get real beer, and then make out on that quilt." She ripped open the bag and took a handful out before she handed it to Brody as he drove.

"You do remember."

"Of course I do," she said.

At the gas station, Brody was almost finished filling the tank when a silver trailer showed up. A much bigger truck than hers was pulling it and an old guy got out.

"Want me to ask the driver if he'll sell it?" Brody asked.

"If he'll take twenty dollars for it, we'll call it an omen and see if my truck can move it down the road. If we bog down, then it's a sign that we should stop right here in this place and find jobs," she teased.

Brody grinned and hollered over the top of the truck. "I'll gladly buy that trailer from you. How much would you take for it?"

"My wife would skin me alive if I sold this thing. It's her pride and joy." The fellow smiled. "She likes to go see the grandkids but she needs her space when it comes nighttime." He lowered his voice. "And sometimes even in the daytime when they get rowdy. Why would you want this old dinosaur anyway?"

"My woman over there." Brody nodded toward Lila, who was only a few feet away. "She's wantin' an adventure and we only got a hundred dollars to spend on it."

The guy chuckled. "Son, if me and Mama was your age and we had a few dollars, we'd go rent a cheap hotel, get us a bottle of Tennessee whiskey, and have an adventure that would be a memory maker."

"Well, thanks for the advice," Brody said.

"Anytime. You kids be careful wherever you're movin' to," he said.

"Yes, sir," Brody said as he got into the truck. "I tried, sweetheart. Maybe the next feller will be ready to sell."

Lila giggled. "What did you offer him?"

"I offered a hundred but I would have given him two hundred," he teased.

She crawled over the console and settled into his lap. "It was too big anyway. You could hide from me in that thing. I want one so small that we can't cuss Duke and Cora without spittin' cat hair out of our mouths. But I appreciate you offerin' him more than the twenty dollars I was willin' to pay."

"I'd give him everything I've got to make you happy." Brody cupped her butt in his hands and leaned in for a kiss.

Happy? The town? Her state of mind? What would it take to make her happy? Being with Brody the rest of her life would be a good start and it looked like he was willing to work at a long-distance relationship. Things would be different this time. They'd call every day, text several times, even Skype, so why was her heart so heavy?

Because you want more than that, right? The voice in her head that morning sounded a lot like Kasey.

Yes, I do, she agreed.

Chapter Twenty-Two

The sun was still high in the sky when they reached Monroe that evening. She picked out a hotel that was pet friendly and got them a room on the ground floor with an outside door. He nosed the truck into the slot reserved for room 131 and grabbed the kittens while she got a small suitcase from the backseat.

She tossed the room key across the top of the truck. "What do you need?"

"Just that duffel bag," he answered.

"I'll bring it with me. Maybe we'll get something delivered for supper. I've had all the riding I want for one day."

"I'm fine with that. I'm ready to stretch these old bones out and rest for the evening." He unlocked the door and stood aside to let her go inside first.

"Thirty is not old," she said.

"Tell that to my bones," he said as he kicked the door shut with the heel of his boot and dropped the key beside the television.

She set down the suitcase and duffel bag, then took the carrier from him. "I'll put them in the bathroom while I run out and get the bag with their supplies in it. Then we can turn them loose and decide what we want to order. The places that deliver are usually listed in the folder on the desk."

It took only a few minutes but when she returned, Brody was singing in the shower. The time had come for her to make a very important decision. Tomorrow morning when they left Monroe, they would turn north to the job interview. Or she could tell Brody to drive west and take Molly up on that job offer to do waitress work at the café. Molly said that she could live in the apartment indefinitely, so she'd have a place to live and a job that paid as well as teaching.

She was reminded of an old country song that her dad used to play called "Old Country." She could imagine the whine of the fiddle as the song talked about a country boy comin' to town and the city girl waiting for him in a motel. Humming the melody, she flipped through a folder on the dresser and found a fried chicken place that delivered. She ran a finger down the menu and called in a family order for four. She had fifteen minutes until it arrived, so she unzipped her suitcase and took out a pair of pajama pants and a faded nightshirt.

The bathroom door opened and two fur babies barreled out, one walking sideways with her tail fluffed out and her back arched as if she were hunting full-grown mountain lions. Duke slunk out like a miniature sleek black panther, belly low to the ground and growling as he attacked the dark green bed skirt.

"Mean critters, aren't they?" Brody leaned on the doorjamb.

Jesus, Mary, and Joseph! Forgive me, Lord, if that's blasphemy but he looks like sex on a stick standing there with nothing but a towel slung around his hips. Lord, even the angels' wings would be seared from this kind of heat.

"If they were as mean as they think they are, they'd give old Sundance a run for his money," she said, unable to take her eyes off him. Her tongue flicked out and moistened her dry, hot lips. He took a step forward and she did the same; then the world stopped turning and they were on the bed. The towel got lost and it was as if he snapped his fingers and her clothing fell off. His hands were everywhere but then so were hers. She wrapped her long legs around him and guided him into her. And soon they forgot all about time and circumstances.

"Sweet Lord," Brody groaned afterward.

"Yep." Lila rolled to the side and laid her head on his chest. "Your heart is still pounding."

"So is yours," he panted. "That was intense but it's what I've thought about all day."

"And just think, the night is young," she said.

A hard knock on the door brought them back to reality. "Who..."

"Fried chicken." She grinned.

He rolled off the bed and jerked his jeans up over his fine-looking butt, made sure the cats weren't near the door, and cracked it open.

"Delivery for Lila Harris. I need a signature if you want to leave it on the charge card."

"How much?" Brody reached for his wallet.

"Twenty-one oh two," the kid said.

Brody handed him a five and twenty through the door. "Keep the change and thanks."

He felt something brush against his bare foot and looked down as Duke headed out the door. He grabbed him by the scruff of the neck and quickly shoved him into the bathroom.

The kid handed him the sack and pointed toward the corner. "Best watch that white one too. It's sneakin' out."

"Thanks," Brody said, and quickly shut the door.

"I was supposed to pay for the food." Lila wrapped the sheet around her body like a toga.

"You paid for the room. This smells wonderful." He let Duke out of the bathroom and the kitten went straight to Lila, sat down on the tail of her sheet, and whined.

"No chicken for you, Mr. Bad Boy. You tried to get outside. I saw that stunt. You would have probably told me that it was Cora's idea, wouldn't you?"

"Kind of like a couple of other kids I could name but I won't. The bad boy who always let the blame fall on the girl." Brody set about taking the food out of the bag and putting it on the table. Then he pulled his shirt on and held one of the chairs for her.

"I liked the view better without the shirt," she said.

"Mama would kick my butt from here all the way home if I came to the table bare-chested with a lady present," he said.

"Lady? After what we just did?" she teased.

"My lady no matter where we are or what we just did," he said with a smile. "You still like the thigh and wings?"

"Do you remember everything about me?"

"Yes, darlin', I do." He put two pieces of chicken on a paper plate and handed it to her. "And you like potato salad but not coleslaw and fries with ketchup. You like corn chips better than potato chips and root beer better than cola but if you have a choice you'd rather have a longneck beer."

"Good grief," she exclaimed.

"I've lain awake many nights reliving the past. But not once were we sittin' in a hotel or were you wearing a sheet while we ate fried chicken with our fingers."

"Oh, really! Well, I had that vision lots of times."

He straightened up enough to brush a kiss across her lips. "They say out of sight, out of mind. Promise me that won't happen."

"I promise," she said seriously.

* * *

Lila slept like a baby until about two-thirty in the morning. She awoke to find Duke and Cora both sleeping on the foot of the bed. She eased out of bed without disturbing either the cats or Brody, pulled a wing-back chair over to the window, and cracked the curtains enough that she could see out.

A half-moon hung in the sky, one side brightly lit and the other side dark—exactly the way she felt as she faced the idea of two pathways, come time to leave. Only a little way on their journey tomorrow there would be a ramp pointing them from Interstate 20 toward Little Rock. That would take her to the job interview. But if she told Brody to go on straight ahead, she'd be making the decision to leave her way of life behind and walk into territory that she was running from just days before.

Which side is the light one and which one is dark? *Daddy, you could pop into my head and give me some advice,* she thought, but there was nothing to help her out.

It might spook the devil out of Brody if she told him to forget about turning north and take her to Happy. Right now he was all for this long-distance relationship thing. Maybe he needed time and space to be ready to take it from a visit every couple of weeks to something more permanent.

At four o'clock she fell asleep in the chair and awoke with a knot in her neck when Brody kissed her on the forehead. "Good mornin'," she said.

"Mornin'. Did I snore?"

"No, I just had a lot of thinkin' to do," she said honestly.

"Want to talk about it?" he asked.

She shook her head. *Tell me you love me and we might have something to talk about but right now it's probably best if I go to Conway and we give this a year.*

"Are we ready to get on the road, then?"

"Soon as I get the cats in the carrier and get a shower. There's not a silver travel trailer out there that's better than this hotel. You want to just stay here for a year?" she teased.

"Yes, I do, but I don't reckon that's an option, is it?"

She smiled and shook her head. "No, but you can't blame the wild child for wishin'."

"Or me neither."

"Well, now that we know we have to check out, then

let's go down to the dining room and have some of that free breakfast they're offering."

Just give me a sign, Lord. It's still not too late for me to change my mind. I'll drag my feet right up until the time to put my name on the contract but he's got to make a move here.

"Aha, hot breakfast. This is great," Brody said when they reached the dining area. "Should we take a piece of bacon back to the children?"

"I'm sure they'd love it," she said.

I don't want to talk about food. I want you to tell me that you won't skitter like a Texas jackrabbit if I spring the news on you that I'm going to Happy.

"Are you okay? Are you worried about this job thing? Honey, I'm sure this interview is just a formality. They've already called your past employers and gotten good recommendations." He heaped a plate with food and carried it to a small table for two.

It wasn't what she wanted to hear but was probably what she needed. She'd asked for a sign and she'd gotten one. It pointed north in a very definite way, whether she liked it or not. She poured batter into the waffle iron. Two minutes later she removed it, dumped a container of yogurt on the top, and then covered that with fresh strawberries.

"Never seen anyone eat a waffle like that," he said.

"I don't like syrup, so I improvise," she said. "I'll come to Amarillo for fall break and Thanksgiving but Christmas always belongs to Mama unless I can talk her into coming to Happy."

"That was a change of subject." He grinned. "But I like that you're plannin' to come home. I've been scared that you'd forget all about me after we say good-bye at the airport."

"Not a chance, cowboy," she said.

He'd said "come home." Was that a sign? Or was the sign the fact that she didn't want to ever say good-bye to him again?

They finished breakfast and went back to the room to get packed and ready for the next four-hour leg of the journey to Conway. The cats carried on with pitiful meows when they had to go back into the cage. The bags were packed and in the truck and she'd made a call to the office to tell the day clerk that she'd left the key in the room. There was nothing to do but get in the truck and make that turn. Brody started the engine and got back out on the highway.

She gripped her clammy palms in her lap. She didn't want to go to Conway, not even to check out the place and interview for the job. Waitress work at the café sounded so much better. *But you worked so hard to be a teacher. You love your job,* her mind argued with her heart.

He caught the exit back onto Highway 20 and pointed to the big sign that said their turnoff was a mile and a half up the road.

Her breath came in short bursts and her heart thumped so hard that any minute it was going to break through her ribs and fall out on the floor of the truck. Visualizing kissing him good-bye at the airport didn't help at all. It might be risky and stupid but she had to listen to her heart and not her mind.

He slowed down and she touched him on the arm. "Keep going, Brody. I can't go to Arkansas. I want to go home and I never want to tell you good-bye again. I can't live with a long-distance relationship. I want it all and if that terrifies the bejesus out of you, then you'll just have to be scared," she said.

He braked and pulled over to the side of the highway. When he turned to her, there were tears in his eyes. "I love you, Lila. Plain and simple, I love you so much that I can't bear life without you."

"You love me?" She brushed away the tear that made a path down his cheek.

"I always have," he whispered. "I was afraid to say it for fear that you wouldn't say it back and my heart would..."

"I can't remember when I didn't love you, Brody Dawson," she said.

"Then let's go home, darlin'."

"I'm ready."

* * *

Brody put the truck in gear and started down the road, then pulled off at the next ramp and parked beside an old vacant service station. He got out of the vehicle, circled around the front of it, and opened her door. "May I have this dance, ma'am?"

She put her hand in his as Dolly Parton sang "Rockin' Years" on the radio. "How did you know this would be comin' on right now?"

"I didn't care what came on as long as I could hold you, but this is a sign for both of us. I need to kiss you. It's important that you know that I love you and that I'll stand by you forever just like the song says." He took her into his arms and danced with her in the hot morning sun with nothing around them but a couple of vintage gas pumps and a building with no windows.

She laid her head on his chest and looped her arms around his neck. "I love you, cowboy."

"I love you, Lila, and I'll never get tired of saying it."

When the song ended, he kissed her tenderly. "I'm glad we won't get home until tomorrow because I want this day with you and only you."

Two hours later, they reached Shreveport and a few minutes past that he pulled over again right near the Texas line. He stopped the truck and got out.

"What's wrong?"

"Not one thing," he said.

He opened her door and held out his hand. "Would you please get out?"

"Why?"

"Because I asked," he said.

She hopped out and he dropped down on one knee. "Dee Harris, I love you. You're my soul mate and the miracle that makes my heart beat. I don't have a ring, but I'm not kidding and I'm very serious. Will you marry me? It can be in a week, a year, or even longer, as long as I know you'll never leave me again."

"Yes," she said without hesitating one second as she dropped down on the grass beside him and wrapped her arms around his neck. "I want to spend the rest of my life with you, Brody."

An old fellow in an older model truck stopped and yelled out the window, "You kids need some help? Everyone okay?"

"She said yes!" Brody yelled.

"Congratulations. Looks like you got it under control," he said, and drove away.

"Yes, we do have it under control—finally," Brody said as he helped her back into the truck.

A mile down the road, he stopped beside the WELCOME TO TEXAS sign and stopped again. He jogged around the back side of the truck, opened her door, and stretched out his hand.

"You can't undo the proposal. I said yes." But she got out of the truck again without arguing.

He dropped on a knee again. "Lila Harris, the wild child who I fell in love with all those years ago, the person who has carried my heart in her pocket for twelve years, will you marry me?"

"Yes," she said again without even a moment's pause as she fell to her knees. "But why twice?"

He cupped her face in his hands and kissed her in a wildly passionate way that was so different from the first one. "Because I want both of you. I want the wild girl I fell in love with and I want the woman that girl has become. I love both of you and I never want you to think that I proposed to one or the other."

"You're crazy, Brody," she laughed.

"Crazy in love with you." He kissed her again. "Let's come back to this very place when we've been married sixty years." He started the truck and headed west toward Happy.

"You mean you think we'll still be kickin' when we're ninety?"

"We'll still be going skinny-dippin' in Hope Springs when we are a hundred," he said.

Nash Lamont's looking for a quiet place to recover after his time in the army. Kasey Dawson is trying to move on from her husband's death. Can the magic of Christmas help these two open their hearts to each other?

Keep reading for a preview of *Long, Tall Cowboy Christmas*.

Chapter One

Nash brushed at the sand stinging his face. He could feel it finding a way past his flak jacket and to his skin, could taste it in his mouth. Thank God tomorrow he would be back in Texas for thirty days. Green trees, fishing in the Big Cypress Bayou, and Grandma's cooking, but today a little boy had gone outside the borders to get a ball he'd been kicking around all day. And there was no one to save him but Captain Nash Lamont.

The whirr of helicopter blades above the base meant that it was time to leave. Three of his six-man team would be going home in flag-draped coffins—two of them had been married and had children. One of those two had saved Nash's life at the expense of his own, but the captain couldn't think about that now. There was a child in danger out there beyond the base perimeter. His mother was weeping and the soldier with the bomb-sniffing dog was out on a mission. That left Nash.

Nash rubbed the sand from his eyes and focused on the child outside the command center. He yelled at the kid but instead of paying attention, the little boy looked over his shoulder in the opposite direction. He kicked the ball, but the wind picked it up and twirled it back at him like a boomerang. Nash couldn't take a chance on the boy running through that minefield, so he took off in long strides and threw himself on top of the little boy. Then he picked him up, kicking and screaming, and prayed that he'd make it back to the command center without stepping on an IED.

When they were inside the gates, he set the boy down and let his breath out in a long whoosh. He'd saved him—this time Nash had saved the kid. The boy might be upset but at least he was in one piece. His mother was running toward them, not lying on the ground with her horrible screams filling the air. Everything was going to be all right. He had failed in his mission and half his team was going home to their funerals but at least he'd been able to save this boy.

* * *

Kasey covered her mouth and nose with a red bandana and bent against the wind bringing half of the dirt in New Mexico across the border into the Texas panhandle. When the storm hit, she'd yelled at her six-year-old son, Rustin, to get inside the house but he was nowhere in sight. He'd been kicking a ball around inside the yard fence the last time she checked on him. She checked the barn first but no one was there. Then she remembered the last time he'd slipped off that she'd found him over at his grandpa's barn on the adjoining ranch.

A quarter of a mile to the barbed-wire fence didn't seem like far unless there was a fierce wind blowing dirt everywhere. When she reached the fence separating Hope Springs from the Texas Star Ranch, she found a piece of Rustin's jacket stuck in the wire and flapping in the wind. She was on the right track. Hopefully he was holed up in the barn and out of the driving sandstorm.

She crawled through two strands of wire and then called Hope, her grandmother, to tell her that she'd be back to the ranch house soon with the runaway. Shielding her eyes, she could see the barn through the sand. Who was that in the doorway? He was too tall to be Paul, her children's grandfather.

It had to be Nash Lamont, the guy who'd moved onto the ranch a few days ago. No one knew much about the man except that he was Henry Thomas's great-nephew and he'd been in the army. She could see Rustin not far from the barn, so she jerked the bandana down and yelled at him. He glanced over his shoulder but before he could take a step toward her, the man from the barn raced outside and threw himself on Rustin. Then he threw him over his shoulder and jogged back to the barn. Adrenaline rushed through Kasey's body like fiery hot whiskey and fueled her race to the barn.

She slid through the half open barn door to find a cowboy with Rustin still thrown over his shoulders like a sack of chicken feed. Her son was kicking, screaming for her, and swinging both fists at the man's back.

"Why are you fighting me, Ahmid? I saved you. You

aren't dead." The man's eyes were unfocused as if he were sleepwalking.

"My name is Rustin and a sandstorm don't kill people." Rustin's yells echoed off the old barn walls.

"What the hell is going on in here?" Kasey dashed across the floor and took Rustin from the guy and set him behind her. He quickly wrapped his arms around her waist and peeked around her side.

The cowboy's brow furrowed in a frown. "You aren't Farah. You have red hair."

She jerked off the bandana, letting it hang around her neck. "I'm Kasey McKay and this is my son, Rustin." She looked into his dark brown eyes. "What are you doing in this barn?"

He looked around as if seeing the place for the first time, then shook his head slowly. "I'm sorry. I fell asleep out here and when I woke up, the sand—I thought I was back," he stammered. "That's classified. I am Captain Nash Lamont. That's who I am and I just saved this boy from—Oh no!"

He shook his head and his broad shoulders sagged slightly. So this was Nash. Everyone in Happy had been talking about how he'd taken over Henry's old ranch. He'd bought twenty head of cattle from Paul McKay and moved into the old house last week but no one had seen him. Not at the café or at church the previous Sunday. Folks wondered if he might be like his great-uncle—slightly strange but harmless.

At well over six feet tall, Kasey had to tilt her chin to look into his face. Black hair brushed the collar of his denim work jacket and those dark brown eyes looked around the barn as if he wasn't sure where he was. His broad chest narrowed down past a silver belt buckle with the state of Texas engraved on it. Faded jeans, cowboy boots, a felt hat thrown over there on a hay bale said he was proud to be a cowboy but that title said that he was military.

"You deserve an explanation." His accent was a blend of Texas drawl and something even farther south, maybe Louisiana or Mississippi. "I was in the army, did some work in Afghanistan, Kuwait, and Iraq. There was an incident involving a young boy. I didn't get there to save him. I fell asleep in the barn—" He shrugged.

"You thought you were back over there, right? The sandstorm and the kid out there in it gave you a flashback?" Kasey said.

He nodded.

She'd lost her husband, Adam, in a mission in what the guys called the sandbox. Before that, she'd held him many nights through the nightmares that his job caused, so she understood. But it didn't take away the fear that had tightened her chest so that she couldn't breathe when she thought he was abducting her son.

"Mama, I'm okay," Rustin said in a steady voice. "Cowboys don't hurt little kids."

"I would never harm a child or a lady." Nash drew up his shoulders in a way that she recognized. Ramrod-straight soldier. Filled with respect. Ready to do battle. No one stood like a military man, especially one who'd been a cowboy before he enlisted.

"Well, then, we'll be going home. Welcome to Happy, Nash." Kasey should invite him to Hope Springs for coffee or supper but she wasn't feeling too hospitable, not with all those memories of Adam flashing through her mind. Not to mention dealing with a son who was in big trouble for wandering off when he was explicitly told not to leave the yard.

She pulled the bandana over her nose again and stooped down to zip Rustin's jacket.

"I'll drive you home. My truck is sitting right there." He motioned toward a new Chevrolet Silverado parked to one side of the barn. "It's still blowing like crazy out there. It's the least I can do for scaring you."

Kasey's first thought was to refuse but it was at least a quarter of a mile between the Texas Star barn and the ranch house on Hope Springs and there was a barbed-wire fence separating them. He was messed up for sure from whatever had happened over there involving a little boy but he wasn't dangerous. She could read people well enough to tell that much.

"Thank you. We'd love a ride home," she said.

He hurried around the end of the truck and swung open the doors. Rustin climbed into the backseat without hesitation. Kasey kept telling herself to trust her son's instincts. Children and dogs knew who to trust and who to back away from—everything would be just fine. She hiked a hip onto the seat and pulled the seat belt across her chest.

He slung open the double barn doors and then hopped into the truck, slammed the door shut, and fastened his seat belt. "Hope Springs? I drive to the end of my lane and turn right?"

Kasey bobbed her head twice.

Nash even sat rigid straight in the truck seat, reminding her again of Adam's actions even if they didn't share a single physical attribute. Adam had topped out at five feet nine inches, and that was with his cowboy boots on. He'd had clear blue eyes and blond hair. He'd always looked so young that he was carded anytime he ordered a drink and he had a smile that would light up the whole universe.

The man sitting beside her with a death grip on the steering wheel was a silent, brooding type who had a lot of darkness inside him. He might be late twenties or maybe early thirties but no one would ever mistake him as being underage.

He drove slowly to the end of the lane, made a right, and then another one a quarter of a mile down the road. It started to rain, water mixing with the dust to create mud that fell in splats on the truck. The wipers couldn't work fast enough to keep the smears from the windows, so Nash backed off the gas and took them the rest of the way at five miles an hour.

"Rustin, you go straight to the bathroom and shuck out of those clothes. And you." Kasey turned toward Nash. "You do not have to be a gentleman and open doors. Thanks for the ride."

"You're welcome," he said. "And thank you, Kasey, for not shooting me. I apologize once again."

"Didn't have my pistol," she answered as she bailed out of the truck and ran through the nasty rain toward the house. Dripping mud, she stopped inside the front door and kicked off her boots.

Wiping her hands on an apron tied around her waist, Hope came out of the kitchen with Silas, Kasey's youngest son, and Emma, the middle child, right behind her. "You look like you've been mud wrestling and lost the match. I was about to call to see if you wanted me to drive over and get you and Rustin when he came through here like a shot and headed toward the bathroom."

"At least he listened to me on that issue. I hear water running, so I guess he's in the shower, which is where he needs to be. I met the neighbor, Nash Lamont." Kasey ran her fingers through her hair and gathered gobs of wet mud into her hands.

"Did he mention his uncle Henry?" Hope sat down in a ladder-back chair beside the foyer table.

"No, but he was nice enough to bring me and Rustin home. Speaking of my son, I think he's going to be on house arrest with no television for the rest of this week. This is the second time he's wandered off. Last time he was restricted to the yard but he's got to learn to pay attention. Tell him to go to his room when he comes out of the bathroom. I'm going to borrow Jace's bathroom and wash this mud out of my hair."

Her grandmother looked a little disappointed that Nash hadn't mentioned Henry but then she would be crowned the gossip queen of the town if she could find out the history on Nash Lamont.

"Why did you ask?" Kasey asked.

"Just wonderin'. What's he look like?"

"Tall as Brody. Dark eyes, dark hair. Military for sure. Reminds me of Adam in his actions but not his looks." Kasey started down the hall.

"Was he talking to Rustin when you got there?"

Kasey stopped and turned around to give her grandmother all the details of what had happened. "Scared the devil out of me. I could just see a big man through the dust storm and he had my child over his shoulder like a sack of chicken feed."

Hope clucked like an old hen as she brushed her short, silver hair back with her hand. She wasn't much taller than her granddaughter, and her green eyes were set in a round face that belied her seventy-two years. "I got to go call Molly and tell her that you almost killed the new man in town."

"Granny!" Kasey's green eyes widened. "I did not. He was having a flashback to the war stuff. Adam did that more than once. I felt sorry for him."

"Might be wise to stay away from a man who's got problems like that." Hope headed for the kitchen.

After that comment, Kasey wasn't going to say a word about the dark secrets she could see in Nash's eyes.

She lathered her hair three times before the water ran clear. She wrapped a towel around her body and peeked out the door before she darted down the hall. She almost made it to her side of the house when the front door opened.

"Hey!" Her sister-in-law, Lila, grinned as she removed a mud-splashed yellow slicker and laid it across the chair where Hope had been sitting. Not a single bit of dirt stuck to her jet-black ponytail and her brown eyes glimmered. "I heard that you had a confrontation with the new neighbor. I also heard that he's quite a hunk."

"Granny didn't waste a bit of time, did she?" Kasey wiped a hand across her brow.

"I was out helping Brody when the storm hit. Thought I'd come get the whole story from you." Lila followed her back to the bedroom.

Kasey told it again as she got dressed.

"So the part about him being downright sexy is true?" Lila asked.

Kasey shook out her curly red hair. “You ever read *Wuthering Heights*?”

“Of course. I used to be an English teacher, remember?” Lila nodded. “Is Nash Heathcliff?”

“Oh, yeah, exactly.”

* * *

Nash opened the garage door with an opener and drove his truck inside. When he got out, he was clean and dry but his poor vehicle looked like he’d been mudding down on the bayou. He left his boots at the back door and padded through the kitchen into the living room in his socks.

His great-grandmother’s influence still marked the place with its lace curtains and those crocheted doily things on every table, along with stuff everywhere. He shut his mind against the clutter and headed straight for his bedroom—the only room in the entire house that was free of junk. Bed made tightly. Table with only a lamp and the book he was reading beside a recliner. His footlocker at the end of the bed and a go-bag still packed and waiting in the closet with half a dozen shirts and a few pairs of jeans hung with exactly the same distance between the wire hangers.

He’d taken down the pink lace curtains and the window shades had been raised to let in as much light as possible—at least on days when the wind wasn’t slinging mud balls against the windows.

Sinking down in the recliner and popping the footrest up, he gazed at the ceiling. His grandma had decided that a nice quiet little ranch in the panhandle of Texas would be a good place to get his head on straight. She'd bought a dozen cows and a fairly decent bull from the guy who'd been leasing the place and sent him to Happy, Texas, to the old family place.

He'd thought that Happy would be the size of New Iberia, Louisiana, where he'd grown up, or maybe like Jefferson, Texas, where his grandmother lived. Talk about culture shock—he'd had a major dose of it when he'd found out that it was practically a ghost town.

One café, a school, two churches, grain silos, and lots of ranches. That was Happy, Texas, and he'd agreed to live there for a year. He was a man of his word but this dot on the map had nothing to hold him. As soon as he could pass the psych evaluation, he was going right back in the army. As much as he loved ranching, that was going to be his retirement job. Men like Nash belonged in the military.

One year wouldn't be easy—not with Kasey McKay living next door—but keeping secrets was part of his job description. He'd known that she'd grown up in Happy, but if his grandmother had told him that she still had moved back to the area, wild horses couldn't have dragged him to that part of the world.

About the Author

Carolyn Brown is a *New York Times*, *USA Today* and *Wall Street Journal* bestselling romance author and RITA finalist who has sold more than 2.75 million books. She presently writes both women's fiction and cowboy romance. She has also written historical single title, historical series, contemporary single title, and contemporary series. She lives in southern Oklahoma with her husband, a former English teacher, who is not allowed to read her books until they are published. They have three children and enough grandchildren to keep them young. For a complete listing of her books (series in order), check out her website at carolynbrownbooks.com

Fall in Love with Forever Romance

TOUGHEST COWBOY IN TEXAS
By Carolyn Brown

New York Times bestselling author Carolyn Brown welcomes you to Happy, Texas! Last time Lila Harris was home, she was actively earning her reputation as the resident wild child. Back for the summer, she's a little older and wiser... But something about this town has her itching to get a little reckless and rowdy, especially when she sees her old partner-in-crime, Brody Dawson. Their chemistry is just as hot as ever. But he's still the town's golden boy—and she's still the wrong kind of girl.

Fall in Love with Forever Romance

UNTIL YOU
By Denise Grover Swank

Tyler has always been a little too popular with women for his own good. Ever since he and his buddies vowed to remain bachelors, Tyler figured he was safe from temptation. Lanie and her gorgeous brown eyes are about to prove him so, *so* wrong. Don't miss the next book in the bestselling Bachelor Brotherhood series from Denise Grover Swank!

Fall in Love with Forever Romance

FORBIDDEN PROMISES
By Katee Robert

New York Times and *USA Today* bestselling author Katee Robert continues her smoking-hot O'Malleys series. Sloan O'Malley has left her entire world behind and is finally living a life without fear. But there's nothing safe about her intensely sexy next-door neighbor. Jude MacNamara has only ever cared about revenge, but something about Sloan temps him... until claiming her puts them both in the crosshairs of a danger they never saw coming.

Fall in Love with Forever Romance

MAYBE THIS LOVE
By Jennifer Snow

Hockey player Ben Westmore has some serious skills—on and off the ice—and he's not above indulging in the many perks of NHL stardom. When a night in Vegas ends in disaster, he realizes two things: 1) it's time to lie low for a while, and 2) he needs a lawyer—fast. But the gorgeous woman who walks into his office immediately tests *all* his good intentions. Jennifer Snow's Colorado Ice series is perfect for fans of Lori Wilde and Debbie Mason!